THE
Eighth
House

Flames of Olympos
Book One

Eris Adderly

This book is a work of fiction. Names, characters, places, and incidents either are products of the author's imagination or are used fictitiously. Any resemblance to actual persons, living or dead, events, or locales is entirely coincidental.

THE EIGHTH HOUSE

Copyright © 2014-2017 Eris Adderly

All Rights Reserved

No part of this book may be reproduced in any form or by any electronic or mechanical means including information storage and retrieval systems, without permission in writing from the author. The only exception is by a reviewer, who may quote short excerpts in a review.

Previously Published on Literotica.com: March 2014
First Print Edition: September 2017

Cover Design by Eris Adderly.

Acknowledgements

Who *don't* I need to thank? The first version of *The Eighth House* (the one that started this whole new life direction for me on Literotica) was the first story I ever wrote. I still don't know the real name of my original editor, because sometimes you don't ever learn these things about online friends. But he is out there, and should know I appreciate him.

For this new version, I have to thank the lovely Myra and Eliya for their beta-reading love, and most, most sincerely, yet another wonderful author friend who contributed so much and has refused any credit, but knows I love her. So much less than three. The unstoppable Jennifer agreed to lend me her eyeballs for a final round of edits, for which I am ever so grateful.

I'd like to thank my EAD friends for their fierce encouragement of me in publishing this story, especially Addison, and again Myra and Jennifer. You ladies had enthusiasm when all I had was doom and gloom. You're the best.

And, as with every book, I will thank my husband and my mom. My two biggest cheerleaders, and the two who have tolerated hearing about my writing *constantly*. I love you.

Contents

I Fulcrum	7
II Promise	31
III Obedience	65
IV Restraint	85
V Trust	123
VI Service	159
VII Pain	173
VIII Submission	195
IX Limits	231
X Equinox	259

I Fulcrum

Amid purpling dusk and the late summer breeze and brine of a secluded stretch of beach just southwest of Smyrna, Persephone wore a false face. And, as she had for ages now, she offered a smile of false satisfaction to the world.

Or at least to Klaudios, her lover for the afternoon.

She turned blue eyes that weren't hers, and blonde locks that weren't hers, to gaze at the sated mortal man, gracing him with a stretch and a little groan of contentment that were not hers, either.

"You see?" he said with a chuckle. "There are *real* men to be found here in the Eastern ports, Euthalia."

The handsome—and still quite nude—sailor gave his manhood a self-aggrandizing tug to illustrate his point. One of his bare feet pushed out to smooth their rumpled blanket atop the sand into some semblance of order.

In her mortal guise as 'Euthalia', she could wound him, if she were cruel. As well-formed as his body was, she could prick his pride by pointing out how utterly forgettable his lovemaking had been. How bland and barely distinguishable from the trail of discarded men just like him stretching back an age.

The faces changed. The languages. The climes. What did not, *ever*, was the handling. So solicitous, eyes on her face as they kneaded and poked, intent on gauging their own prowess. Secretly worried about the size and performance of their cocks. Their endearments, whether sincere or calculated, so soft, so toothless.

It was enough to bore an immortal to tears, and yet what alternatives did she have?

"Real men, indeed," she said, running absent fingertips along the lines of Klaudios's chest.

They lay propped up on elbows now, facing each other, though she made a mental note of where she'd laid her sandals, preparing to take her leave.

This was the last time Klaudios would be enjoying the company of the enigmatic Euthalia.

"Will you be gone from the port long this time, my wandering pearl?" He reached out to toy with her nipple while she suppressed a roll of her eyes at the name.

"I'm not sure," she lied. "I never can predict these things."

The shush of waves beyond their extended legs repeated to him the truth, but the mortal man was too blinded by pride to listen.

Persephone came to her feet and reached for his chiton, slipping the too-large garment over her head, fibulae still in place.

"What are you doing?"

"My peplos has washed out to sea," she said, her smile too innocent.

"And what do you expect *me* to wear?" He grinned up at her, waiting for her to admit the jest.

She tied the second sandal in place, repressing a chuckle. "Will you not go naked before the gods?"

"Euthalia, wait."

She was already on the narrow path up and away from the sand.

"Euthalia!"

The corners of her eyes crinkled in mirth. Sailors were adaptable. He'd figure it out.

Poor Klaudios, she thought later, as she made her unhurried way back through the busy streets of Smyrna. He'd never see his fair-haired, eager lover again.

Poor him? Poor me. He'll be disappointed for a few weeks. I'll enjoy my disappointment for an eternity.

But her discontent hadn't started in Smyrna. Nor had it originated from any of the other cities of men. Those were only where it had gone to fester.

As she meandered, always toward her goal, Persephone let idle fingertips touch the crisp leaves of potted rosemary, gone dead in a drought year, outside this door and that. Bursts of new growth sprang up in her wake and morning would find the palest of blooms, impossibly full overnight. An unintended benefit for mortal gardens, grown from her inexplicable compulsion to touch everything.

No, flirtation was never simple as all her green and growing things, was it? Well. Perhaps among mortals. On Olympos? She made a low noise in her throat.

Persephone made her way through a netting of streets arrayed without any apparent plan or reason in that particular way of coastal cities, taking no care to avoid watching eyes. In her mortal guise, unless she willed it, the gazes of men would find an inexplicable reason to slide elsewhere. Unobserved, the goddess knew the lightest wrinkling of her borrowed brow.

Somehow—*somehow*—in a way she could not put to name, there had been something essential lacking in Klaudios. By the Fates, something lacking in the *scores* of mortal men with whom she'd amused herself. She couldn't take them seriously. So many of them had been almost … *too* gallant and bright. Was it possible to possess too much of what others prized as desirable qualities?

Down and away from the mount to the southeast she went. Away from the agora, away toward the eastern gate, away, away, away from all she'd reached for that had left her wanting.

If all their so-called charms did so little to keep her attention—let alone fever her dreams, as the songs and poems all claimed would happen—what then, was wrong with *her*? If traditional appeals failed, should she what? Search for their opposite?

Maybe you should seek out just that, Persephone. A darker, more wicked partner.

But who would want such a thing? More irrationality. Answers were nowhere, and yet here she was. On the mortal plane, resorting to *this*. Again.

Yes, my most bountiful thanks, Mother.

She grimaced to the *slap-slap* tune of her sandals on the hard-packed earth.

Her solitary path led her at last to her goal and she put the thoughts to one side. Here, now, was a final familiar haunt before she returned to the realm of the deathless gods. It had been too long.

One low house of baked earth, indistinguishable from any other on a dim street crowded with windows and doors and awnings, was what held Persephone's eye as she approached.

Warm light showed itself from a tiny window, shoulder high against the blue-black of evening shadow. Here was the other indulgence the goddess allowed herself while she walked among mortals.

She rapped on the door, three times in just such a way. After a moment, a voice came muffled but firm from the other side.

"What flower blooms this evening?"

Persephone smiled, the clouds of her mood parting. "The eternal one, Good Mother."

The door swung into the house on generations-old hinges and a woman stood in the golden light, beaming.

"My goddess! Come in, come in!"

Polyxene stepped back into the nest of her rooms and Persephone entered, releasing her intention from the blonde, mortal façade and reclaiming her true form.

The woman before her, perhaps just beyond her childbearing years but still full of feminine life, hurried to prepare a tea while her unlikely guest soaked in the surrounding room. There had been minor changes, but the feel was the same as ever. Humble. Honest. Good.

"It has been at least a year, has it not?" Persephone said.

"I have counted five, Green One." The woman didn't accuse, but Persephone cringed all the same. It was all too easy to lose track of mortal time. More strands of wiry white, she noted, threaded their way through Polyxene's dark curls than had at her last visit.

Every wall and beam in the cozy space bristled with hanging herbs in various stages of drying. Earthen jars and tight-woven baskets littered every available surface, and some of these the woman reached into for pinches of this or that for the tea.

Polyxene was the only living woman to have seen the goddess undisguised more than once.

Persephone had only just arrived on the mortal plane during one of her secret excursions. She'd stepped from the æther just outside a sunlit copse of cedars, anticipating a private entrance into the world of men, only to find a teenage Polyxene trembling and staring wide-eyed back at her, a basket of gathered boughs scattered across the ground.

After a series of stammering promises extracted from the girl never to speak of the presence of the goddess that day outside the temples, Persephone had calmed and taken an interest in the flora the mortal had been collecting.

For a mere bud of a woman, Polyxene had impressed even the Goddess of Growing Things with her knowledge of and enthusiasm for the same. She had been learning from her grandmother the ways of healing. Persephone had been so delighted with this mortal after her own heart that during her returns to Smyrna over the years, she'd become a sort of silent matron.

The woman with the greying hair before her now, who moved about her home with such a quiet confidence, had become the only mortal to whom Persephone dared show her true self. Eyes too green, hair too lustrous, skin too eerily luminous to be human. There would be no way to slip among the streets and markets of men without attracting unwanted attention. Recognition would cause a riot.

And it was a relief.

A relief not to have to lie, and hide, even if her lies bought her some semblance of her own pleasure when she used them to lay with men.

In exchange for the gift of this unlikely and infrequent friendship, and out of sheer admiration for the woman's dedication, Persephone would bring her the occasional cutting from the deathless realm. A blossom, a branch, a tuber, all superior to their mundane counterparts.

It was these rare gifts that had grown Polyxene's reputation over the decades. Polyxene's cures worked better than anyone else's, the people would say. *'Take your mother to Polyxene. She will know what to do.'*

Persephone smiled as the woman offered the steaming cup, taking a step back to clasp work-worn hands in anticipation.

It was, as always, hot perfection.

"Mmm," she said. "What have you today, Mother? Ginger?"

Polyxene tried to hide the making of a face. The woman had objected before to Persephone's use of the fond name out of fearful respect for Demeter. The goddess, however, felt more warm sentiment toward this mortal, despite their dizzying inversion in age, than she had for her own mother in decades.

"And citron, is it?"

"Yes! You are right on both, my Goddess!" A flush of pleasure colored the tanned cheeks. Oh, how Persephone had fought to win such an easy discourse from the woman.

So much insistence, so many assurances to do away with the bowing and scraping.

There was a movement at the edge of her vision and Persephone glanced to see a sleeping cat stretch its striped legs and send a yellow basket toppling. Polyxene rescued the container on its way to the ground, muttering at the small beast, and Persephone smiled.

"I'm sorry to say I have no cutting for you this day," she said to the woman between sips of her tea. "My mind was elsewhere, I'm afraid."

"It is nothing. Nothing." Polyxene made some habitual supplicating gesture, always uncomfortable with immortal apologies. "That you bless such an insignificant home with your presence is more than any could pray for."

Persephone was less impressed with herself by far than were mortals, but made yet another attempt to remember that anything might become tedious if one were to see and live it every moment.

"How fares your home these last years?"

"Well," the woman said, folding her hands at her waist. "Perhaps as I get older, the years fly for me, too. It is much the same. I enjoy an ease, my Goddess. Thanks be to you." A wistful smile. "People need healing. Green things need tending. My son returns from the sea with news and wild tales every few months."

And, after a pause: "I do miss Iacob. It can be lonely, of a night."

Persephone saw just the lightest dusting of fatigue over the woman's features. Her husband had made his journey to the Underworld perhaps ten? Fifteen years ago, now?

"It *can* be lonely," Persephone said. "Can't it."

Her own weights burdened her words.

The surface of her tea rippled under her breath in the lamplight. When would she be in Smyrna again?

"And how do *you* fare, *Karporphoros*?"

Bringer of Fruit. Somehow she didn't mind the epithet when it came with Polyxene's warmth.

"We are too alike, you and I," she said, perching on a tall stool and holding her cup on her lap. "Little changes. My mother will not relent. I expect she feels some relief that I have stopped asking." Persephone's eyes went unfocused, working at knots beyond the clutter of the little room.

"Will this be my immortal life?" she said. "To come and go, dissatisfied, alone, from now until … until …?" Her free hand made a vague fluttering and Polyxene bit her lower lip. "And were I to fall in love with one of these *men*, what then? I watch them fade and die, a flickering of a candle while I go on and on?"

"My Goddess …"

Worry creased the woman's brow and Persephone felt instant shame. There was no excuse for putting this mortal in such a position, to pose questions in front of her which had no answers. Polyxene only wanted to do good, and had such a short time in which to do it.

Persephone's gaze waded around the room. So much gathered in one place. From seed to stem and rind to root, such deliberate cultivation. Who, of the two of them, was making the best use of her available years?

Her eyes landed at last on Polyxene and, again, her hands. Something at her center became very still. Very quiet.

"Mother," she said, "will you lend me your ring?"

"Goddess."

With wide, sober eyes, the woman slipped the jewel of black onyx and silver over a weathered knuckle. She offered it in an open palm and dipped the sort of nervous bow Persephone hadn't seen in decades when the goddess took it.

The stone was long and narrow, meant to span half the length of a finger; the bezel and band worn worry-smooth over most of a life. The young Polyxene's face when Iacob had given it as a gift had been the warmest sunrise in spring. The two had known such love.

This was useful. This was better than unchanging eternity.

Persephone let it well, and the room dimmed away, at least for her.

The dormant, still thing inside her woke. Stirred. A sleeping hive coming alert to the call of its queen. The soles of her feet, her lips, the crown of her head, buzzed with a tingle, electric.

Just how much did I inherit from the Lord of Lightnings?

Her fingertips grew cold as the humming force gathered. Then her forearms, the tops of her ears.

The ring grew hot.

Scalding.

The black stone knew the opposite of becoming. It trembled on the cusp of something ... else.

Could they feel it? On Olympos? Would any of the deathless ones sense some subtle shift?

Did she care?

It could have ended with some dramatic burst, but it didn't. When Persephone opened her clutching hand and now heavy-lidded eyes, she only felt ... scoured? The slightest bit raw? It was the sort of sensation that would heal, she sensed. Like a mortal sunburn.

Polyxene stood frozen, fingers gripped her own crossed arms from a few paces further back than when the goddess had closed her eyes.

Persephone held out her palm, the ring in it almost seeming to breathe now, like a live thing.

"Come," she said. "Look."

The woman stepped forward, cautious, as though she held an adder. She leaned to peer at the ring, but only for a heartbeat before coughing and turning away in a hurry, a palm bracing herself on a high table.

"Goddess!" Polyxene wiped at her mouth with the back of a hand.

The shape of the onyx remained, but it was now formed in a stone of such a vertiginous and unearthly green the mortal woman couldn't bear to look upon it without being vibrantly ill.

"Do not worry, Mother, I will not ask you to look so closely again, this night."

"*Karporphoros*," the woman said, regaining her balance. "What is it? What have you done?"

"I haven't decided yet," Persephone said. She contemplated the altered jewel. Placed it on her own finger. "I will return this to you," she said. "I promise this."

"Will it ... will it dizzy my head again when you do, Green One?" The unspoken part remained, of course. *If it will, you can keep it.*

"It will not if I make a new gift of it in the way I intend."

Dark, expectant eyes returned to the goddess, pleading to understand.

"You will do so much for so many," Persephone said. She turned the ring this way and that in the lamplight, allowing the inception of such a deed to settle on her. "I will take some time. I will not choose in haste, my mortal friend. But an eternity is going to waste in my hands, and it would not in yours."

"Goddess." A mere whisper.

Was the ichor still gold in her veins? Or would Persephone bleed red now, if she cut herself?

"If I return with this stone unchanged," she said, "my immortality is yours."

After several incredulous blinks, Polyxene stammered. "But I am a—an old woman! Well. Perhaps not *old*, but"— she made a helpless gesture—"but, *Goddess*."

Persephone reached for the woman with half a tired smile.

"Then I will not make you wait long, worthy friend."

The unnatural green gem sang in the light. The goddess would have to begin paying heed to the time.

♦

It was not unusual for the Goddess of Lust to slink everywhere she walked. It was not unusual for her to glide familiar fingertips along the columns and doorways of immortal palaces. It was not even unusual for her to smirk and sigh out of boredom, oh no. Reputations were not born out of thin air.

It *was* unusual, however, for her to be doing these things in the Underworld. Whether she would still have done them, if she knew the Lord of the Dead watched her, remained a mystery.

Hades was not amused.

He stood at the head of the great hall, the Helm of Darkness concealing him altogether as he assessed his uninvited guest.

The moment one of the Olympians had entered his realm, he'd felt the familiar pressure. It shared a hint of sameness with a state of submersion in water, though subtler, more airy somehow. When he'd traced the disturbance to its source, and discovered Aphrodite, of all immortals, circumspection had banded with irritation and Hades had followed her, hidden.

Now her steps carried her around the floor of the great hall, her footfalls producing no echo, despite the size and relative emptiness of the chamber. A dozen or so of her acolytes clustered together just inside a vaulted doorway the lot of them could have passed through three times abreast. The windowless corridor outside it loomed like a void. Breathing as one, they stood without a scrap of clothing to share among them. Hades curled an unseen lip.

She brings living mortals into my domain? Arrogant.

The goddess stood out as a gewgaw on an ash heap amid the cool, dry black of the hall. As it remained always, at his preference, a diffused glow lit the chamber from nowhere and everywhere all at once. He could see the distaste radiating from her like heat from her unfortunate husband's forge as she eyed the broad, twisting columns that marched the length of the space. He suspected her unaccustomed to a place so bereft of ornament. But Hades would not soften hard lines with draperies or mosaics. It was not his way.

She sauntered toward the Throne of Tears as he watched, circling it as she stepped up onto the dais. He felt his jaw tighten, but waited. The most opportune moment would come.

The severe, black granite seat, on which Hades alone had the right to sit, spanned the space between a pair of towering, glossy stalagmites, eternally forming on the very spot. The goddess traced a delicate fingertip through the moisture on one of the dark columns, taking a license too far. And, as anticipated, she turned her back.

He removed the Helm, appearing some paces behind her. The herd of acolytes gasped.

"You imagine you can meet the demands of this Throne?"

Aphrodite turned, unflapped, toward the flat rumble of his voice and greeted him with a smile that told him this meeting would only get worse.

"Hades." She acknowledged him with the slightest of nods; familiar and brazen in a way only the Goddess of Lust would dare respond to a Lord of one of the three realms. "A grim throne for a grim ruler, yes? I had no idea you favored a style so"—her eyes flitted around the hall—"bare bones." She flashed teeth at the tasteless jest.

"For what purpose," he said, taking a deliberate step, and then another in the direction of his throne, "are you in my domain? I am certain my realm has never been considered a destination of *pleasure*." He sneered at the word. "And I know you to make efforts when it comes to only one other pursuit."

He came to stand on the dais, and turned to look down at her, allowing his height to speak about which of them had precedence here. Some of her smirk deflated, only to reappear inverted in his own scowl.

"So. *Goddess*. What matter of *business* brings you beneath the Earth?"

Olympians did not travel to the Underworld if they could avoid it. Even Hermes, and that one was familiar with the landscape.

Whatever she's about, you won't like it.

Aphrodite stepped down onto the floor of the hall, waving a hand as though she found him tiresome. Hades took his seat.

He rested his elbows on the arms of the chair and steepled his forefingers together, awaiting the nonsense. The goddess bothered with no preamble.

"It is time for you to take a wife, Rich One."

And nonsense it was.

He exhaled scorn in a quick rush of air.

"Are you not *lonely* under the Earth, my lord?" Her voice turned to honey, as though a solicitous course would be effective with the Lord of the Dead.

"Bah." He made a dismissive gesture. "Do be serious, Goddess."

Lonely. Did Olympos believe him so weak? He had ruled alone for ages without the need of another.

Perhaps they deserve a reminder of who resides here.

"I am quite serious, my Lord Hades." And by the Fates, if her eyes did not say it. Did the others send her, or had she come under her own impetus?

"The Throne of Tears is not a burden to be held by one who pines for companionship like an unweaned pup," he said. "I need nothing of wives."

His brothers hadn't brought up the subject in an æon. They knew better after the last time. So why, then, was Aphrodite here, raising the issue again now? Her feigned concern for his solitude was merely a first gambit, of course. Olympians didn't bother themselves with happiness in the Underworld. He waited for the rest, features blank.

"Do you not even desire a partner who can satisfy your particular"—she rolled her eyes up to search for the word she wanted and came back with a mocking arched brow—"*needs?*"

Insinuation flowed heavy and florid as the goddess swayed a path over the stones. In a chamber of linear black and grey, Aphrodite cut a shocking figure. A mass of coppery hair tumbled forward over fair shoulders. Pale green linen, sheer as mist, draped over her curves in a mockery of discretion. Nipples and navel unnecessarily on display, though to what end in his presence, Hades could not determine.

Aphrodite might have been a perfect distraction for mortal men. Her wiles might even ensnare other gods from time to time, more the fool Ares. But the Underworld was *his* realm. It respected no power save his own, and visiting immortals soon found their familiar abilities most useless until they returned to the sea or sky.

The goddess's charms were quite impotent here, and Hades found this suitable to his purpose.

"And what would you know of my 'needs'?" he said.

"I know enough." Something kindled, secret behind her eyes, and she toyed with an emerald pendant the size of a bird's egg that rested between her breasts. He didn't care for secrets.

"One can only imagine." He drummed slow fingers on the arm of his throne and continued, dry as ash. "A deathless god may have his pick of mortal bodies, if he wishes to quench baser thirsts, *Goddess of Lust*—a fact of which I am certain you are *intimately* aware." A shadow of a smirk appeared. "I have no need to alter my circumstances. Marriage is a fruitful endeavor. It has no place in the realm of the dead."

"I see." Some of the bold assurance had drained from her eyes, but something with a hard edge moved in to replace it.

"Allow me to approach this proposition from another angle, *Lord of the Dead*," she said, slinging his name back at him in an equally taunting manner. "There is a particular flower I wish you to pluck up in marriage, and you will do this thing for me because you owe me a debt." She folded her arms across her breasts and met his eyes in challenge.

"What debt." The word fell heavy and deliberate, a bitter mouthful. "And what flower?" Hades frowned. His patience had limits.

"Ah, what indeed?" Satisfaction returned to her drawl.

Tiresome. And wasting his time. Minos will have been waiting.

"Do you enjoy vexing me, Goddess?"

Aphrodite ignored him and scanned the room from one end to the other before making a face. She raised a graceful hand at the elbow and made a languid motion to her acolytes. A buxom young mortal broke from the huddle near the door and approached her goddess, eyes glazed in euphoria. Bouncing to obey, the woman dropped to hands and knees on the stone floor, head erect and proud in her service. Aphrodite nodded an approval and took a seat on the arched back of her devotee and, furniture thus arranged, returned to her original pursuit.

"There is the little matter of the *Elaionapothos*," she said. "You did not create it without help, as I recall."

Hades narrowed his eyes.

"What was it you said to me?" she asked. "When you and I finished perfecting that little toy? An endeavor, I might add, for which you approached *me* for assistance."

Ah yes. That *little project.*

And now Aphrodite had come to see him make good on his word. Though he ground his teeth, he would not be able to sit silent indefinitely.

"I said I was in your debt," Hades answered. "And I would grant you a favor, should you ask it."

"Yes," she said, "I see you *do* remember. And now I am calling upon it. I want you to take a wife. You're one of the last of us, *Polydegmon*, to be otherwise unattached. Your realm is ideally out of the way." She made an encompassing gesture. "And that is where I need this little distraction moved. Out of the way."

He regarded her in silence, waiting for elaboration. None was immediate.

She made another subtle curve of her wrist and two more stepped away from her entourage, both male, both aroused. Aphrodite's presence on Olympos turned heads. Among mortals it intoxicated, indiscriminate. The acolytes approached their goddess from either side, eyes locked on her face, fevered with lust, each with a hand absently stroking an erection.

Ignoring the human tableau in favor of checking his temper, Hades pressed her. "And this … *wife*," he said with distaste. "An immortal, I assume."

"Of course." She smiled. The advantage was hers now, and the goddess preened. At a nod of her head, the mortal man to her left knelt, ready phallus in hand. He pushed and found entry, taking up a leisurely thrusting, thighs kissing the upturned rump of Aphrodite's human bench. His eyes never left the goddess, hungry as they were for approval. The worshipper-turned-seat began sounding her thanks for such a reward, and the usual stillness of his hall fled before earthy moans.

Hades took a long, full breath, and let it out. Slowly.

"Will your plaything be making a burdensome amount of noise for the duration?"

Aphrodite smirked and tilted her head toward the man on her right, who moved to kneel in front of the now panting female. Like his counterpart, he found an eager entrance and began a slow plumbing of the woman's throat. Moans now reduced to quiet mewling, the goddess met his eyes, pleased with her crude ingenuity and daring him to veer off into petty distractions.

"Is that better then, Lord? Not so loud now?" she said.

He lifted an impassive brow.

Hades was no stranger to pursuits of the flesh. In fact, some of the 'entertainments' he enjoyed might have been beyond even Aphrodite's tolerance for perversity. *His* pleasures, however, he took in private. The lewd public performances the goddess demanded of her followers felt crass and amateurish. A complete waste of time, but Lust Herself was ever inclined toward spectacle.

"Your theatrics grow tiresome," he said. "Name names. Who would you see as Lady of the Underworld? Satisfy my morbid curiosity."

"I didn't imagine you had any other kind," she said. "I name the maid Persephone. And I do not suggest. I demand. As payment on your debt." She laid her hands atop her knee, a look of sober calculation underlying the outrageous display around her.

He snorted in mild amusement. "It is unwise to make demands where you are not the highest authority. A daughter of Zeus, you say? Have you considered that I have chosen to remain unwed for these many ages expressly to avoid becoming further embroiled in Olympian politics?"

"There are advantages to strengthening your ties to the Lord of Lightnings," she said, her words melting into a purr that might have worked on other immortals. "Persephone's voice advancing her husband's agenda—*your* agenda—into her father's ear, could help to ease relations between the realms. *Basileus*, our king, has not always decided matters in your favor in the past, if I recall correctly. Wedding his daughter could only provide leverage for your side in the future."

"Your logic is not unreasonable," he said, "but I find it lacking. The only one in this hall concerned with my political standing is me, yet I know you seek this match for your own benefit."

Aphrodite tilted her head just to one side, patient for the rest. He asked the question.

"Why Persephone *specifically*, and not some other daughter of Olympos? We both know there are plenty." His brother's reputation for spreading his seed was not what one would call 'discriminating'. "Not that it matters," he said. "I've heard rumor of Demeter rejecting any immortal suit to come her daughter's way. You know she will never allow it."

"Ah, but this is the very meat of the thing," she said. "Demeter has kept her exiled from the palaces. From Olympos *itself*. Even the Lord of Lightnings has been complicit in preventing the male gods from seeking Persephone's attentions elsewhere."

Hades gave a minimal shrug and Aphrodite took the hint to come to the point. The goddess swayed with the subtle rocking of her bench, and her lips turned up at one side.

"You see," she said, "your nephew, Hermes—that fickle deity—has been *ignoring* my charms of late. He persists in his obsession with Demeter's daughter, despite the edict to keep her sequestered from the lot of you." Her eyes looked him up and down, and Hades knew whom she meant: any god with a cock.

"I grow tired of his preoccupation with this immortal he shall never come to know. It is time for his attentions to return to their proper place."

So there it was. Jealousy.

The base emotions are to be found at the root of all designs. Do you not know this, Clymenus?

"And I assume the 'proper place' for his attentions is on *you*, Aphrodite?"

"Of course," she said, as though he were being obtuse. "I'm the mother of his children. And his lover. The Goddess of Love allows her consorts' interest to wane when *she* chooses." Her lips came almost into a pout and she stroked the damp chest of a still thrusting male acolyte with the back of her hand.

Hades couldn't help but laugh.

"It appears he has *already* chosen, Fair One! And what do you suppose Hephaistos thinks about all this?" A rare bit of mirth warmed his chest. She wanted *him* to go to the trouble of taking a bride—a daughter of Zeus, no less!—

all because *she* wanted a lover's attentions back on herself. The weaknesses of the other immortals never failed to entertain him.

"Hephaistos is none of your concern," she said. "My husband and I have an 'arrangement'."

He observed the smug lines of her face, the musk of coupling blooming in his throne room.

An 'arrangement'. I do not doubt that at all.

"Let us say I entertain this absurdity of yours," he said, altering his tactics. "You claim some knowledge of my 'needs', do you? What will I do then, with a *maiden*, hmm? Or do you believe the generous patience I'm showing you here extends to my lovers?"

Aphrodite showed her earthy side and snorted. "What *won't* you do, you filthy immortal?" It was enough to make him bark out a laugh. "And I suspect you create worries where none exist. I think you'll find Persephone's temperament quite suited to your little 'proclivities', should you make the effort. After all, there's someone for everyone, isn't there?"

"Not for me. Not here."

He'd tried to slice through with a note of finality, but it did nothing to affect Aphrodite's knowing smirk. "That remains to be seen," she said.

"And what of Demeter's permission?"

You're not giving this serious consideration, are you?

It was a mad idea. Preposterous. But a primitive, inexorable part of him had awakened at the scent of blood, as it were.

An immortal companion. The notion rolled around in his mouth, savory and crimson. His experiences with mortal flesh had been entertaining enough over the ages, but perhaps another of his own ilk might prove …

No. He pushed the thought down with an internal grimace.

Here you are, getting caught up her machinations.

Aphrodite went on, oblivious to his internal debates.

"First of all," she said, "Demeter's edict prohibits her daughter from consorting with any of the gods of *Olympos*. But you are *not* a god of Olympos. Are you, Lord of the Underworld?" Clever white teeth flashed in the light.

He inclined his head to acknowledge her point.

"And second," she said, "Demeter's consent becomes irrelevant when I have already obtained approval for the match from her father. Zeus."

Indeed. The goddess had been busy.

As if orchestrated to coincide with this last revelation, to which she had no doubt been building the entire time, her trio of vassals was now grinding toward a climax, and they found it increasingly difficult to keep quiet. Aphrodite rose from her makeshift seat and turned to watch the final throes of their performance from a few steps away.

The woman's face was flushed and damp from her efforts to accommodate the men. Fingers tangled in the gold of her hair, kneaded the pink curves of her bottom. The three pushed and worked, building to a crescendo and then seizing to a halt in the grip of their shared climax.

Three pairs of glassy eyes remained on their goddess, begging for approval. Aphrodite nodded and granted a dreamy smile of approbation. Enraptured mortal faces beamed thanks, and the two men bent to help the woman rise to shaky feet before they half-walked, half-stumbled back to wait with the others.

Aphrodite turned back to Hades, aglow with the high of worship. It was an addiction the others had. The Lord of the Dead needed no such displays from mortals. Not when they all came to his realm in the end.

But what of *im*mortal devotion?

"Why has Zeus deigned to give permission after all this time championing Demeter's cause?"

A rich chuckle. "Our Loud Thunderer wouldn't be shackled to a *feather* for any longer than he absolutely must," she said. "Zeus grows tired of such constant vigilance. He grows tired of constant *anything*, as Hera will tell you. It was a simple matter to convince him to abandon it."

And here the goddess was. Convincing another ruler of the Three Realms to abandon reason.

"So." His grip on control faltered. "Her father's permission. And you expect me to approach Persephone with an offer of marriage, is that it? You do know we've never met."

"No," Aphrodite said. "You will not be able to come near her without Demeter learning of it. Your powers above the earth are insufficient."

"And if I have other means?"

"Oh?" Copper brows ascended. "Means you'd like exposed? No? I didn't think so. The Goddess of the Seasons will thwart your advances. No. One does not entreat a flower to leave its soil and come live in a vase. One plucks the bloom and has done with it. Particularly if the Lord of the Skies has already given consent to the plucking."

"You suggest I do what? *Abscond* with her then?"

"Precisely," she said. "So pleased you understand, at last."

"Ridiculous. You are well aware a deathless god cannot be forced into a marriage. She must speak the vows of her own will. You expect her eager to give her eternal hand? To the Lord of the *Dead*? After I've *abducted* her?" His voice had risen in incredulity to an unacceptable level. His fingers gripped the arms of the throne.

The goddess only smiled, predatory and eerily sweet all at once. "I am certain you possess the ability to 'persuade'."

"How in the name of the Three Realms do you expect me to accomplish such a thing?" He leaned forward on the throne, flinging one hand wide in exasperation. "Does her mother not watch over her every move?"

"Ah, Hades." Her sigh was just this side of patronizing, and something twitched at his temple. "You imagine I am ever filled with desires and this leaves no room in my mind for forethought. But I have thought this venture through very thoroughly indeed. Listen a while longer, and I will tell you *exactly* how you will be able to snatch your bride away to your own domain, without interference from her mother or any of her other companions."

And so, whether out of exhaustion or sheer morbid curiosity, he listened to her plan.

And it was very thorough.

It was so airtight, in fact, Hades could see almost no possibility of a failure. *If* he decided to go through with it, that was.

Stealing the daughter of another immortal and 'persuading' her to wed? This was not a mere favor Aphrodite asked of him. This was not a gift of riches, nor the return of a mortal soul to the living world, nor any other act he might wash his hands of afterward. This 'favor' would result in his having a partner here in the Underworld. And unlike his promiscuous brother, he would be loyal to *one* wife, if he married at all.

What was the likelihood he would want to share his immortality with Persephone, a goddess he only knew of by the fame of her birth, and had never seen with his own two eyes? And more unlikely still, that she would want to share it with *him*?

Especially when she sees what you really are.

What good could come of it?

But an escape hatch might free him to explore some of the potentials. Perhaps he'd see word slipped to Demeter, after the fact. The goddess would demand the removal of her daughter from the Underworld, and this would absolve him from blame while curtailing the situation with Persephone, as the inevitable need would arise.

He could play his games without the fear of a loss.

"I will think on this plan of yours," he said at last, settling back in his seat. "And I will inform you of my decision before the next time Selene's crown shines full in the night. Be grateful, Goddess, as that is more consideration than

I was willing to give when I first found you in my hall, caressing the Throne of Tears as though it were your own."

Aphrodite moved to stand before him and cut him an insolent brow. "Think for however long you like, *gracious* Lord," she said, "But you will do this thing for me.

"It has been a great many years since I aided you in bringing about the *Elaionapothos*. A creation, I might add, we both know would not be entirely *permitted*, were its existence known among the other Powers That Be. I imagine you would like to continue to keep your little 'plaything' to yourself?" She waited for his acknowledgment.

Of course, he had no intention of giving up his secret to the other gods, his brothers Zeus and Poseidon in particular. It would upset the balance. He forced a nod and she continued.

"You see, that is why you will follow through with this plan and make Persephone your bride. Then Hermes's attentions will be back where they belong, and I can put my lovely mouth to better uses than telling tales of what Lord Hades has been up to, hidden away down here in the Earth. Do you see it now, *Polydegmon*?"

He exhaled through his nose and faced down the goddess come to do business in his halls.

She has you. There is nothing else for it.

He could almost respect it, in a grudging sort of way. He couldn't remember the last time someone had tied him in such a tidy manner.

"I see *quite* clearly," he said.

"Splendid." Aphrodite was all smiles now. "You have a week to prepare. Always a pleasure, I'm sure, my Lord Hades."

She turned from him to glide across the room, but when the green swirl of sheer linens brought her to the open doorway, the goddess looked over her shoulder.

"Seven days," she said. "You know where you must wait. I will make good as to my part; see that you do yours, as well."

The Goddess of Love flowed from the hall, her entourage following without a backward glance for the Lord of the Dead.

Persephone had no idea what was coming.

And when it came right down to it, neither did he. All because of the *Elaionapothos*.

What in creation's name had he brought upon himself?

✦

II Promise

Persephone knew what was coming, and it didn't stop her. The weight of Polyxene's ring, transformed now on her finger, somehow lifted the burden of words like 'forever' and left her bold. Heedless.

The infamous Question, asked anew after a tree-fattening number of years, did nothing to stop her mother from scowling, either.

"Much has been said, Daughter, about those who persist in repeated endeavors with the hopes of new, different outcomes each time."

Demeter's barley-crowned cattle flicked their ears as their mistress stood beside her chariot. Her eyes meandered over the rolling swells of Nysa on a humid, windless afternoon, late into summer. Fat honeybees hummed from perch to powdery perch at the center of the season's last blooms.

"Ah," Persephone said, gaze also conspicuously avoiding her mother's, "new outcomes such as their elders seeing reason?"

"I have seen *every* reason," Demeter said, "and with far more clarity than have you." The Goddess of the Seasons placed the wide basket her daughter refused to take on the ground between them. "They will never be faithful. You know this. Not Apollo, not Hermes. Not any of them."

It had become something of an art form, the way Persephone and her mother could have entire, stiff-backed conversations without ever making eye contact. The ring might have made her reckless enough to start flinging open old doors, but she had no interest in the wake of scorched earth that followed behind the locking of eyes on this issue. And so she remained, lacing her knuckles together for patience. Chin high.

"They're no threat to me, and I'm sure *you* know *this*," Persephone said. "Most of them are clamoring after Aphrodite these days, from what I hear. Ares, Hephaistos …" She shrugged. From a distance, their conversation would look casual, even bored. The tone of their words remained low, but a tension strung them together, pressing the mother and daughter pair so tight into their long-held roles the very earth beneath their feet felt ready to erupt at any moment.

"That bearded anvil pounder." Her mother made a low noise of disgust. "Be thankful the Fates saw fit to bind him to that faithless wife of his and not set him hungering after you."

But Persephone had not heard Hephaistos's rare and sudden bark of laughter in an age, nor Ares's crude jokes. Compared with the mortals, their kind were but a few. Eternity was daunting enough with such a limited number of peers; reducing that number by half had her wanting to wail. A prison with spacious rooms was, after all, still a prison.

"I have no interest in the Artificer *or* the Stormer of Walls, nor they me," Persephone said. "Surely it's not necessary to keep me sequestered from *them*."

Her mother's words grew a shade darker with ferocity. "You believe you understand the nature of immortal men?" she said. "You do not. They will *ruin* you, Daughter. And for what? To satisfy their lusts? I will not have this for you. I will not."

The great and subtle voices of the mountains sang a more moveable song than Demeter's words at that moment. It was no use, and never would be.

The muscles under her eyes tightened and Persephone felt her nails making delicate, crescent shaped cuts into the backs of her knuckles.

The others were arriving in the distance, by chariot. Artemis's hound leapt to the ground and went tearing through the grass, flushing out an explosion of small birds.

Persephone wanted to explode with them.

The metallic weight of Polyxene's ring as she let her hands fall to her sides was what kept her in one piece. She inhaled. Held it. Exhaled.

"I understand," she said. "I will not trouble you with this matter again."

She felt more than saw her mother's curt nod and it took everything Persephone had to maintain her placid composure. A black tide swelled in her veins, filling her to the rim with the urge to lay waste to the fields. To draw back into herself every last drop of growing life from leaf and branch and root, and leave Nysa a rolling heap of ash.

Which of her parents she'd inherited her temper from remained a mystery, but it was this wordless gesture of Demeter's that set Persephone seething.

"Some wisdom at last," said her mother. "Perhaps your time with Athena has begun to bear fruit. Now go on." The goddess gave the basket a nudge with her foot. "Your friends are here. If I know you, by the time you've filled this, you'll have forgotten this whole idea."

But that was the marrow of the thing, wasn't it? Demeter didn't know her at all. No one did.

By the time her fists relaxed, her mother's chariot had dwindled to a gnat-sized silhouette above the hills. Persephone's gaze fell to the fate-cursed basket and she scowled.

✦

Gold touched every stem and leaf in the field as Helios the All-Seeing drove his blazing chariot toward the western horizon.

Persephone stood at the edge of a tiny stream with her eyes closed, taking in the warmth of the titan's disc, the sun turning the inside of her eyelids an amber red. The first knuckle of her right hand brushed against the second, the feel of Polyxene's ring there a continual reminder.

She sighed. Opened her eyes. Clutched in her hand was the infamous basket, bearing a shallow layer of greenery. If she'd been there alone, there would be no need to pretend interest.

Her companions made sport far enough away that she would have to yell if she wanted their attention.

Persephone turned an eye over her shoulder to find Artemis playing games, as usual. The Goddess of the Hunt had something dark and unidentifiable in her hand, and was chasing Athena who—in a rare moment of irrationality— was shrieking in half-feigned terror and darting about to avoid her sister's grasp. A laughing circle of Oceanids cheered them on while Artemis's hound tore and leapt between the pair, wild with canine enthusiasm.

In truth, the three of them were half-sisters: Athena, Artemis, and Persephone. They all shared Zeus as a father, but a common mother was not to be found between any of them.

Of course. The Lord of Lightnings may rain on as many fields he chooses, but am I allowed one—one!—from among my peers?

Her sullen thoughts were ill-matched for the lazy serenity of the day. Would her mood be obvious to the others? Persephone couldn't see how their skies deserved darkening over *her* personal concerns.

She looked down at the basket she held by the handle. The size of a large serving platter and flat-bottomed save the slightest curve, the reed-woven burden was yet another reminder that her current state of affairs could not continue.

It in no way surprised her how little Demeter knew about what Persephone considered a worthwhile day. For the sake of appearances, however, it was best to go along with her mother's suggestions from time to time. At least if she wanted to forestall the arguments. And it was a fair enough excuse to gather new gifts for Polyxene. Not only had she failed to arrive with anything on her last visit, but she'd left with the woman's ring.

After her mother had placed her once again among female immortals—glorified chaperones, is what they were—for a day of 'flower picking' in the fields of Nysa, Persephone had decided. She would be returning to the house of the mortal healer sooner than the woman expected.

There were those who would kill and die for what Persephone had now, and here she was, ready to do at least one of those things, at some point, to be rid of it.

Of course, the fields sang with beauty. The sons of Man would swoon and compose ballads. Blossoms in white and blue and purple dotted the sweep of foothills, and the occasional grove of trees, mainly cypress, but here a cedar and there an ash, punctuated the glowing afternoon landscape.

And of course, her sisters were pleasant company, no matter how different they all were. Artemis in particular. The goddess's sense of adventure always spurred Persephone to attempt feats when she probably shouldn't. Not that she had any desire to try leaping from the top of a waterfall again.

And yet here was her mother, so vigilant, so concerned. The goddess expending vast reserves of energy to harass, bribe, or bore the gods out of her presence. Demeter walked the eternal fields confident her daughter remained a maiden, untouched. Perfect. Artemis, her closest friend didn't know. Athena—astute as she might be—didn't know. They all rolled through the ages under their pretty illusion.

Among the cities of men, as she'd been doing since shortly after Demeter's unprecedented edict had gone into effect, Persephone had allowed her resentment to bubble into one of the best kept secrets on the immortal plane.

No, the Goddess of Growing Things was no maiden.

If her mother had an inkling of what she'd been up to on her last visit to Smyrna—or Argos, or Kornithos, or any of the others—well … there were only so many nightmare scenarios she was willing to entertain.

It was one thing for Persephone to resent her mother's interference. Any of her immortal companions could have explained her ill temper away with such an obvious irritant. Which of *them* would be content with their choices forfeit?

It was because Demeter professed to care about her *so* much. Because the Goddess of the Seasons was willing to hide her daughter away, while at the same time knowing so little about her. Her mother was oblivious to reality. Persephone's increasing boldness in her travels to the mortal plane were proof enough.

When Demeter sent her to play in a field like a child, with the naïve belief her daughter was well under control, it made Persephone's eternal golden blood boil. And it would go on and on, wouldn't it?

All the more reason to return to Polyxene.

Artemis had given up her chase now, and she and Athena had collapsed on a grassy incline to stare up at the fierce golden sky. Athena pointed to something overhead, some bird or cloud perhaps, and Artemis nodded in agreement. The Oceanids had wandered toward a point further downstream to dip their feet in the clear water. Her companions allowed her and her peevish temper plenty of space.

Can you blame them?

She brought a hand up to shield her eyes from the sun and surveyed the field once more. There had to be *something* out there worthy of her time.

And so there was. She never knew if she was simply adept at prediction, or if these things manifested themselves from her thoughts. Either way, just beneath the gentle rise of a hill to the west, a bloom stood out on its own. A lone green stalk topped by a vast number of yellow blossoms.

Narcissus. Perfect.

Poison, certainly, but also medicinal with the right preparations. A rare and exceptional gift. The thought of Polyxene's inevitable clapping hands made her smile.

Persephone stepped across the stream and made her way toward the lonely flower, her path heading straight into the blinding arc of the setting sun. Her bare feet pressed into damp grass and dark, loose earth with each step, and she angled her body forward now to compensate for the subtle incline.

As she neared her goal, a perfume grew heady on the air. The narcissus? It had to be, but it was strong. She found herself swaying in place and had to stop and lock her knees for a moment to ward off a stumble.

Sweet Fates, this thing is potent!

A treasure indeed, for her mortal friend. Had she ever come upon one like this before today? Was the near giddiness jangling her nerves an effect of the beckoning scent, or merely excitement at a potential discovery?

At her arrival, dozens of yellow blossoms burst open at the crown of the stalk, each with six-pointed petals arranged in a star around proud trumpets. She bent to inhale from the source and had to put hands on her knees to keep from swooning.

If Polyxene bottles this, she will earn her fortune.

Persephone laid down the basket and, righting herself, began to tug at the stalk, ready to pull the whole thing up, bulb and all.

The narcissus remained stubborn and so did the goddess. She persisted and it resisted, as willful a pair as there ever was. She was about to give over and borrow a blade from Artemis to dig her tenacious adversary out of the ground, when she felt it. The faintest of rumblings, under her feet.

Then: chaos.

A sudden jolt.

The hillside spasmed, horseflesh beneath a swarm of summer flies, and Persephone tumbled, scraping hands and knees.

An awful grating of stone welled up from the deep. Eyes rolling wild, she turned to her sisters but ended up looking at sky. The land convulsed, terrible and violent, rending the earth at her feet. Where there had been gentle hills, a gaping chasm ripped Nysa wide.

She did not remember losing her footing, but as stones and clods of moist soil bounced and spun away into the yawning depths below, Persephone saw her only support.

That thrice-damned narcissus! You just had to have it, didn't you!

The defiant stalk was in her grip. The goddess held herself at the scarred rim of the earth, knuckles white, grasping at the mercy of a singularly unfortunate flower. A glance backward showed her black oblivion.

Quiet yourself. Panicking will be of little help.

She took a deep breath, and then another, slowing her heart, pushing down terror.

One thing at a time. One. Thing.

She planted her right foot on the wall of earth in front of her.

Now the next thing.

She levered herself against the freshly broken soil, testing the stability of the stalk.

It held.

With a grunt of effort, she brought her left foot up, ready to hoist herself over the edge of the gap.

The defiant narcissus chose that moment to compromise.

The bulb broke free and consigned Persephone to fate.

Her heart stopped. Then erupted in terror, her fingers clawing, desperate. She tore at the ledge and tore at the ledge, and then didn't.

The goddess fell backward for a small eternity. The afternoon sky fled, shrinking from an infinite dome to a jagged, receding crescent of light.

She almost laughed through the horror.

You did this, Mother. This is what happened when you tried to protect me.

And poor Polyxene. She would never get Iacob's ring back.

Persephone fell and fell and fell. A swallowing darkness separated living from dead, thought from form.

For a time, she thought no more.

✦

Hades stood at the base of the chasm and watched his intended struggle with the narcissus. He watched the Fates give her to him; watched her tumble from her home above the earth. A patient hand rested on one tall wheel of his chariot, and a harnessed pair of black mares waited with him.

Persephone fell and he was there to catch her. He scooped her unconscious form from the last of its plummet with a swing of his arms, reducing the impact as he cut her fall short.

What Hades was not prepared to shield himself from, however, was his first glimpse of the goddess, Persephone.

Whatever tentative plans he'd thought he had burned away like so many shadows before the path of Helios. Hades was in unfamiliar territory.

Immortals came in all sizes and forms: homely, handsome, hideous. He'd prepared himself to receive any manner of goddess into his realm, despite Aphrodite's assurances. *You won't be disappointed, Polydegmon*, she'd said with that smirk of hers.

But this? This might be more than he knew what to do with.

Persephone lay draped over his arms, her knees in the crook of one of his elbows, her neck in the other, head lolling back, unconscious. Such was the consequence of a direct passage into the Underworld from the Earth above, rather than entering his realm by the more customary and gradual means across the Styx. Kharon would not approve.

It was not her limp body that gave him pause, however. No, Hades swallowed to wet his throat for a more unexpected reason.

Here, in his black grip, was the embodiment of divine creation itself—at least if the Lord of the Dead were to try to describe such a thing. Petal pale skin all but glowed, even this far from the light of the sun. A dark waterfall of hair spilled over his arm, framing a face which—even at rest—compelled rapt attention from an infamously cynical god.

Her eyes were closed, the black fringe of her lashes brushing her cheeks. What would those eyes look like? Would they be light? Dark? Would they dilate with fear at the sight of him? He wanted to shake her. To jar her to consciousness and see for himself.

No. Control, Immortal. Master yourself.

It was true. How would he retain power if their first interaction consisted of him staring down at her, slack-jawed, like some awestruck Son of Man?

Reining in his urge to rouse her for the moment, Hades allowed himself instead the indulgence of gathering the goddess higher against his chest. He lowered his face between neck and pale shoulder and inhaled.

Damnable Fates, what have you brought me?

Had the scent of springtime ever been known in the Underworld? All things dewy and green flooded his senses in that one breath. It was as if Persephone was made of budding life itself, the antithesis of all that went on in his realm.

Something small and dangerous flared to life beneath Hades's ribs, and he clutched her body close. His thoughts began to spin with unspeakable possibilities.

A stone skittered across the rocky ground.

"What foolish thing have you done, Clymenus?"

Kerberos padded toward him out of the darkness as Hades ripped himself out of his reverie.

As always, he heard the ever-surly guardian's voice in his head. Far easier for the great beast to form words by thought than with its three canine tongues. And what better way to taunt Hades than by greeting him with one of his epithets: *Notorious*.

"A god cannot fulfill his desires?" It was not the entire reason for Persephone's presence, but Hades couldn't resist the amusement of needling the guardian in kind.

"A Deathless One may rut any mortal bitch he chooses, and sire pups as he will. Why bring an immortal female here? You will roll in the stink of complications."

He shook his head at this admonition. Kerberos was right, of course, as he often was in that uncanny animal way of his.

Hades was, without question, the lord of his realm, yet he could hardly call Kerberos a servant. The imposing hound and he had cultivated a mutual respect, but unlike the dogs of men, the Guardian begged at the heels of no master. Of a height with Hades himself and nearly as old as the shores he patrolled, groveling before even a god would be laughable. Each was loyal first to his duties in the realm of the dead, and an easy familiarity had grown between the two from ages at work under the same purpose. Calling it a friendship, however, would be carrying the sentiment a bit far.

"There is more at work here," Hades said, "than a desire to 'rut', Kerberos. Unfortunately, matters are *already* complicated. Olympian complications are exactly what has brought this female here to me." He turned with his explanation to lay Persephone across the floor of the chariot, taking care not to jolt or bruise her. "Barring interference from any injured parties above," he continued, "she is to be my ... my mate, if you will."

He'd almost said 'wife', but that was a thing of Aphrodite's wishful imagination. Demeter's daughter would never speak the vow of her own will. Not to the Lord of the Dead. And 'mate' was closer to something the Guardian might understand than 'lover'.

Kerberos snorted, one of his three heads shaking itself with dour mirth. The sound of flapping ear leather echoed along the crevasse. *Sometimes I think you immortals are as soft in the head as the humans when it comes to mating.*

The horses stamped and chuffed in the presence of the great hound, their liquid eyes rolling with unease. Hades needed to be away from this place before the added disturbance woke Persephone.

"Why have you come here, Guardian?"

My eternal charge, what other reason? I felt the rift open between realms. Kharon and Minos had not seen you, and the breach was significant. It falls to me to ensure no soul gets out. Or in. At this last, Kerberos cut at least two pairs of disapproving eyes at the goddess.

Hades lifted a brow at the beast. "And are you satisfied now that all goes on with my knowledge?"

Perhaps a poor choice of words, Unseen One, but yes. I see our realm shifts at the whim of its ruler, and not some external force.

"A relief, I'm sure." Hades pronounced each word with all the slow weight of his annoyance.

The Guardian ignored his peevishness, as always. *I'll leave you to your female, then. I must return to my place at the river.* Kerberos turned his heads as one and trotted away into the darkness, his attention for the affairs of gods disappearing as smoke in a breeze.

Hades turned to calm the mares with pats to their arched necks and a few murmurs of reassurance, but the goddess lying unconscious stole his focus. He could see the shallow rise and fall of her chest as she slept, her lips slightly parted. His placement of her in the chariot had rucked up her skirts to reveal a length of pale thigh.

So vulnerable she was here in the Underworld. So exposed.

Yes, the Underworld.

A molten hunger welled up from somewhere as abyssal and deep as time. Everything in this realm belonged to him, from the waters of the Akherôn to the very souls of the mortal dead.

Everything.

✦

The scent of wet stone was the first thing to tell Persephone she was awake. Something soft lay under her prone body, and she tried to crack her eyes to see, but the lids were swollen as though she'd slept for an age.

She rolled to her back and rubbed at her eyes with drowsy knuckles, blinking at last into a dim, diffuse light.

Everything was grey.

Her head fell to the side and she saw violet. *Not everything.* Violet and red. And black. An orgy of cushions supported her, somehow sinister in their opulence. As she pushed herself up on unsteady arms, Persephone saw the grey was stone. Everywhere. All around.

Where in the three realms …?

Panic stretched and began to wake alongside her. She levered her body out of the sea of pillows to stand. Arms clutched to her waist, she turned to find the unexplained nest atop a knee-high platform of still more grey stone.

This is not Nysa.

Persephone made a slow pivot on one heel to survey the space and understand just how much the sunlit field this new place wasn't.

The cushioned platform fit in the contour of a wall at one end of a long, ovoid chamber. Floor, ceiling, and walls all met with irregular curves, as though the cavity in the rock had been grown, rather than built.

This is not my mother's palace.

She paced the room to investigate on careful feet—sandals intact, she noted—as though the slightest misstep might spring some trap. Her heart reported a thudding tattoo.

Overlapping rugs, plush and patterned, lined the floor. At the opposite end of the chamber from the bed of pillows, a wide slab bench in formidable granite stood alone. A pace or so behind it, a waist-high outcropping jutted from the wall like a stone shoulder blade. A basin made of the same granite as the bench sat on the ledge and, when she approached to peer in, Persephone found it contained water. The liquid surface was a still mirror for her held breath.

How am I—

Nysa.

The earth splitting wide, that awful fall. But to awaken in *this*? This … wherever?

Her focus traversed the dimly lit space. No torches bracketed to the walls? No standing braziers? No one could make light without flame except—

An immortal.

And another conspicuous absence, now that her frightened perception began to expand: doors.

Neither wall nor ceiling harbored a single opening through which a body could enter the room. The pattern of tiny vents pierced into the rock overhead might give passage to no more than an insect.

This was a prison.

Fates, what is happening?

Leaden feet carried her back to the platform and she sank among the cushions again, lost.

Which one of them had done this to her? And why?

Maybe your mother knows. Everywhere you've been, everything you've done. Maybe this is her way of—

Darkness. Black and complete.

It didn't matter where the light had come from, because now it was gone. And in its place, terror.

✦

The ambient light drew back into the surrounding stone at Hades's will, retreating before his entry like the sea before a tidal wave. It had been a long time indeed since he'd been interested in such games, but if he partook at all, it would be on his own terms. Another deathless god was on the other side of the rocky barrier, and she would see him when he deemed it most advantageous.

By means only the Lord of the Underworld could manage, he passed through the stone of his realm and into the enclosed space. The heartbeat he heard in the darkness was wild with alarm, but shot through, as well, with an intriguing thread of fury. Perhaps this Persephone would prove herself a bit more 'sporting' than the daughters of men.

The goddess sat among the cushions, feet tucked underneath her, back straight, eyes wide. Did she hope to find even the thinnest sliver of light? There would be none.

To Hades, the absence of light was simply another way to see. The ability came like the working of a muscle, over time and with repetition—something for which his counterparts in the other realms never had need.

True, he could have entered unseen wearing the Helm of Darkness as he'd done with Aphrodite, but Hades preferred the disconcerting effect the complete loss of vision would create.

"Who is here?" she asked the opaque silence. "I feel you in the room, coward."

Why toy with her? Do you wish to forfeit her tolerance so soon?

It was a finely-honed edge to walk, wasn't it, to engage in subtle cruelty for his own amusement? Could anything intended to be a marriage begin this way and survive? And yet a wedding had been Aphrodite's goal, not his.

Still, indulging his depravities with Persephone as he had with the line of mortal woman stretching back through time ... well. It was a risky gambit to say the least. Especially with a partner not so easily discarded after the inevitable end of his games.

"Did my mother send you?" she said. "Has she found some way to isolate me further?" Her voice came smoky like obsidian, yet building in upward momentum like the first green blades of spring, pushing past the ash and death of winter. The sound of it went straight to his cock.

A suitable opponent, yes?

Oh, yes. Aphrodite might have cornered him into this arrangement—this *burden*—but now, seeing and hearing and *breathing in* the arresting Daughter of Olympos, Hades forged his intentions anew.

He would take what satisfaction he could before matters became dreary. Might she tolerate his attentions? Possibly. But if she met him with horror ... Well. Resistance and fear had that potent tang he always liked, didn't they.

You could stop all this and simply explain what has happened. Let her make her own choices.

But where would be the fun in that?

And when will you again have the opportunity?

Hades turned his attention to the waiting goddess and began.

"Persephone."

He poured her name into the void, each slow syllable a stroke of oblivion. At her stifled gasp, his smile widened in the black.

◆

"Where am I? And why?"

Persephone tried to cover her start with demands. Fates be damned, she'd *felt* the presence. Why had the other's voice shaken her so?

"Well," it said. *He* said—the tone was deep, and male. And self-satisfied, she noted with a downturned lip. "You're not on Olympos, are you? Nor under the Seas."

Two of the three realms ruled out, and none of the beehive hum of mortal activity stirring on the periphery of her senses. Only one possibility remained, and it made the fine hair stand up on her arms.

"The Underworld."

The earth had opened up and swallowed her whole, and now she was beneath it. Some bizarre logic made this ring true, but it was a fact she would deal with later, once there were others to place beside it. She set it aside for her next question.

"I'm neither mortal nor dead—as far as I know. What am I doing here?"

"Oh, you will be *delighted*, Daughter of Zeus." The male voice couldn't have sounded more smug. The male *immortal* voice. "Your father has commuted your sentence of eternal maidenhood. You're here to marry, by *his approval*." Each sentence came as a shifting purr in the dark. As soon as she thought she'd ascertained his location, the sound came from somewhere else. Her eyes still sought light, but there was none.

Persephone ignored the absurdity of the word 'marriage' for the feel of her heartbeat in her throat.

"My *father*," she said, rolling the bitter taste of incredulity around in her mouth. Her back slumped, confusion distracting from indignity. "Who in the Underworld would he have …"

"You know who I am, Persephone."

The words were a deep velvet caress, so close in front of her now she might reach out and find a body with her fingertips. Her sightless eyes lifted to where she imagined he stood, and the blackness around her whispered the only possible truth.

"Hades."

All reasonable avenues eroded to dust. Every rumor she'd heard about the most elusive of the gods gibbered about her in a black, flapping gyre. And then the cushions gave under his weight.

"Exactly right." His answer came slow and deliberate, a serpentine tail coiling into place, and so close the vibration of the sound heated her ear. "Your father has given you as wife to the Lord of the Dead."

Panic rose up, but she bound it down, securing it for the rough road to come. His proximity might have made her breath hitch, but his message brought a scowl.

"Zeus hasn't the power to 'give' me as *any*thing, *Polydegmon*. I fail to believe this realm is so far removed from the rest as to render you ignorant of the nature of immortal marriage vows. Even Aphrodite had to choose Hephaistos of her own will."

Of all things, this made him chuckle, and the sound had her thighs clenching back an entirely unhelpful hum of awareness.

Male. Immortal. Forbidden.

And was he ... was he leaning in to breathe her scent? *Damnable Fates!*

"So she did, Flower of the Earth, so she did." She could *feel* his smirk. "Not a detail escapes you, I see. Perhaps it would be more precise to say he has given his blessing for a courtship."

Had there been light, she might have looked him up and down in disgust. "Is that what this is supposed to be? A courtship?"

"The Lord of Lightnings failed to define terms. It has been my privilege to do so in his place."

Persephone's hold on sobriety fled. "Why am I in the dark?" Her cheeks and the tops of her ears heated in outrage. Outrage and something ... else? *No.* "This is *your* realm, *Unseen One*, why do you hide? Is this how you earn your name?" Spite served as a distraction from the disturbing new warmth.

"It might be one of the ways, yes." That *voice* stroked her again. If that weren't enough, something came in contact with her upper arm. Persephone bit back a gasp. When what felt like a knuckle went sliding along her prickling skin down to the inside of her elbow, the start grew into a shiver.

The Lord of the Underworld is sampling me like an exotic wine.

If Hades knew how her world wavered amid the surreal, he acknowledged none of it.

"You are in darkness," he said, "so you understand who holds the power beneath the Sea and the Sky. *Do* you understand?"

There was no need to affirm the obvious. Persephone snapped at him instead.

"*Will* you show yourself? Or am I to remain blinded indefinitely?" She played a tune of defiance, loud and brash, if only to cover up a second, lower harmony trilling along now. Would he hear it anyway?

"Oh you will see me, little flower."

Hades shifted closer still; there couldn't have been a finger's breadth separating her shoulder and what was probably the wall of his chest. The space between them roiled with heat, but Persephone was frozen stiff. A whisper of movement on her left and a hand was brushing the mass of her hair behind her shoulder, exposing her neck.

Creation spare me!

"Perhaps," he continued—and had he just bent his head to place his words against her *throat?*— "perhaps tomorrow we'll have a look." There were lips dragging along the skin beneath her ear. "Would you like that? *Persephone?*" Hades growled the last of his offer low against her flesh.

He can see it! I know he can!

Her brief flirtations with Apollo and Hermes had done nothing to prepare her for the attentions of a ruler of one of the three realms. The Lord of the Dead was another sort of force, altogether. His language, his movements: they all seemed to see past every veneer.

Persephone wedged her palms between her knees to quiet herself. The inside of her lower lip knew the bite of her teeth, a warning against any sort of pathetic whimper.

Is this who you are?

Was it? Was this all the better she could do, confronted with one of her own at last?

The most infamous of the gods let out a lazy laugh, a crimson leaf floating to an autumn floor.

"Tomorrow then," he said, uncoiling from the platform to stand again. Despite her attempts to retain control through scornful words, he was leaving her with parted lips, abyss-wide eyes.

Before Persephone had time to win back even the narrowest of advantages in the moment with perhaps more questions or insults, Hades *Nekrodegmôn*, Receiver of the Dead, had willed himself out of the room, taking his unsettling shadows with him.

✦

"Why do you deceive me, Artemis?" Demeter's words for the immortal were poison darts, fired into the too-innocent breezes of Nysa.

"I may be many things," the tall goddess said, the arrows in her quiver bristling a warning over her shoulder, "but 'liar' is not among them. Perhaps you should seek out Hermes if you want to deal in those sorts of insults. We don't know where she is."

"And you, Athena, will you pretend ignorance as well?"

"I pretend nothing, Daughter of Kronos," Athena flexed irritable knuckles around the shaft of her spear, its butt planted in the field where they'd reconvened. "We've explained several times all we saw that day—it is you who refuses to listen. What reason could we possibly have to hide our sister?"

Demeter eyed the pair she'd tasked to accompany Persephone to Nysa. *Let my daughter enjoy the flowers and trees that are to her as children*, she'd said to them, *but watch over her*. Now they stood before her, in the shade of a stand of cypress, overlooking the same hilly terrain her daughter had walked only two days before, trying to tell her stories of tremors in the earth, of a great rift splitting the meadow in two. Of Persephone disappearing.

"Perhaps I should be speaking to that tawny brother of yours," she said to Artemis. "Why should I believe he hasn't convinced you at last to aid him in carrying her off?" That golden peacock had laid the foundation for her worries in the first place. Him and that silver-tongued Hermes. She saw through their games, the pair of them.

"My brother can attend to his own wooing," said Artemis, "he doesn't need any help from *me*. Tread carefully with your accusations, Goddess of the Earth. Your concern for Persephone is not without reason, but there are only so many barbs I am willing to tolerate." Artemis's jaw flexed, and the sleek hunting hound at her feet rose with the beginnings of a growl in its throat. The warning did little to blunt Demeter's questions.

"So where is this 'great rift' in the earth *now*?" she asked. "The field appears as it always has. You expect me to accept your account, but where is the evidence any of this took place?"

Athena leaned down to take up her great shield from where it leaned against her hip, shouldering it in her readiness to put an end to the conversation. Her face had grown redder than usual. "It is as we've said, Demeter. The hillside healed its own wound only moments after it tore itself in half. You may choose to believe us or not as you will—stranger events have shaken our realm in the past— but as for myself, I will stand here and bear your insults no longer."

The Goddess of War turned on her heel then and strode from the shade of the cypress. A pair of dappled grey horses tossed their heads at her stiff-backed return to her chariot.

Artemis ran a calming hand over the head and haunches of her dog, lowering its protective hackles. She hefted her bow and painted Demeter with a final assessing look. Her features softened, but only just.

"We know you speak with such fire out of a Mother's desperation, but—"

"Is that what you know? Two virgin goddesses with not a child of their own between them? So much experience, I'm sure."

"—but she is Zeus's daughter, as well. Our father is unlikely to have let any harm come to her, Demeter. I'm sure she is well, and I am sure you will discover where she has gone. If we learn anything new, we will find you."

With this, Artemis jogged away, her hound trotting at her heels, to join Athena at her chariot. Demeter watched the pair mount the cart and, with a flourish of the reins, Athena's horses thundered from the field, carrying the goddesses who should have protected her daughter with them.

Now she stood alone, knuckles popping one by one, a scowl fit to blacken acres of grain to the root carved between her nose and chin. Like everything else, she would have to take care of this herself.

This had better not be your own doing, daughter of mine.

✦

Hades made his patient way through the bare stone halls of what others might call his palace. His formal dwelling in the Underworld could claim only the most distant kinship with its cousins terracing the slopes of Olympos. Any signs of frivolity—those curtains and tassels and busts preferred by much of the pantheon—were too ashamed to even *begin* manifesting in his domain. Fripperies and distractions, the lot of them. Austerity helped him to focus.

And focus he did.

His legs knew their destination. He might will himself there, but walking allowed him time to plan.

He'd given *her* time. A whole night—as it were—for her thoughts to run rampant. More games? Hades sighed. Yes, but he did so enjoy them, didn't he?

The wall of the corridor he moved through opened on his right to overlook one of the greater caverns. Here it became more of a recessed walkway, and the molten line of the Phlegethôn glimmered far below in the dark.

Something of interest among all this sameness, hm? And why not?

How would he present himself? Simply appear in the room? Hades grimaced. No. He wanted her many things, but startled was not one of them. And how, for example, would that help if he found her asleep? Perhaps darkness again, if only to begin.

The speed at which his motivations had changed was troubling. He'd gone from irritation to lust at the mere sight of Persephone. And at the sound, the scent of her? The way she'd dared to upbraid him all while trembling away in that darkened room? Hades had moved straight past lust to something far worse.

Interest.

You have to retain the upper hand, Immortal.

The walkway tunneled back into the rock, a corridor once more, and Hades clasped fingers around the opposite wrist behind his back.

She didn't have to know what he was. Not right away. A god could take whatever form he chose, could he not? There was Zeus with all his bulls and swans, for whatever sick thrill that got him. And Hades had disguised himself as a mortal to appear to the daughters of Man on many occasions.

Perhaps some unruly golden curls; wholesome, tawny limbs? Blue eyes like one of the sky-dwellers? He smirked and only stone walls were there to see it. An entertaining choice.

Persephone might drop her guard when met with a more familiar breed of immortal. He could buy her instant ease, perhaps even ready affection. Who knew how badly Demeter's edict might have made her hunger by now? His steps slowed as he lost himself in it.

There she was, lidded eyes, parted lips, embracing her false God of Light. Hades would cast off his fair façade in the midst of it and she would shriek at the truth. The sound of it would finish him off then and there.

And after? What then?

He turned left down the last of the vacant hallways and exhaled, shaking off the remaining images of a mere few moments' amusement. Since when did he fail to consider the long game?

The idea of Persephone's submission was tempting, her dread a useful tool with which to bargain—if that was the way the wind blew once she saw him—but everything between them would be clear and straightforward.

To entertain fantasies of trickery? Was he no better than Hermes, that flighty charlatan? No. Ruses and tricks were mere sleight of hand, and even the audience knew them for lies. The real sorcery lay in honest, naked power, which enthralled without doubts or dispute.

And one of your own kind deserves better from you, Clymenus.

Yes. He would show her his truest self, physically and otherwise, and judge her reaction. This was no delicate mortal he prepared to sport with: this was a goddess. She had earned, at least, the respect of sincerity.

He came to an iron glyph set into the deep grey of the corridor wall. A circle above a crescent, bisected by a cross: his personal mark stretched an armspan wide, gleaming against dull surroundings. On the other side of the stone was the first challenge Hades had looked forward to in a very long time: Persephone.

✦

The light Hades left behind might have been worse than its absence at their first meeting. It forced Persephone to relinquish denials, to confront reality.

She walked the length of chamber, restless after a fitful sleep of indeterminate length. Who could account for time without Helios or Selene riding the skies overhead?

So. The Underworld.

She was in this place at the blessing of her father and the will of a monster—or so other immortals were wont to name the Lord of the Dead down here in his hidden realm.

A monster whose words had curled against her skin under the veil of darkness, whose voice had taken license with her body's reactions where she gave none. Persephone's arms condensed around her in a shudder. The way he'd established power, blinding her in shadow ... Was it fear that made her cringe? Or something ... worse.

But why necessarily worse?

Why, indeed. Her knowledge of Hades came only from whispered tales, passed among gods and men alike as so much contraband.

Harsh. Cold. Unfeeling. His reputation on Olympos hardly spoke of a desirable partner. Her mother would be ... horrified? No. There were no words hyperbolic enough for what she would be. Zeus had to have given permission without Demeter's knowledge, but why? Why now, after all this time?

Persephone went again to the basin on the ledge, taking up the cloth and wetting it to scrub away dirt from her fall yet another time. Any traces were imaginary now, but between nerves and a severe limit on distractions in the sparse chamber, her obsessive cleansing knew no difference.

Why had Hades chosen *her*, of all the goddesses to pursue? He wanted to … to *court* her? Persephone made a little *huff* of disdain in the silent space. What sort of courtship started with an earthquake and proceeded to imprisonment? And, more important, could she escape if matters became more ridiculous than they already were?

She stopped her scouring and pacing long enough to stand in the center of the room. As she'd tried several times already, Persephone reached within to touch that part of her godhood so inextricably tied with every growing thing in the realms. She let it fill her, churning and green and immense, and cast it up and out through the rock surrounding the chamber.

Again, she felt nothing. The will of living growth was enough to push apart stone and, amplified by an immortal, could have served to wedge open a crevice into the sealed space. The beginnings of a way out, if only she could find it.

Persephone had never experienced such an absence of life. Not a stem, not a root, as far as her will could reach.

And what did you expect? This is the realm of the dead.

The Underworld was either too far below the surface—if indeed its location was as literal as all that, which she doubted—or divine abilities flowed by rules of their own in Hades's domain. Either way, it was one more failsafe she couldn't rely on to—

The ambient light fled the room. Again.

Something almost imperceptible had changed in the quality of the air.

He was with her.

"In the dark again, are we?" Did she sound as jaded as she hoped? Anything was better than nerves, weakness.

"For the moment."

"You promised yesterday to show yourself. What has changed?"

"I said *perhaps*." His voice was moving, but in which direction she couldn't tell. The space, along with its lord, was playing tricks. "You've had a night to change your mind," he said. "Are you certain you wish to see?"

"Games," she spat. "Does my Lord Hades still intend to court me for a *wife?*" She heard his hum of amusement at her insinuation. "Then face me, *Nekrodegmôn*. The Sons of Man have managed to do *that*."

"Hah!" Her challenge earned a bark of laughter. "Very well. Meet your fate, Persephone."

In the space of a breath, he restored the light to the room.

The gods of Olympos were, with few exceptions, a tanned and golden lot, or sometimes sanguine and ruddy, depending on temperament. They spent their immortality basking in sea or sky, kissed by the light of Helios.

Hades, Lord of the Dead, was *not* a god of Olympos.

Before her stood a figure so pale it might as well have been carved from marble. If it wasn't for him speaking to her moments ago, Persephone couldn't have said whether life flowed in his veins at all.

Despite the chilly façade, Hades stood with a casual smirk, inviting her continued scrutiny. One muscled forearm rested between the prongs of his infamous bident; the rest of his weight centered on the adjacent leg. The phrase 'body of a god' was not lost on Persephone.

He might have said something then, but whatever part of her heard him was subordinate to the part of her that was staring.

That Hades was the color of a thing grown underground only made sense when she considered the realm he called home. What she couldn't explain away, however, were his extremities. They looked as though he'd dipped them in ink and his limbs had absorbed it like a sponge. Hands and sandaled feet were the deep grey of doused coal, and the dark coloring crept up to forearms and knees until it faded away to match the rest of him. The stained flesh had a lustrous quality about it that brought to mind the skin of a snake. Persephone slapped away an urge to reach out and sample its texture for herself.

You embarrass yourself. You don't need to touch everything.

He arched a midnight brow in her direction. "Do you wish for darkness again, Green One?"

No, there would be no mistaking Hades for any of the others. Not even the slightest chance.

"Lord Hades," she said without breath, "I don't—that is, I've never seen—"

You're stammering now? Are you a mortal spying their patron at a temple? Fates!

"Stilled that salty tongue of yours, have I? Come, now, you've nothing to say?"

Persephone snatched up her wits like a fumbled weapon. "You intended to shock with your theatrics, yet now you're cross when you achieve your end?" This earned her a smirk and a subtle dip of his head, which only served to further irritate her. "Why, then," she said. "Why me? Because I'm the *one* daughter of Olympos forbidden to any of the other gods?"

"You know, I'd never thought about it from *that* angle before, little flower." Hades flashed white teeth. "Forbidden fruit *is* sweeter than all the rest, isn't it?"

"Be careful you don't bite into the apple of discord," she said, folding her arms in front of her breasts.

Did his grin widen at that? Was he *enjoying* her rude mouth?

"I shall attempt to look before I bite, goddess," he said, "but no. You can thank Aphrodite or perhaps even Hermes for your 'invitation' to my realm."

"Vague is not a color that suits you, Rich One."

"I suppose not," he said, "but I do enjoy watching your lovely face twist around."

She blinked at him, unimpressed, and congratulated herself on not turning a violent red at such a comment. Hades continued.

"It's all one big vicious circle, you see." As if to illustrate, he hefted his bident mid-handle, cutting a practiced swath through the air, like the arc of a scythe. It condensed at the end of the stroke into a bulky iron ring, which he popped onto a finger.

"Hermes tried to court you," he said, beginning a leisurely pace around the room, "and Demeter wouldn't allow it so she hid you away. I'm sure you're more than familiar with *that* part of the story, yes?"

She eyed him in silence as he moved off to her right.

"Once your mother denied him," Hades went on, hands clasped behind his back, "our fleet-footed friend has been pining for you ever since. You'll have to give him credit—the Messenger normally has the attention span of a gnat. Well. You can imagine Aphrodite was none too pleased with her lover's wandering eyes. Rather glorious a concern, when you think about it."

Persephone refused to turn and watch him as he walked behind her, but she imagined those eyes glittering in dark mirth at this notion.

"What does any of this have to do with me?" she said to the cushioned platform.

"Ah, this is where the Goddess of Lust asked me to 'remove' you from the equation. And now, here you are." He arrived in front of her again and spread his hands. "The beauty of it is, if Demeter hadn't bothered to make an unobtainable prize of you, Hermes's favor would have wandered back to Aphrodite by now on its own. Your mother thought to save you from the gods of Olympos, but delivered you to the most hated of us instead. Poetic, don't you think?"

She might have thought so, were it happening to someone else. And would that smile have been ... *handsome*, if she weren't so unnerved?

Handsome in the way of a tiger, before it leaps at your throat.

"How would Aphrodite convince you to do such a thing, if the idea wasn't yours in the first place? You don't strike me as the sort of immortal whom others lead about by the nose."

"Yes. Well," he said, smoothing a hand over the top of his head. "I owed her a favor." The curtain of his hair shifted under the idle motion to fall back over his shoulders. Like his oddly colored arms, it grew silver from the roots, but was inky black by the time it reached its end. Her fingers might run through it after a—

Stop it! Fates!

The rational voice in her head brought the thought to heel, but the dangerous, unpredictable part of her only unleashed new ones in its stead. The part that sent her in heat down to the cities of men had begun walking a curious circle. A lion discovering a wounded antelope.

The Lord of the Dead was not the only immortal in the presence of someone forbidden. Who was in the Underworld to enforce her mother's edict? No one. And here was a god who claimed an interest in courtship, however unlikely. Persephone took in fine limbs, an arrogant smile. Shoulders and chest, deep from … from what? Wielding that bident?

What would he be like?

No! Enough!

"And how did you come to *be* in the goddess's debt?" she said through a tight jaw, trying to steer her questions back on course.

Another low chuckle, but his eyes were on something distant. "I think that will remain a story for another day." He focused again and Persephone did her best to hold her ground as he stepped toward her.

"Why would my father allow this?" she said, bold notions fleeing where her body refused. "My mother will be a tempest when she finds out."

"There was no reason for him *not* to allow it," Hades said. His hand rose to separate a sable lock from the bulk of her hair and examine its texture between a thumb and forefinger. Persephone swallowed. "Zeus is more familiar with my nature than most. He sees that I would not be an unfitting husband, despite the exaggerations the others spread about me. It isn't for Demeter to decide, really. You've long been of age. She cannot keep you sequestered against your will, indefinitely."

"Oh? Because it's your turn to bind me away now, is that it?"

This earned her a throaty noise of amusement; a joke to which she wasn't privy. His steps took him slowly around her while Persephone stood stiff and still. The question loomed large, as it had since his arrival.

"What is it you expect me to do?" she said.

Hades completed his circuit. Eyes as black as the night of a new moon looked down into hers and infinity spun away into their depths. She saw there possibilities both sublime and terrible.

"I expect you to *obey*, Persephone."

Her breath caught, suspended at a lungful. The silence stretched. An unblinking stare worked to remake her world, and in it she read volumes. Realities to which she did not want to give name.

"And why," she said, "would I do that?"

"Because you wish to *leave* one day."

To leave? He intends to ...

The furious labor of her heart began to drown out all else.

"You don't recall me visiting Olympos much, do you?" he said, closing the short distance between them. "That's because I am not a god who wastes time in gilded palaces, drinking and feasting. Gossiping. No. I am a listener. I observe. I plan."

Much like the lords of the other two realms, Hades stood at least a head taller than Persephone. She had to tilt her head back to meet his eye, and swore a silent oath over the obvious imbalance of power this mirrored.

He drew the knuckle of his first finger over her collarbone. Something akin to panic rose in her chest, but it did not make her want to run.

"Because I observe," he went on, "I can see that once Demeter discovers your whereabouts, and how you've come to be here, she will petition your father to have the matter 'remedied'. He will deny her at first, but your mother holds more power than he would like to believe. Zeus might be king among us, but he will relent, I know him."

The ghost of a touch had made its way to her shoulder now, drawing her eye as it went. Onyx nails extended just past the tips of dark fingers, serpentine, claw-like. He ran one down the side of her arm and she hurtled toward a precipice.

"You'll be sent for, Persephone. Probably that imp, Hermes, will come with demands from Olympos—he knows his way in and out of my realm better than any of the others. Whether I release you to him is another matter entirely."

Her eyes jumped back to meet his. *Creation take me, he can't be serious.*

"Those are your choices, Daughter of Zeus." His face was very close to hers now; his words painted her skin. "Abide by my wishes for a time and return to the upper realms. Or"—he shrugged with a dangerous elegance—"do neither."

Arms snaked around her shoulders. There were palms gliding down her back to catch her at the waist, to crush her to his chest. Persephone angled her head back to read in the lines of his face a single hungry purpose.

Possession.

She saw the edge of the cliff in her mind, in his eyes. *Fates, this is it. It's happening. Now.*

Hades brought his mouth to brush over hers and it was not cold, as she'd expected from the Lord of the Dead.

It was fire.

He spoke his damning words against her lips: "Will you obey?"

Without waiting for a response, Hades seized her in a kiss.

Liquid heat surged through every extremity, welled in every junction, lit every nerve aflame. Her upper lip felt the sliding invitation of a tongue and, consequences scattered to the abyss, she opened to him. He growled at this and pressed his advantage, exploring, savoring. Persephone had a taste for him now: warm and faintly metallic.

... a darker, more wicked partner ...

The thought she'd dismissed at Smyrna came bubbling up to confront her. A small noise of recognition rose in her throat and, pressed close as they were, she felt Hades's body respond. He sealed off the kiss with a nip of his teeth before pulling back to take in the turmoil he'd wrought. There was no hiding her flush, her parted lips.

Persephone stood reeling. He'd already begun to take from her without permission: his mouth on hers, his hands still at the small of her back. His very kisses seemed to know her every humiliating, unrecognized need. Why bother seeking her assent at this point?

But to speak the words aloud? There would be no turning back.

When he'd caught her against him, her hands had come up in a gesture of defense and there they'd remained: palms against his chest, fingers curling against the black of his chiton. It was a posture of resistance and submission both, and she raced in her mind toward the leap from one blind height or the other.

Resist.

Or submit.

Two possibilities, each terrifying. One stood defiant, a noble exercise in futility, chin up, but at what cost? The other beckoned with a crooked finger, whispering dark promises, for the mere price of surrender.

Eyes that turned on seasons of destruction and resurrection bound her to the spot, and Hades asked her again.

"Will you obey?"

No no no No No NO NO! This is madness! You can't!

"Yes," said Persephone, turning the key in a fateful lock, "I will."

✦

III Obedience

Thunder rumbled beneath slate-bottomed clouds as Aphrodite mounted the steps to join Zeus on one of the absurdly grandiose balconies of his palace. The god snapped his wrist forward again and a finger of lightning ripped the air from sky to rain-dark soil.

"Hah!" Mighty hands went to his hips as he barked a laugh. "Look at him!"

"I'm afraid even to ask," she said, tone conversational at her approach.

"Mm?" He turned to see who joined him, orange chiton rippling in a breeze of his own making. "Ah. Goddess. Not much that's more entertaining than a startled mortal, eh? That last one almost fell off his horse."

"You're terrible." She shook her head, suppressing a grin.

"And wondrous," he said, surveying the landscape. "And powerful, and generous, and rude. Wise. Unfaithful. So many things besides 'terrible', if we're being honest."

"Oh, now stop, or I won't have any names left to call you." Aphrodite placed her hands on the white marble of the balustrade, enjoying the smell of damp and the subdued blue and green vista spread out to the south of Olympos.

Zeus squinted at something distant and let loose another bolt, grunting in dissatisfaction after a moment. Perhaps no one had been startled enough.

"I gave permission for him to court her, you know." He turned to Aphrodite. "Not nab her from a field like an exotic pet."

She waved a graceful wrist and made a noise of dismissal. "How else would he have had his chance with her? Her mother had her chaperoned at nearly every moment, and his powers are nothing more than a laugh in our realm."

"My realm."

"*Your* realm, my Lord."

"Demeter will not be patient," he said, flicking several electric streamers into the sea to the east in rapid succession. "She will dig, and she will discover. And then we'll *all* have to hear about it."

"Then let us hope, *Basileus*, that by such time, it shall be too late."

Silver brows descended in doubt. "If he can convince her."

"Have you no faith in lust?" The goddess's face warmed as her smile spread. "Persephone has been denied any thought of romantic 'company' for ages, and now here she is, free to test the waters, as it were. And Lord Hades is, well … *Hades*. He will persuade."

"Provided he wishes to do so."

"Oh, he will wish," she said, "I assure you."

"Who will wish?"

Like a shadow upon the lighting of a lamp, Hermes had appeared on the balcony.

Aphrodite gave an undignified yelp. The base elements of her body all seemed to fly apart and snap back together in a startled instant.

Zeus chuckled, holding a hand over his midsection. "*Im*mortals might be even more fun to watch jump in the air!"

"Sorry," Hermes said, "just popped in. Who's wishing what now?"

Her fingers rose to the emerald she wore around her neck, their touch gentle, renewing her focus. "It doesn't matter," she said. "You came all the way up here?"

"Oh!" Hermes raced an excited and instantaneous path around the balcony, returning to his spot in an eyeblink. "Have you heard? Either of you? The Lord of the Dead has *abducted* Persephone!"

Zeus cut a glare at the goddess, and she returned it in kind, sure he shared her thoughts. The greatest gossip among them was aware now.

Hades had better use every trick at his immortal disposal, and fast.

"Have *you* heard?" she said, recovering at an impressive speed. "The Lord of Lightnings has given his brother permission to court. He's down there wooing her right now."

"*Wooing* her? *Hades?*" The Messenger's eyebrows leapt. "After all I offered, you approved a marriage to *that* pale Lord of—"

"Your tongue," said Zeus. "Control it." Thunder rolled in ready irritation. "Or I'll start to think you're losing respect for rulers of realms."

"Ugh!" Hermes rolled an exasperated eye and turned in a futile circle, throwing up his hands. "I'd *just* come upon the perfect argument to convince Demeter. Now she's down there with that"—he flicked blue-grey eyes at Zeus—"Lord of the *Dead*, having the-Fates-know-what done to her."

And isn't he tempting when he's frustrated? She let the emerald be, choosing instead to admire the way his nimble fingers raked back through pale gold hair. Aphrodite would ease out that little crease of displeasure between his brows, oh yes she would.

"It's all a bit of a disaster for you, isn't it?" she said.

Hermes blinked at her, thrown from his parade of misfortune. The goddess continued before he could sidestep her momentum.

"I know the very thing we must do in situations like these."

"What's that?" Zeus and Hermes both said at once.

"Drink."

The Messenger's features arced upward in interest and Aphrodite's smile grew teeth. The Lord of Lightnings only shook his head, moving his attention back to the amusement of his storm.

"Drink?"

"Oh *yes*," she said, slipping an arm through his to link them at the elbow. "I have wine. And my palace is only just there."

"Who am I, Dionysos?"

Now there was a thought. The three of them one day? *Perhaps.*

"Of course not," she said. "You're not nearly mad enough." Her steps guided them away from Zeus and toward the ends she'd so carefully orchestrated. "Come. You can either drown your troubles or share them. Or both."

"Have I told you about the last time I was in the Underworld?" Hermes said. "You'll never believe it …" The god's attention skipped to another subject as fast as his winged heels moved him across the skies.

Aphrodite tossed an unrepentant wink over her shoulder, to which Zeus merely rolled blue eyes and turned back to his entertainments. Her challenge now was to keep all the virulent rumors Hermes was sure to spread away from Demeter, at least for long enough.

She glanced at her recaptured lover and smiled. There were ways of keeping his tongue busy.

✦

The wall of basalt between Hades and Persephone aligned itself to his will, choosing to occupy the available space in a manner that allowed him entrance to the chamber.

She whirled to face the sound of tumbling stone. Cushions scattered in her wake, bouncing from the platform where she'd been sitting with her back to him. The wide-eyed look of surprise—however fleeting before she controlled it—had Hades envisioning *such* schemes to provoke its appearance again.

The doorway knit closed behind him and Persephone nodded, composure returned. "So, that's how you come and go," she said.

His arrival in the light had been intentional, just as the darkness had been at their first meeting. Every part of his domain, down to the very bones of the earth, was subject to his wishes. She would see it and take heed.

"*Stones* part for me, little flower," he said.

The way she sat up straighter told him the unspoken question had been clear enough. "Trees grow at the touch of my fingers in the upper realm," she said with a shrug. "We all have our gifts."

Quick as shadow, this one. And impertinent. Hades all but wrung his hands. He did not, however, because his hands were full.

"So we do," he said, extending an arm in mock formality. "Goddess."

Her eyes went to the bundle of scarlet linen he offered, but she made no other move.

"What is this?"

He hefted the folded handful again, gesturing for her to take it. Irritation painted her features, but she relented, pinching the material between two fingers of each hand so its length fell over her lap. She held up a long chiton in bloody crimson, and Hades wore a ghost of a smile.

"I believe the journey to my realm was rather unkind to your other." One of her hands let go the new chiton and fingered the pale grey fabric of her old, where it held itself together by naught more than good intentions over her shoulder.

"Do you have an array of garments set aside," she said, "for all the immortal women who come tumbling into the Underworld?"

"No," said Hades, "only for you."

"Well," she said, words coming clipped at his sobering response, "thank you." She refolded his offering and lay it beside her. Hands returned to her lap and waiting green eyes held his.

And Fates, such eyes.

"You don't wish to wear it now?"

Her lips made a thin line.

Ah. She doesn't want to undress with you here.

And where was modesty when her mouth had been accepting his at their last encounter?

She hadn't fought his kiss like a frightened mortal, nor did she shrink away when he pressed their bodies close. When Persephone had agreed to obey, there had been fear, but it was only a solitary note. The overwhelming chorus singing in her gaze, her pulse, her breath, was of something Hades hadn't anticipated.

Want.

There was more to the goddess's story than 'sequestered maiden'. He wanted her secrets. He would have them.

Hades turned from her and, clasping one of his wrists in his other hand behind his back, took up an idle pace across the room. "Tell me, Persephone, when your mother decided to keep you from Olympos, were you grateful? Did you fear the intentions of the gods who pursued you?"

She made a noise of dismissal behind him. " 'Grateful' would not be the word I would use, Lord Hades."

So. He'd made an accurate guess at where to dig.

His steps brought him to the granite bench at the opposite end of the chamber. He faced her again and sat.

"And what word would you use, then?"

"I don't know what *word* I would use," she said, a sourness ripening in her tone, "but the choice in how I might deal with the Olympians should have been mine, not hers. And not yours, either."

When he'd caught her at the end of her fall, a singular sort of blinding drive had risen to place its demands. At the new heat in her words, it began to simmer again. This was *his* realm. The Goddess of Growing things would soon find he'd be making *many* choices for her. The idea she might still resist made his skin prickle.

"Stand up," he said.

Her lids closed. She let out a breath through her nose. Elegant wrists unfolded from her lap and Persephone stood. Compliance given to the letter, she waited with a blank stare.

Hades rested an elbow on his knee and cradled his chin on his thumb, curled fingers in front of his lips as he appraised her stance. The silence stretched. She began to fidget with the folds of her dress.

Test her.

He sat up straighter and bent three of his dark fingers toward himself in succession, beckoning. "Come."

A blink, but no more. Persephone remained still.

"You agreed to obey," he said. "Or have you forgotten?"

Her jaw tightened and he saw color come to her face. She had not forgotten. Hades gave a smile and shrugged, turning his palms up to show she'd left him no other choice.

Cracks spiderwebbed beneath her feet. She yelped and hopped forward as the earth fell away at her heels. Behind her now, a dark crevasse yawned from one end of the room to the other.

Persephone swore and clutched at her chiton, and Hades held back a chuckle. Did she think some horror would ascend from the pit and drag her down with it? When she risked a terrified glance back to the abyss, he knew she would not see the bottom.

The goddess turned back to him, eyes wide. He saw fear there, and anger, of course. But something richer. Far more valuable. Gold, immortal blood surged through his veins.

She wants you to save her.

He'd been the cause of her peril, but it didn't matter. Those eyes begged for protection. How was she every sumptuous flavor at once? Ever more complex than the cringing mortal women he'd tasted, by the Fates, she would be his!

"Will you come to me?" he said. "Or will I have to make you come?"

Her chest rose at the shameless innuendo. With a look over her shoulder at the alternative, she picked her way over the carpets.

Then stopped a full pace from where he sat. He ground his teeth.

Flames of creation, she might match you for obstinance.

Hades let the remainder of the floor behind her disintegrate, sending rugs fluttering to the abyss.

No hesitation. Persephone leapt without thought and pressed urgent limbs against him; stood rigid on tiptoe between his knees. The black wool of his chlamys bunched in desperate fists—anything to prevent a fall.

As she caught her breath and realized where she stood, her eyes came down to his. He did nothing to hold back the smug grin when she relaxed her grip. There was nowhere left for her to stand but in extreme proximity.

"Now." He traced nails down her arms, reveling in the first opportunity for touch. When Hades arrived at her palms, he laced their fingers together, dark and light. "What were we talking about? Ah yes, your lack of experience."

His eyes painted a licentious trail to match his words, from her thighs wedged between his, to the curve of her hips and breasts, up around her slender neck. By the time he arrived at her eyes, only one word swelled in his mind.

Devour.

She was so … so …

Consume. Possess. Own her. You must!

Perhaps more than one word, then.

He inhaled. Exhaled.

Control yourself, immortal.

Hades moved backward on the bench, creating a vacancy on the granite between his legs.

"Since we'll be here until I decide otherwise"—he tugged on her hands—"why don't you have a seat?"

He saw something break in the way she held her shoulders. Something small, almost unnoticeable, but with it came resignation. Persephone extracted her fingers from his, turned, and sat. His thighs knew a delightful pressure from the body they now surrounded, but the goddess sat upright, arms folded once again. She would make him work, but he would enjoy it.

He leaned forward, hands on his knees, making contact between her back and his chest unavoidable. This close, her scent rose to him, woody and damp, and he fought to remain collected.

"I think I may disappoint," she said, ignoring his attempts to fluster her. "The prize you hope to claim has long been given away."

"Oh? And what prize is that?"

"A *maiden* goddess for your bride."

"So your mother *didn't* hide you away in time. A rumor proves false," he said near her ear. "Interesting. It wasn't Hermes, of course. Apollo then?" That pretty face and regal manner—Phoebus may have had enough to succeed where another hadn't.

"No," she said, and now he could *hear* the clever smile. "My mother has been as vigilant as any gossip you've heard, I'm sure. No immortal has managed to touch me."

His brows rose to look for the rest. "And yet ..."

"Demeter spent her efforts keeping me out of Olympos. She paid no attention to my travels among the cities of *men*." The last word carried a note of triumph. She thought to deny him some thrill, did she? Dampen the heat of his conquest? She would find herself mistaken.

"So," he said, sweeping her hair away from her neck, "you're familiar, then, with the things a man will want of you?"

"Oh yes," she said, ignoring his tactics for her own. "Athenai. Thebes. I know their streets. The sons of man have amused me for ages."

"Have they." Hades shifted closer. "I wonder how that compares," he said, "to what a god will want from you?"

"I imagine if they're anything alike, the amount of fuss my mother has made has been all out of proportion."

He couldn't help a chuckle at this.

You've never taken an immortal lover, either.

It was true. He had satisfied those urges he couldn't meet on his own by ascending to the mortal plane to play out his lusts with the daughters of men. Disguised as a handsome mortal, he could convince and coax; make them giggle and squeal at his touch.

Or, during darker moods, he would show himself for who he was: Hades, Lord of the Dead. Their cries and pleas to the god they feared filled a hidden well in his soul. There were times he felt shame after such nefarious exploits.

There were times he did not.

It troubled him not to know which road he would travel today.

He turned his hands palm-up on his knees.

"Persephone," he said, "will you allow me to touch you?"

"What?" Of all things, this broke her calm.

"Will you allow me"—he let his chest slide against her back—"to touch you?"

"Why bother with permission now?" Her heart thundered through her ribs and into his.

"You agreed to obey," he replied. "I never said every *single* interaction would involve a command. Perhaps only when you need a nudge, yes?"

Why it was so important at this moment to persuade and not force, Hades couldn't have said.

"May I?"

He felt her body expand in a controlled breath. A single nod was her only answer. Restraint took every effort he had.

His right hand rose to a wrist she had tucked into her folded arms. She allowed him to tug it loose and draw it away from her breast. He did the same for the left, and hooked thumbs under both her palms, turning them to face the ceiling. With the backs of her hands cupped in his, he returned them to rest on his thighs.

Her muscles were tense; no doubt prepared for crude handling to come, but he met her with none. Her upturned, open hands rested in his, and he left them there. A more significant lesson lay in his choice.

His arms and hands would remain open, as would hers. This had happened because she had allowed it.

"Goddess."

She gave a start. Such was the point to which the moment had tightened.

"Before your mother's edict," he went on, "Apollo and Hermes sought your eye. Did you find their attentions flattering?"

"Of course"—he felt her swallow and try again, having to work hard to speak above a whisper—"of course I found it flattering. I'd never been courted and here were two of Olympos's favored sons. They had songs, they went on and on about my beauty …" She shrugged against him.

"And had Demeter not intervened, you would have considered them?"

"Perhaps to enjoy a flirtation. Beyond that?" A small shake of her head. "They weren't for me."

"Why not?"

She sighed. Relaxed into him the slightest measure. "I suppose Hermes might have made an entertaining lover," she said. "He was witty enough. And a tongue like that *outside* the bedchamber?" She let out a *huff* of rueful amusement.

Hades let his thumbs fold back over the sides of her hands. He began to trace circles in the center of each palm.

"You didn't wish to sample his offerings? Not even once, to see for yourself?"

Even from the side, he could see she made a face. "Do we have time for me to recite a list of his lovers? No, the only thing constant about that one is his ability to lose interest. And for him I have none."

So, she preferred an attention span. A mark in her favor.

"And Apollo? He was never so fickle, was he?"

"I see you leave no stone unturned," she said. "No, he might have been faithful. Perhaps."

"What was wrong with him then?" Hades made his caress into a momentary squeeze.

"Oh, nothing."

His brows rose. "Nothing?"

"He was charming," she said. "Generous. Handsome as the day is long. Everything a goddess could want." Persephone began to lean into the curve of his chest now, somehow negating the frustration her answers brought him.

"You must know how thrilling it is," he said, nuzzling the side of her face with his jaw, "for an immortal to have the goddess he's attempting to seduce sitting on his lap, listing the better qualities of his rivals."

Persephone stiffened, but didn't pull away her hands. "First, he is not your rival. Second," she said, words cutting the air, "this is not your lap, it's a stone bench. And third, is *that* what this is? A seduction? I thought you were attempting to 'court' me."

His grin widened at her fire to the point of showing teeth. "That you assume a distinction between those two things is evidence the Sons of Olympos have done you a disservice." He took hold of her hands and flipped them face down on his thighs, covering her fingers in the pressure and heat of his. "If I still have your obedience,

Persephone, I will show you what it is to be courted by a lord of a realm."

She tugged to free herself and, for a moment, he held her in place, making his point. When he let go, she drew back her hands, but once he restored his to their former place at his knees, palms turned up, Persephone surprised him.

With no little trepidation, she laid her hands back in his.

Hades steeled himself against a reckless pace.

"So Apollo was a shining example of godhood, was he?" He took her right hand and lifted it to cover her breastbone, his fingers splaying to flatten hers against her own heartbeat. "And I'm to believe you don't pine for him?"

"As I said, *nothing* was wrong with him." She gestured with her free left hand. "He was so gallant and *so* blinding bright. I'm to take someone like that seriously?" The goddess gave a shake of her head. "I can't put a name on it, but he felt ... wrong. There was no *friction*. He was so smooth you would slide right off!"

Hades let go the hand at her chest, only to come up from under her arm and seize a new grip at her shoulder. She gasped as he hauled her close, his next question low and dangerous.

"And you would have liked it a bit more ... rough, Persephone?" He laced their left hands together, squeezing to a point just the wrong side of friendly warmth.

"I ... don't know?"

Sweet Fates, could he be the one to show her?

"Tell me what your mother was so afraid of," he said.

"That you would ruin me."

Her head had fallen back onto his shoulder, the dark waves of her hair spilling over them both. She recited Demeter's fear of Olympians in general, but somehow the words seemed tailored for none but the Lord of the Dead.

"Ruin?" he said. "Oh, no. Never that." The wood fibula holding her chiton in place was just beneath his fingers. He tugged it loose and the linen fell away from her shoulder.

"Challenge, absolutely." Hades bent to press his lips against the silken skin there. "Has anyone ever tested your limits, Persephone?"

She shivered. "Limits?"

Did her imagination run in frantic circles, as he hoped?

"Those boundaries beyond which you refuse to cross." His mouth moved to the column of her throat. "When we discover them, little flower, you will tell me to stop."

Her pulse fluttered under his mouth, but her right hand had risen to rest over his at her shoulder. Hades let his teeth graze her neck, and when she hissed in response he wanted to abandon every careful plan he had.

Instead, he spanned her collarbones with his fingers and brought her back full against his chest.

"Can you feel that?" he said.

"Feel?" She sounded hazy and faraway. Was it *her* lust clouding perception? Or his?

"My heartbeat. Do you feel it?"

Two breaths later: "Yes."

He let go her left hand to trace nails along her thigh. When he met the curve of a hip, he pulled her to him at the waist.

"And this?" His arousal pressed between them. "What do you feel?"

The goddess nearly choked on her breath. "Hades!"

"That's right," he said, grinding further against her backside. "That's. Right."

Could she know how his name on her lips affected him?

"A seduction works in both directions," he said, "or weren't you aware?"

A distracted hum was all the answer he received, but she rolled her head to lay her temple along his jaw. The flushed pink of parted lips bloomed close and tempting. All traces of tension had gone from her limbs. The Lord of the Dead sat with a Daughter of Olympos draped in his arms, and she made no moves to fend off his advances.

Were he not able to feel her weight, breathe her scent, he might have written off the whole of it as nothing more than a fantasy with which to torture himself.

"I was told this was a courtship, *Clymenus*," she said from behind closed eyelids. Her backside shifted against his groin. "Or is my obedience not sufficient?"

For the love of— Is she ... is she goading me?

"Shall we find out?"

His hand rose to her nape. Fingers splayed up into her hair; made a fist near the scalp. She gasped at his pull but didn't struggle, and green eyes searched the ceiling for reason as he branded the hollow beneath her jaw with lips and tongue and teeth.

The undone right side of her chiton beckoned. A dark hand slipped past linen to find a ripe swell of pale flesh. At the cup of an assaying palm came a plaintive sound and furrowed brow. At a thumb's brush over a nipple: a whimper. An arch of her back. It would be nothing. He would only have to lift and carry her to the cushions, lay her back ...

Damn your eyes, stay with your plan!

Yes, one thing at a time. And already *such* things, why be greedy? A breast was a lovely distraction, but not the goal.

Grey fabric hid his sliding palm as it moved past ribs and soft belly to the crease where her thigh and hip met as one. From there he traced a path to her pleasure and dipped a pair of fingers into the heat of his own weakness.

She was soaked, swollen. Thighs smearing his knuckles in it. The throb of his cock demanded he do heedless things.

"Hades." It came on a ragged breath this time, the downfall of his whispered name. A plea, but not for him to stop.

Test her. Do it.

He let go her hair. Yes. It was time to measure her response to his ... 'other' inclinations.

"What happened to 'Lord' Hades, hm?" He found her left wrist in a fierce grip. "Too many distractions?" Spring green eyes flew open and he hauled her arm behind her back, trapping it between them.

Again, she could have balked. Could have yanked her arm away in livid protest. It wouldn't have been the first such reaction he'd seen.

But Persephone slid her right knee over the top of his, leaning back into his threats, defying their execution. Against his assumptions, his casual restraint had opened her further. He wouldn't waste the gift.

The strokes he painted between her legs were an art begotten of devotion and greed. Unlikely bedmates to tease out her desperate sounds, to map out the unspoken wants.

He found her entrance slick with need and curled the tip of a finger to sate it. Her moan hummed under his mouth on her throat, and he made it two, knuckles twinning in a curve, to push her.

Dusky lids fluttered and she tilted her hips, parted her thighs. Eyes born pale of Olympos turned to lock with Underworld black as he worked at razing her wits, at stealing those soft, soft sounds. It was only the beginning.

Oh, what we will make together, you and I.

As though privy to his thoughts—impossible—she raised her mouth to his, demanding. Was it only their second kiss? Now, with his hand beneath her linens, fingers wet with her lust? The nudge of her jaw, her tongue insisted, urging him to roughness. Hades obliged, bruising, taxing with teeth.

To the edge and back. Now.

He withdrew buried fingers in favor of a more obvious treasure. When he grazed it between fingertips, her gasp tore their kiss as he'd done the earth at Nysa. Panting and closed eyes met his worrying of her little pearl.

"Please."

The single word had him marble hard, and aching. From stubborn pride across the room to senseless and begging under his touch, it was more than he'd hoped for. More than he could tolerate.

"Please?" he said, toying as her brows drew together in frustrated effort.

You are cruel, Polydegmon.

True, but a small cruelty would prove its worth.

"*Please*, Lord." The titles came back as she squirmed, entreating with her hips.

Hades withdrew his hand, straightening the linen over her lap. Upturned eyes searched his, lips parted in question.

"My Lord, what—"

"Tomorrow," he said, drawing a nail under her chin.

Her features were as flushed with red as her breath was heavy with need. "Tomorrow?" she said. "You intend to leave me like this?"

He traced dark nails, glossed in her surrender, along the swell of her lower lip. "Leave you like what?" The fingers slid into her mouth. "Like you're not the immortal in power?" He couldn't hold back a predatory smile.

Persephone held his eyes and beaded the seam of his fingers with a slow lap of her tongue, a cynical lament for the pleasure he'd forsake by taking his leave. The spiteful move had him crackling with unspent glee.

She wishes to play against, *it seems, and not just play along.*

When had he given up searching for a partner like this? But Hades outpaced himself—a single interlude was but a season. They had years to explore before the story was whole.

On impulse, he leaned forward and pressed his lips to hers, internal appeals to reason doing no good at all. Was it possible he'd gotten the better end of Aphrodite's bargain?

He would see. Tomorrow.

He shook off the fog of desire and raised his palms once more. From oblivion, the stone floor rose with a rumble, restoring itself between the bench and the platform. The chamber might have never yawned in a jagged pit, for all the difference visible now. Aside from, of course, the rugs, most of which had gone missing.

Hades rose from the bench, hauling a disoriented Persephone with him by her upper arms. She stood with her back to his chest and he brushed a final light kiss over her cheek before stepping away from temptation.

In three long strides, he was on the other side of the room, a basalt doorway forming at his will. He turned to the goddess, her face aglow with furious want, unforgettably denied.

"Enjoy your last night in this room," he said. "Tomorrow we'll try something a bit more … fitting." She opened her mouth, perhaps to fling some barb, but Hades held fast to his edge.

"Good night, Persephone." He turned then and left her standing, the stone growing shut at his back. It was a necessary barrier indeed, if he were to compose himself at all.

◆

Demeter shifted her jaw and scowled out over the agora in front of her temple in Thebes. To the passing sons and daughters of Man, scurrying here and there on their mundane little errands, she appeared as nothing more than another old woman, come to leave her offerings for the Lady of the Earth.

Not one rumor, one sneeze. Athenai, Messenia, Tegea; she had scoured their places of offering all to no avail. None of the mortals she'd questioned in her gnarled body had a word to say about Persephone.

The goddess stepped from under the temple's eaves and squinted into the bright noon light. Broad, limestone steps moved away under her feet in descent and the sun painted the square in a shimmering heat that made her eyes water.

Someone had *to have seen.*

Her daughter couldn't have mastered the art of disguising her appearance; she hadn't nearly enough experience. If Persephone had run off—a far preferable reason for her absence than any of the possible alternatives—there would have been signs of her passing. An immortal on this plane would *not* go unnoticed. There would have been a swell of offerings, a rise in fervor at the sighting of a goddess, however brief.

Demeter made a noise of frustration, startling a scrawny boy as he jogged past her out of the temple. The youth eyed the crone he saw over his shoulder before dodging off into the square, the glare of sunlight watering her mortal eyes as she followed his bouncing path.

And then the Goddess of the Fruitful earth swore a violent oath.

A woman herded a tiny girl away, cutting the guised immortal a disapproving eye as she went, but a wash of cold epiphany prickling her skin was the only thing holding Demeter's attention now.

Yes. Someone *had* seen. Hadn't they.

Shadows followed the bodies of men as they busied themselves about the agora. They arced transient echoes from dawn to dusk at the foot of each beast, tree, and building. At the noon hour, they pooled at their smallest, hiding from the face of the sun.

The Sun.

Helios.

Nothing that moved on the earth could escape the blazing eyes of Helios. The titan's daily course showed him gods and men, alike. And he was infallibly honest.

He will know. He will know and he will tell me.

His chariot straddled the midheaven now. She had half a day to reach his evening palace at the River Okeanos.

Her steps carried her from the temple and away from Thebes at a pace only an immortal could set. Helios would quit his resting place at dawn, but Demeter was determined to have answers well before then.

Her own chariot awaited on the deathless plane, and her lips came into a hard line as she goaded her cattle to a westward trot.

Pray, Daughter, this is some foolish misunderstanding. Whoever has done this will surely need it.

✦

IV Restraint

Persephone found it difficult to discern direction in the Underworld without Helios's chariot arcing high overhead, but it was simple enough to see Hades was leading her somewhere far from the chamber in which she'd spent the past three days. Somewhere 'a bit more fitting' was the only inkling he allowed as to their destination, and she couldn't decide whether this was ominous or thrilling. The backs of her arms prickled, either way.

The god who thought to 'court' her for a wife—an ephemeral excuse, they both knew—set a leisurely pace through the halls and hollows of his unusual palace. His right hand rested at the base of her neck as they walked, a warning against bolting or other foolish choices, or a reminder, perhaps, of her promise to obey. Both were effective. Both summoned thoughts of where that same hand had been.

Her fury that night had been as bright and blinding as the house of Hades was not. How *dare* he leave her that way!

Yet the greater outrage Persephone reserved for herself, for allowing the fiend to draw her along to that point. The moment the rock had grumbled closed in his wake, she'd thrown her frustrated body to the cushions and taken the matter into her own hands.

And he'll never hear how you breathed his name in those final throes, will he?

She grimaced even now, as the corridor around them became a bridge underfoot, spanning an abyss between outcroppings of the structure. When she hazarded a sideways glance, he was ready with one of those smiles.

Beast! Is this it now? Is this the problem with immortals?

In her excursions to the mortal plane, *she* had been the aggressor. The seductress. Here she was something else, something that taxed her nerves.

Here, she was prey.

Was this what her mother understood? Why she'd been so determined in her protection? The way his face had been there, waiting when she closed her eyes. When her fingers had tried to recreate the intensity of his strokes, that dark gaze had come searing into her thoughts. That smirking mouth, the drape of hair over his shoulder … What further sordid things *might* he have done? The very idea had brought her climax exploding from the one direction she'd failed to anticipate, destroying with it a whole field of assumptions at once.

The Lord of the Dead was neither cold nor repulsive. She did not abhor his attentions.

She could not control her responses in his presence.

A thumb brushed over the nape of her neck and she barely avoided a gasp at the interruption of her thoughts.

He was driving her to distraction.

"Is the third realm so unnerving, Green One?"

She blinked into the cavern surrounding the stone bridge. "No, I was only wondering"—*anything! Now!*—"about those lights." She nodded to the irregular smattering of glowing shapes piercing the blackness far, far overhead.

"Ah yes," he said, pausing to follow her eyes, "the lakes."

"Lakes?" *Yes, encourage him.*

"Mortals call them 'bottomless'," he said, shifting his touch to her shoulder, "and invent all manner of wild tales." Hades cast her a sideways eye and his mouth twitched in the shadow of a grin. "If they only knew."

Persephone stopped to stare, shepherding hand be damned. "*Those* are lakes of the mortal plane?"

"Some of their lakes, not all of them."

"But ... where is the water?"

He made some nebulous gesture with his free left hand. "The mortal and deathless realms come together in odd ways," he said. "For them, they are lakes. Here, perhaps you would call them *paráthyra*. Windows."

She eyed the faraway, shifting lights, their blurred edges eerie; so many misshapen lanterns hung above nothing.

"Is it so literal, then?" she said. "Is your domain truly *under* the earth?"

"Odd ways," he said again with a shrug. "Insofar as we'd like to mark the passage of time down here, it is."

Her brows came together, not understanding.

"Did you begin to wonder how many days had passed in that chamber?" he asked. She nodded. "I discovered for myself when I first claimed this throne how a lack of measured daylight begins to drive a mind mad. You would assume such things would have no effect on immortals, and you would be wrong. But"—he cast an eye to the unlikely portals—"I was able to come to an agreement with Tethys."

"Why not Poseidon?"

"I don't bargain with the other two lords." For an instant, his voice turned grave and it was a sound that made Persephone swallow, but casual grace returned with the same speed. "But no matter. I only needed a few lakes, and our dear Tethys was happy to oblige."

Persephone had only crossed paths with the titaness once, and the ancient water mother had exuded nothing but nurturing love and care in every direction. What deal could such an immortal need to make with the Lord of the Dead?

"And those?" She pointed down now, to a lit pair of tiny orbs, ruddy and flickering above the vast cavern floor. "Another of your bargains?"

"Oh, no," he said, "no bargain. The distance plays tricks on your eyes, but those lights spring from *Enodia*. The Underworld is her home, as well, though I find it best if you don't—"

"Hekate?"

"—speak her name," Hades finished in disappointment.

The stone on the bridge ahead of them shimmered, as if under a sweltering heat. Red as Hephaistos's forge, the same twin lights whorled to life from the void not three paces from where they stood, large now, and free-floating. Nothingness condensed between them, and out of the black stepped the Goddess of the Crossroads.

Persephone's stomach lurched and, without thought, she shrank to Hades's side for protection. The god had no qualms about circling her waist with a possessive arm.

"*Enodia*," said Hades. What was that in his voice? Irritation? Uncertainty?

Hekate held up a hand and Persephone steeled herself to tolerate the motion. "I havve not come ffor you, *Polydegmon*," she said. "Though you could havve told me of thiss developmennt."

It took all of her will to make her eyes linger on the three faces of Hekate. A first so frightening it might silver mortal hair overnight preceded a second so beautiful it made Persephone's bones ache. A third, no words could describe, save they bend and shear away from the agony of effort. Each of the three slipped and slid, one becoming another, sometimes two or all at once in sickening impossibility.

The Underworld goddess stepped in their direction, the golden-red orbs floating with her.

The twin torches. So the rumors are true, if skewed.

"You havve come a long wway," said Hekate, approaching within an arm's terrifying reach. The susurration of her voice came as many-layered and hair-raising as her faces, its sibilances sliding past her ears like layers of an onion skin. Even the dark fabric of her chiton, her hair, roiled about in some disconcerting, immaterial way, as though they stood there on the bridge under drifting seas.

Eyes a match for the hovering globes burned into Persephone's for an unsettling amount of time. A moment before she abandoned courage to look away, the corners of Hekate's lips turned up in a smile. Three smiles at once, really.

And they tell us Medusa is hard to look at. Fates!

"I approve of thiss mmatch, Lord Hades," Hekate said. "You havve made a wise choice." It was a pronouncement, and he opened his mouth for some rebuttal, but the goddess spoke over him, this time addressing Persephone.

"Consort of my Lord, you may ssummon me by the call of mmy name," she said, "annd I will come to you and sserve. May your crossings be well-lit, alwaysss."

Persephone hardly had time to become aware of her blush, let alone ask questions, when the tri-form goddess vanished in a whirl of dry air and a cryptic smile.

Hades's arm remained at her waist, and she surprised herself by not stepping out of the unexpected feeling of security. The Lord of the Dead, a comfort? A long way to come, indeed. Her eyes traveled his chest, throat, and jaw, leaning back into that steadying grip.

"Consort?" she asked, meeting his eyes at last.

"*Enodia* is … dramatic," he said, shifting an errant streamer of hair away from her brow with one of those wicked nails of his. Her pulse fluttered and she cursed herself for it. "Still," he went on, "she sees much in the Realm of the Unseen. I would be a fool not to consider …"

Something in that dark gaze as his own thoughts rolled him under made Persephone ache in an unfamiliar way.

"Consider what?"

He cleared his throat, eyes focusing again.

"Regardless," he said, "I think you see now why you might avoid calling her true name." Some of the smirk had returned. "The goddess makes quite a sight for the unprepared."

Nervous laughter was the best she could do as he released her to walk at his side.

The last of the bridge joined the palace proper once more, carrying forward to form yet another corridor. Real torches guttered past as they went, Hades leading them and Persephone having to trust it wasn't to slaughter.

"I forgot to thank you," he said, trouble billowing behind as he walked.

"For what?"

"For wearing it."

There was a brush of a hand at the small of her back. Her eyes fell to scarlet linen, eddying around her feet with each step. Just like obedience, it had been another choice. Where would she find herself with her next?

✦

At the end of a wide, high-ceilinged corridor, a pair of doors at least twice Persephone's height stood closed at their approach. Panels in some dark, burnished metal she couldn't name hung with the weight of ages from hinges as long as her leg. Inlaid in milky quartz, crossing from one door to the next, was a symbol she knew from before her descent into the earth. She'd seen it carved into mortal tombs.

The mark of Hades.

It would seem he makes a habit of placing his mark on entrances, wouldn't it?

He halted before the doors and turned to her, assessing.

"Before we go further, you will recall your promise to me," he said.

How in the three realms could she manage to forget? "I recall, my Lord."

"And what did you promise?"

Of course, he would make her say it aloud. It would only drive home the point. Persephone swallowed.

"I promised to obey."

A phantom of a smile stirred that stern expression. "Yes you did."

Three words could not have weighed more.

After all his displays of bending the earth to his will, the sight of Hades taking one of the sturdy handles to open a door struck her as oddly pedestrian. He gestured for her to go first, and Persephone stepped through into more uncertainty.

The chamber beyond resonated in such a perfect pitch with the god at her side, she wouldn't be surprised to learn he'd manifested it himself.

They were standing in what had once been an active, limestone cave. As in the other chamber, a sourceless light banished shadows in every direction. There was no sign of moisture or sounds of dripping now, but well overhead, a forest of stalactites bristled, somehow both decorative and threatening at once. At least a dozen impressive stalagmites rose like sentries around the perimeter of the chamber, but the rest of the spacious floor lay cleared of formations, leveled, and polished to a low sheen.

A wide, unlit fireplace dominated the furthest curving wall. Before it sat a low table and a pair of heavy walnut chairs. Perhaps out of nerves more than anything else, Persephone clapped hands over her mouth in a laugh.

"Where do you get wooden chairs in the Underworld?" she asked. "I feel no trees here."

"You receive them as a gift." His voice, along with the sound of a door latching, came from behind her. "Perhaps an unintentional gift, but no matter. Aphrodite insisted on bringing them when she tired of standing."

"The Fair One was here?" Lust and the Lord of the Dead? In this private place? She was both surprised and not, at the same time.

Do your eyes grow greener so soon? Perhaps the god knew more about 'courtship' than she'd care to admit.

"She was," he said, "a very long time ago. It was when we made this."

Persephone turned to follow his voice and almost took a step back when she found him.

Hades stood in front of an enormous black sphere, half again his height, hovering an arm's length from the floor. It bobbed in place, the motion as subtle as breathing, and she could see their reflections in the gloss of its surface. Something indefinable in its looming presence promised and tempted, yet made her want to cower in fear.

Or was it Hades who did those things? Or both?

"What ... is that?"

"That," he said, "is the cause of your presence in my domain."

"But what *is* it?"

"It is the *Elaionapothos*."

"Oil of Desire?" She cocked her head. "I don't understand."

He smiled and held out an arm for her to approach, which she did while keeping a cautious eye on the ink-dark globe.

"At the touch of a deathless god, the Oil forms itself into that immortal's deepest desires." His arm slid around her waist as she came to his side, a confusing distraction as they faced the ominous thing.

"And this has what to do with my being here?"

Hades ignored her and leaned down to bury his face in her hair. She felt him inhale and hum an approval, his presence as intense and flustering as the hovering mass before them. He cleared his throat and returned to her question.

"The *Elaionapothos* obeys any god with the practice of its use, regardless of which realm he occupies. You feel your power weakened in my domain, yes?"

She nodded.

"Even with your abilities hobbled, the Oil will be as you wish it," he continued. "Were I to take it above the earth, or to Olympos, where *I* am naturally weak, well ..."

He shrugged, stepping away from her side. "It will take whatever form I desire."

He moved around the thing now, and it began to do just that: descending, flattening. "How do you imagine Zeus would react," Hades said, "if he knew I possessed such an advantage? Do you think he would allow me to keep it here for myself, when under my command in his realm it might be a chariot? A ship? A storm of swords?"

As he moved around the Oil, it morphed from one black version of those things to the next, as quickly as the words left his mouth, and Persephone felt her eyes widen.

A weapon like that ...

It settled into a circular, knee-high platform on the floor, as wide as it had been tall. A glossy lake with no vessel to contain it, the *Elaionapothos* now stood between them, defying logic.

"And what of Poseidon?" he asked, "Or Fates forbid, that hot-head Ares? If one of them were to discover it? I'd have half a dozen gods making plans to infiltrate my domain and seize it for themselves. Until now, there have only been two aware of its existence. You are the third, aside from myself."

"Who is the other?"

"Aphrodite."

Persephone raised her brows.

"She had a hand in its creation," he said. "I was able to draw the raw oil from deep below the earth, and she was able to imbue it with the properties of desire. Each our particular gifts, you see." Hades inclined his head. "We merged our powers into the Oil to give it the ability to read the deepest of wants. The price of her help was a favor."

Her tongue grew heavy in her mouth at this.

So. His original intent hadn't been to take a wife at all. She was here because of a blackmail demand: he could do as Aphrodite asked, or she would reveal his secret to the other gods. Her shoulders slumped the smallest measure.

Are you ... disappointed?

"See for yourself?" he said, nodding across the *Elaionapothos*.

She stepped forward, cautious. "How do I …?"

"You'll need to be touching it."

She held her new chiton away from the black oil and peered down at the thing in distrust. "*You* didn't have to touch it."

"That comes with æons of practice," he said. "Go on." His smile promised nothing good.

Or everything good.

Ignoring the screaming doubts in her head, Persephone lowered a hand to the Oil. Her touch met with a flexible resistance, firm yet pliant, and not at all the liquid it appeared. The surface dimpled like a slick, dark skin under the press of fingertips.

"It's not really an oil at all, is it?"

"Not anymore," he said, sounding far too satisfied.

Was it her imagination, or was it warming to her touch? Her eyes rose to meet his.

"Why is this in your private rooms?"

His grin widened. "Imagine a place of rest that conforms to your every desire." Black eyes glittered in suggestion. "But more important, the location of this room is known only to me. And now you, of course. No one will find this place unless I lead them here."

Which also meant no one would find *her*.

The air in the chamber between them fairly crackled with portent as they faced off across the *Elaionapothos*. Hades crossed his arms over his chest and took some silent measure with his eyes. Persephone withdrew her touch from the Oil.

He lifted his chin in half a nod. "Come here."

And it began, again. The price of her heavy bargain.

"I expect you to obey, Persephone."

"And why would I do that?"

"Because you wish to leave one day."

She closed her eyes for a moment, inhaling and exhaling, before starting around the Oil.

"No," he said. "Across."

The words halted her like a blow.

"... you will recall your promise to me."

Was it fear that tightened her jaw?

The point of no return loomed large and she stepped up to meet its threshold. What purpose would arguing serve when her opponent could withdraw the very earth beneath her feet, the light itself from the space around them? The inevitable—whatever that was—lay across, and the sooner she faced it, the sooner it would no longer be a threat.

Persephone hoisted her chiton to keep it from tripping her up, and bent a bare knee up onto the black platform. The surface held. She put weight on it. Then it didn't.

The Oil swallowed her knee, liquid long enough to close around the back of the joint. Her palm shot out to brace for a fall, to lever up and out, but the *Elaionapothos* consumed that as well, solidifying after it like clay in the sun.

Her eyes leapt to Hades, mouth coming open to match their panic. His chuckle rolled out in a wave the color of midnight, and he was no longer watching from across the platform. He was at her side.

She yanked at her arm, but the Oil held fast, gripping her wrist like a manacle while her fingers splayed and clenched, futile in the indescribable texture beneath the dark surface.

"Oh no, love," he said, sliding his left leg between hers, one angled up and mired within the Oil, the other holding out hope of supporting her upright on the floor. "I have far more experience with the *Elaionapothos*—it will respond to my desires before yours." Fingertips traced her shoulder now, contemplative. "I don't think you'll find them terribly unpleasant."

She must have made a pathetic sight, partially bent over what amounted to a bed, straining to right herself, neck craned around to raise wide eyes to the god trapping her in place. The arrangement prickled her skin.

Prey. You are prey.

The question was, did she like it?

"Hades, what do you want?"

A smile unfurled on his face. "I want you to play my games."

"Games?"

"Oh yes," he said, leaning down to curl the heat of his body around hers and speak near her ear. "The game where I take your choices away and replace them with mine. As we began last night."

She had to lock her elbows to prevent a collapse. That hold on her wrist, the way she'd splayed herself to his touch … The promise of pleasure under Hades's hands had been great, but to what further limits would he push her?

"When we discover them, little flower, you will tell me to stop."

Would he, though? No one would hear her protests otherwise, down here in this secret place. Just how much trust could she place in the Lord of the Dead?

"What is it you fear, Persephone?" His thumb brushed the back of her unembedded right hand, where it held her as upright as it could over the Oil. A caress for the prisoner. When the trembling began, did he feel it?

"You'll hurt me." She prayed the confession wouldn't put her in more danger than its absence. Hades only chuckled.

"I won't hurt you," he said, tilting her jaw toward his with a knuckle. "Not until you ask me to."

The naked impossibility of such a thought drew in Hades's kiss on the tide of her gasp. That warm mouth made her reckless, the hot tongue urged her to forget. All those delicate parts of her hummed with want by the time he let her breathe. While she reeled from the nature of his argument, a dark hand slid to her elbow, drawing it back, toppling her last vestige of support.

"Come," he said, and bore her down to the Oil without a fight.

His body covered the right half of hers, trapping her free arm beneath his weight and causing her untethered right leg to cantilever out over the edge of the platform, useless. The surface of the *Elaionapothos* molded to accommodate her curves. With her left knee crooked up onto the platform, secured in place for whatever 'games' were to come, Persephone knew her own vulnerability in the most unprecedented of ways.

Fates, I can do nothing to close him out! He will have whatever he wants!

He will have whatever he wants.

When the thought streamed by again in a different tone, she felt the heat rise in her face, and a hint of dew seep between her thighs.

Fabric tugged against her neck. Though she faced away from the god at her back, she could feel him pulling the fibula loose from her shoulder, coaxing it to release its hold on her chiton. The tension in the linen went slack and she froze, a silly attempt at prolonging the inevitable.

"Let me see you."

Did his words try to assure as he peeled away the garment? The chiton opened on the left side of her body and Hades gathered it toward him, revealing the curve of her spine, her bare bottom. The heat of her secrets exposed burned against the cool air of the room like a blush.

She heard a hiss and some other sound of barely-restrained indulgence, but caught no sight of his face, no matter how far she twisted in the attempt. Charcoal-dipped fingers slid into view over her left shoulder, only to disappear and shift the mass of her hair behind her neck. Not one veil would he leave intact.

The silver crown of his hair tilted into view, and a mouth was on her throat. A surveying palm skimmed the length of her, from shoulder to thigh, pausing to weigh breast and buttock.

If his goal was to disorient her, stirring one new sensation after the next, crossing boundaries in rapid succession, he'd done more than achieve it. And the moment her breath couldn't decide whether it wanted to come or go, the mass of his body left her.

Fabric rustled. The platform shifted beneath her.

Wha …?

Weight, once more, pressing her into the Oil. Hot weight. *Naked* weight.

Hard, muscled chest molded to her back, a heavy thigh draped over her hip, and—Fates help her—the intense heat of an erection wedged in the cleft of her ass.

"Hades." A plea to the god unseen, but for what?

That purposeful hand returned to curve over her hipbone, to pull her back against him, stretching her trapped limbs against the hold of the *Elaionapothos*, so he might grind the promise of his lust into that warm press of flesh.

"Hades!"

She'd found no such heart-fluttering confusion on the mortal plane. Not once.

"I enjoyed the pretty sounds you made last night," he said in that voice that turned her wrong-side-out. Some of the pull abated, but only for the gripping hand to snake over the swell of her backside, down between her cheeks. "Do you have more of them for me?"

Fingertips brushed pouting lips; slid into moisture. Persephone whimpered.

"It seems you do."

His touch was everywhere, kneading, pinching, sliding. Each stroke carried with it instruction; Hades *Nekrodegmón* teaching her body to beg.

And beg she did.

Forsaking all pride, Persephone tilted her hips, eager to learn. Somewhere behind her, a male rumble of lust thrummed against her spine. A pair of slick fingers curved and her teeth closed on her lower lip, reining in a moan. In her mind's eye, she saw it: those dark knuckles, glossy and wreathed in the pale pink of her sex. Sweet pressure built in a way she wanted to both squirm away from and toward at once, insistent fingertips pushing firm and deep into the sticky meat of her fruit.

She made *every* sound for Hades. Some involuntary, some humiliating, and some she didn't know she *could* make.

And then the fullness subsided, along with his touch.

Again? Again, he will deny me?

"Please."

"Please?" A kiss marked her shoulder blade, and she could all but feel the mocking smile. With her neck twisted as far as it could go, his profile only just darkened the line of her sight.

"Not like last night, my Lord," she said. "Please."

Listen to yourself!

"Do I have something you want, Persephone?"

The pads of his fingers settled over swollen flesh, warm and still. Torture. She rocked against his touch, shameless. "Don't."

"Don't what?" His words were a breath on her ear, and everything ached with need, straight through to her bones.

"Don't leave me."

What? Why would you say something like that?

Quiet laughter answered like steel over stone. "I think that's the least of your troubles," he said, making no moves to satisfy. "Tell me, Daughter of Olympos, if your hands were free, would you cure your own ills?"

She whined at the truth of it. Until he chose to let her up, the hunger would go unsated. Hades was undeterred.

"Have you done so already? Here in my domain?"

Persephone nodded, the bite on her lip becoming painful. Was it Hades making her want to offer up her secrets? How far did his powers in this realm extend?

Her hips wriggled for friction.

"Are you in need again?"

"Yes!" She wanted to cry! *Fates!*

Hades chuckled. "I'd make you ask me, but another game for another day, hm? Your body pleads sweetly enough."

Her moan of relief mirrored sounds of pain when his fingers returned to work. He settled for no longer than a moment on any single approach, each lasting until she began to tense before it gave over to the next in a disorienting bazaar of pleasure.

The fervor built. Her eyes couldn't stay open, but purple and white lights banded behind fluttering lids. Nonsensical sounds bubbled in her throat as she jerked like a blind thing, seizing.

The throbbing came at intervals, and those intervals decreased. Faster, faster, that florid pulse thundered a crescendo in her ears, her sex, until there was no silence between its ruddy beats at all.

It overtook her.

There was nowhere to hide, no way to delay, held wide and fast by the *Elaionapothos* as she was. Her mouth came open to choke on the enormity of feeling, the helpless rush as she surged her completion around Hades's fingers.

Even before the convulsing subsided, Persephone knew the pang of a terrifying truth.

It will never be enough. This. Him. Never.

A hand was smoothing hair away from her face, kisses made tracks up the damp line of her neck. Her muscles were limp and euphoria rang in her ears. For a time, there was nothing but the sound of her slowing breath and the Lord of the Dead petting her cooling skin with a feather's touch.

When the silence broke, it was with his voice and, at the same time he shifted against her back, she remembered he was very naked.

"Tell me the truth, Goddess," he said. "Have the Sons of Man served your needs?"

There was something about the question more intimate than the cries he just pulled from her body. It was a truth no other knew, save perhaps, in some small part, Polyxene. And what about him kept compelling answers?

She shook her head. "They haven't."

He moved again, higher, almost caging her upper body with his. She could see his face now, and those black eyes held her as surely as the *Elaionapothos*.

"We have something in common, you and I." Hades traced a thumb over her lower lip. "We've tried to slake our desires on mortal flesh and skill, but it hasn't quite satisfied, has it?" Another tiny shake of her head.

Part of his very presence uncoiled her instincts to defend or prevaricate; charmed them into a placid line, the subdued and weaving will of a snake. It was a dangerous lull—she might answer anything. Agree to anything.

"Let me share with you my own truth, Persephone," he said. "I have known no immortal flesh."

How naïve does he imagine me?

"You're the lord of a *realm*."

"I've made it no secret," he went on, "though I doubt anyone on Olympos bothers with talk of *me*. Not when *your* maidenhood has been such an intrigue all this time." His smile curved and grew, teasing with the lines at the corners of his eyes.

"But Aphrodite," she said. "She was here. In your rooms."

And where Lust goes …

His hand moved to cup her jaw, eyes focused and grave, once more. "There has never been a shred of interest on either of our parts," he said. "Aphrodite's very essence and mine are in complete opposition. She would never tolerate my demands, nor would I hers."

"What are your demands?" A whispered question, coming more wide-eyed than Persephone would have liked.

"Discipline," he said. "Surrender." He let the backs of his fingers slide down her trapped arm to where it sank into the Oil. Parts of her tired from bliss began to warm again with want. "The nature of lust is not control of the self. It pursues pleasure for its own sake, of its own will."

"You've"—she swallowed, wetting her throat—"you've strange ways of showing me I should go without pleasure."

"I never said that." He leaned down for a kiss, which she gave, her stomach tightening at the hard length pressing at the small of her back. Hades pulled back just far enough to speak.

"I've asked for your obedience. I've asked you to give over your will to me." *Sweet creation, those words!* And was she arching against him? "Your pleasure is mine now, to allow or deny, but this"—he rolled his hips—"is too important. It is beyond my games. Will you make with me, Persephone, the only union the deathless plane has ever known between the Sky and the Underworld? Shall we be one another's first taste of our own kind?"

Hades spun enticing words, but the goddess teetered on a knife edge, grasping for signs of certainty that might tip her.

"If I say 'no'?"

All motion ceased.

"I will not force you, Green One. Is that what you want? To stop?" She could read it in the tilt of his brows, the tension in his arms. He did not deceive.

"No," she said, "I don't want to stop."

The rough kiss came as a relief. She couldn't have stared into those black eyes any longer without losing something of herself. The cost of this bargain was already high enough.

A cost you don't seem to mind paying so very much, do you?

A heavy erection slipped between her thighs, sluiced through new wetness.

No. No she did not.

His fingers closed over her wrist, just above the Oil. "Shall I free you?" he asked.

Persephone took a full breath in and out while some gathering force thickened the air between them. Her lips parted. Did her pupils dilate when she decided?

"No."

A hiss and a growl. His hand disappeared and she felt wrist and knuckle bumping and rotating between her cheeks, streaking her own fluid lust over his cock. The blunt head nudged, ready to end an age-long ignorance for them both. Consequences hovered.

"Goddess."

The one word signaled the last of his restraint.

In the silent space between thought and deed, a sliver of clarity opened against the haze of want. Neither of them had gone seeking this. Abandoned hope and blackmail had brought them here, but they both saw a new path and took it. And Hades didn't chase, as the others had done. There was no fawning or posturing. There was only his call, which she'd chosen again and again to obey.

Come to me. Come to me. Come.

The Lord of the Dead hilted himself, filling her, and Persephone gasped.

And gasped *again*. The loud crack of stone hitting stone broke the heady spell in the chamber, and something inside her jarred loose with it. Something marrow-deep, familiar and unfamiliar at once. She could almost grind it between her teeth.

Hades froze, impaling her from above. Where her line of sight came into focus out over the plane of the *Elaionapothos*, a stalactite the size of her arm had fractured away overhead and fallen to the limestone floor. Behind her, a grunt as the god both acknowledged and chose to ignore. The distraction lasted a breath, maybe two, and then Hades began to move.

He drew back and pushed home again, this time deliberate, slow as luxury, to the tune of a measured groan. Persephone stretched around him, the last of the day's reservations scattered on the wind. Here was the most forbidden of forbidden things, and she would have it. Her choice. *Hers*, and there was nothing anyone could do about it.

"Hades." His name was everything. A cry of victory, a demand, a preening affirmation, all ground out in a voice she hardly recognized as her own.

He answered her with a slow roll of hips, his weight and pressure bearing her flat, pillowing her cheeks against his groin. There was no way he could touch her in enough places at once. Chest to her shoulders, lips at her cheekbone, the firm hold of a thumb at the small of her back—never enough.

And the Oil. Fates, the *Elaionapothos*. It held her indefensible; spread her for him, yet made her secure. The restraint at her wrist and knee removed all worry over decisions, all choice but to accept into her body the god who would court her for a wife.

Submit and be free, was the seductive song it sang, and Persephone found her arousal twisted up into a tight knot of intensity she'd never known.

A trio of percussive cracks interrupted them this time, and the goddess jerked at the sound of more stone hitting the floor, somewhere out of sight. There was a rumble of more rock grating against itself, and Hades slowed to a near standstill.

"Is there something wrong?"

"I don't ... *think* so." Uncertainty stowed away with his assurances and Persephone's brow furrowed.

"Is this ... usual?"

"No," he said after a pause, "but I don't care."

And he didn't. Dark fingers gripped her at the waist and fitted her down onto his cock. They did this again. Again. *Again.*

Persephone moved with him as best she could, her back arching to take as much of the god as would fit. When his rolling gave way to the more primal need to thrust, Hades hunched to capture her mouth, their bodies now mirrored arcs. A circle made whole on the deathless plane, decay feeding into growth, the fruit of the grave nourishing spring-white buds and pumping the veins of green leaves until they withered and gave suck to death again.

They moved and worked together now, every push and flex rougher than the last, as though the coupling were a war. More of the cave formations fell, but it was nothing, now. All around them, impossibility frolicked. Stalagmites grew from the ground, glistening, building in sweaty heartbeats proportions meant to take ages, before crumbling and forming again. The air was thick, humid. Limestone glittered. Crystallized. The Oil of Desire held her and Hades had her.

The approach made her eyelids flutter. The drag of his cock, the shifting of swollen flesh—it was just out of reach, always one more push away. She grimaced, straining.

"Hades! Nnnh!"

"Makes two of us," he slurred against to the top of her ear. The hand at her hip crept around, fingers seeking, finding. She made an angry sound of amplified pleasure, the infuriating ache so much closer to relief.

"I'm close, love," he said, working her from inside and out. "Come for me now."

The words did as much for her as any dancing touch, any filling cock. Her eyes snapped open.

"Come for me."

Lungs filled. And filled. Her muscles tensed and burned.

"Come!"

Come to me. Come for me. Come.

Everything burst in a pulsing gush. The tightening of her belly forced out her held breath. The grip of her sex pulled at the length he fed her and Persephone came around Hades with a wail.

Chips of shattering stone pelted the Oil around them. There might have been a jolt to the floor, but the goddess couldn't be sure under the pummel of hips, the staccato of profanities as Hades reached his limit.

"Persephone!"

He bottomed out, lancing his need with a growl. The pressure on her furthest places bordered on pain, but it didn't matter. Too much of Hades was exactly the right amount, and he gave her just that, in jet after scalding jet. Filling her with ages of unspent need.

For a moment, nothing could be still. The *Elaionapothos* rippled beneath them. His cock twitched and she throbbed around him in the reckless wake of orgasm. Even the light in the room flickered from bright to dim, for it, too, required Hades's control to maintain and the god had lost his grip on such things.

There were kisses along her cheekbone and Persephone felt the tremor in his arm as Hades tried to hold himself upright. With a final push, as though he might summarize all that had just taken place, he slid a hand down her arm and drew it from the Oil. The black non-liquid relinquished her knee as well, like dark soil pushing up a spring shoot. The Lord of the Dead collapsed behind her, heaving an exhausted sigh.

Her freed fingers flexed and clenched, testing their own use after time spent amid the inexplicable hold of the *Elaionapothos*. She straightened her knee, stretching, and felt her thighs slide together, the proof of boundaries leapt.

At least a dozen of her long breaths strung themselves end to end, making a line along which Persephone could pull her mind back into same plane as the rest of her body. Parts of her wavered in a dizzying way she'd never encountered among the Sons of Man. Her head was clear of noise, of the oppressive, listless chatter that at other times kept her just off balance. Here now, at last, she'd had the thing Demeter had assured her was so ruinous, and she was cleaned out, calm, and floating in unblemished peace.

He had brought her here.

Hades, the Unseen One, god beneath the earth, had done this for her. He and he only.

Persephone blinked, seeing the chamber around her for the first time in what seemed like hours. She pushed herself onto her back, and then rolled to her other side to find him.

I'm in bed with the Lord of the Underworld. Light of Creation, look at him!

It was true. There he lay, face, chest, and thighs as white as the Oil was black. A dark hand sprawled over his belly, and she followed the lines down to the curve of his cock, where it fell lax now in the sheen of their coupling. Every bit of languid nudity begged for the touch of her hands, from the charcoal arch of a foot to the mist-pale temptation of an exposed throat. So what kept her from doing just that?

He had to have felt her staring, because he turned his face to look up at her from under heavy lids. The haze of completion softened the trouble in his smile, and his arm fell wide away from his body, inviting.

And why not?

She nestled into his side, fingertips fanning along his ribcage, one bent knee draping over his. Discarded chitons were a joyous catastrophe beneath them.

What n—

Cold! Something wet popped her on the shoulder and she gave a little gasp. Hades's eyes opened at her jerk and she looked to the ceiling just as another drop of water *pocked* down against her skin.

The overhead landscape of the chamber still hung heavy with descending stone, but there was no way to mistake it for the same dead cavern she'd seen on her way in the door. There were stalactites and stone curtains, yes, but they were new, and in different locations. Where before, there had been dry relics of the space's forming, now there were wet inverted spires of living stone, dripping humid life onto their knobby counterparts rising from the floor. Onto her. The bones of the earth in Hades's private rooms almost seemed to *blossom*, for lack of a better word.

"My Lord, is this *normal?*"

He huffed amusement and gathered her close at the hip. "Little flower, not a single piece of this is normal. Not you, not this"—he made a lazy gesture around the room with his free hand—"not any of it."

She cast a wary eye around the altered space, the potential violence she saw now in the columns of stone. "Will it"—she bit her lip—"will it happen every time?"

The hand at her waist moved up into her wild hair, gripping and drawing her down near his face. "I have no idea, Persephone," he said, awakening to mischief again. "But your assumption there will be other times is most encouraging."

So was the hot tongue in her mouth, the scrape of nails at her scalp. If this was the 'ruin' to which obedience brought her, Persephone would obey and let him raze her to the ground, then beg to be remade so he could destroy her again.

✦

It was a very different thing to put clothes back on with another immortal's eyes on him. It was not the absentminded formality that came after bathing or sleeping. Hades wanted to liken the feeling to *something*, but there was nothing to which he could.

A daughter of Olympos was in his *bed*—well, atop the *Elaionapothos*, the nearest thing—stretched out on her side, head supported on her hand, green eyes following his every move. She'd thrown the red linen of her own garment in a haphazard drape over her curves, whether from some inexplicable modesty or mere habit, he didn't know.

There appear to be any number of things you don't know.

He fastened the remaining shoulder of his chiton with its fibula and moved to tie off his belt.

Why had he thought the occasional mortal woman would be an acceptable substitute for *this*? For *her*? Would he go on with the affairs of his realm, behaving as if nothing had changed?

And the cavern, lurching back into a formation cycle the moment their bodies had joined. An unnerving sight, yet the ichor in his veins sang with the seductive melody of growth and decay.

This whole arrangement should have been an inconvenience, but he'd accepted it might become entertainment, instead. An amusement to pick up and put down at his leisure, for a time. What it would not—*could* not—become was a need, an ache.

Persephone blinked at him through languor and a lazy smile. "Had your fill already?" she said.

Hades swore to himself. Had his fill? Had his *fill*? She ought to be beneath him again and squealing right now, but the Lord of the Dead kept his face under control.

"The Underworld is a demanding realm," he said, coming to stand at the edge of the platform. He trailed fingertips over her ankle, but she pulled the limb back, moving to sit upright instead. Fabric threatened to slip below her breast.

"And you'll be abandoning me again for how long?"

Did she sound ... eager?

"Provided I find my duties as I left them," he said, "perhaps a day."

"A *day*." Eager became annoyed. "You're going to lock me in here to stare at your furniture until you return?" He raised a brow, but she anticipated his doubts. "What chance would you say there is of me finding a way out of the Underworld on my own?"

Hades smirked. "None."

"So," she said, coming up to sit on her heels, "why not let me explore? Or are you afraid of a single, powerless immortal running loose down here in your caves?"

The sight of her disheveled on her knees had him biting back a snarl. Powerless? Hardly. But there was no need to be a tyrant, not when she'd agreed to his terms.

"Very well, Persephone," he said. "As I am more than capable of finding you no matter *where* you may disappear to within my realm"—he paused to watch her face for understanding—"you have leave to wander." Something in her shoulders relaxed at this, and he nodded, satisfied.

On his way out the door, he ran a hand up one of the damp stalagmites and rubbed slick fingertips together, frowning. It made no sense.

He turned to her before slipping into the corridor. The goddess hadn't moved.

"Maybe not *quite* a day," he said, narrowing his eyes at all the possibilities draped in scarlet linen. "I will find you."

◆

Minos and his brother Rhadamanthys argued over the fate of a single mortal at such length Hades could no longer be still. The Judges of Men kept up with their charge in more or less the expected manner and, now that he'd marked nothing out of the ordinary, he could move on to the next of his routine visits.

In the wavering light of the largest of the *paráthyra*, the orchards of the Underworld grew in regular rows. The trees and their fruit served no other purpose than the vanity of nostalgia. The souls of Man had no need to eat and neither did he, nor any other immortal residing under the earth. He had not always been Lord of the Dead, and the solitary plot of green on the floor of the Great Cavern stood as a lasting memento of his ages before the War.

Ah, but now there's something else green in your realm, isn't there?

He pushed the thought aside with a frown, steering his focus back to finding Askalaphos. The orchard keeper rarely had anything unusual to report, save the occasional complaint of Menoites's oxen wandering loose, trampling new growth.

It was neither the herdsman nor the arborist, however, who came rustling between the trees.

"Your immortal 'guests' arrive with more frequency, Polydegmon."

The surly presence of Kerberos did nothing to raise his brows, but the smaller figure following the beast did.

'Guests'. Bah.

"Goddess," he said, looking Aphrodite up and down in disdain. "I hope you haven't come seeking more favors. You'll find you've exhausted your supply."

The Fair One's smirk ignored his disapproval outright.

"Well," she said, "if your lapdog's warm reception wasn't overwhelming enough …"

Kerberos snarled but padded away to the orchard's outer rows, leaving the deathless gods to their privacy.

"What is it you want?" he said. "My end of the bargain is complete. Persephone is here and out of your way."

"And so she *is*." The goddess swished past him in a cloud of sheer yellow linen, the mischief in her tone enough to make him want to grind his teeth. "It seems you've wasted no time at all, *Clymenus*."

"Except perhaps the time I'm wasting now." He had nothing but dry scorn as they began a slow course down the length of a row.

"Do you know," she said, ignoring his jab, "the first time Poseidon took Amphitrite to his bed, it was said the Aegean multiplied with such numbers of fishes the Sons of Man could drive an oxcart from Athenai to Smyrna without ever sinking their wheels in water?"

"Wasting. Time."

"Zeus and Hera?" Her lecturing continued, and Hades gathered his patience. "When your brother first claimed his consort, the lightnings raged about Olympos for a day and a night. Selene gave up and stabled her horses, the skies blinded her so. The chariot of the Moon sat idle for *two* nights that month."

"You will come to a point, Fair One, or I will open a rift here and now and cast you back to Olympos."

"So testy." She waved a hand. "I'm sure your poor bride-to-be is smitten already." The goddess stopped walking and turned to face him. "When I heard tell of earthquakes, my Lord, one right after the other for the better part of the night …" Aphrodite shrugged a graceful shoulder, smiling as though she'd said something clever.

"Earthquakes," he repeated.

That madness with the cave. But surely …

"A realm recognizing its master's consort." She could not have sounded more smug. "Persuasive indeed. Has she agreed to the vows?"

As though a wedding were a possibility. Hades scowled. "What business is it of yours?"

"Of mine?" she asked, all feigned innocence. "Oh, none whatsoever, Lord of the Dead." Pale fingers plucked a fruit, ripe, from a pomegranate tree. The goddess examined her take with an arched brow while she continued to speak. "I've only come to forewarn you."

"Forewarn me of what?" Did she dare makes threats in his realm?

"Hermes has become aware of Persephone's whereabouts. And if the Messenger knows, it won't be very long before Demeter knows, as well."

"And from whose lips did he learn this, I wonder?"

"Be serious." She brandished the pomegranate at his accusation. "That would defeat the purpose of our bargain entirely. I don't know *who* told him. What I do know is this: time grows short. If you want a bride without interference from Olympos, you'll want to act, and soon."

"You assured me Zeus had given his approval." Hades forced his features to neutrality, but something in his chest roiled. It should have been weeks before the inevitable demands from the Sky. Persephone had only *begun* to surrender, and the way she responded to his touch, his mere presence, told him she had far, *far* more to give.

"Oh, you know how this game will be played, *Polydegmon*." The goddess met his eye, cynicism bright green beneath copper lashes. "Demeter will insist, The Lord of Lightnings will laugh, then the threats will come out, and then he will bend. And *then* our dear Hermes will be down here to fetch her from your 'villainous clutches'." She punctuated her thoughts with a roll of her eyes.

"Your bargain with me is complete," she went on, "but the look on that very serious immortal face of yours tells me you're nowhere near prepared to end your time with Persephone. I did promise you'd find her suitable, did I not?" A knowing flash of pearly white teeth accompanied a flick of a delicate wrist. Aphrodite tossed him the pomegranate and he caught it with a grunt.

"What I say to you, my Lord Hades is no more than this: unless you wish to hand back your new consort"— she waved away his frown at her choice of words—"you'd best find a more permanent way of binding her to your side. Marriage vows will do, but in their place …?" The goddess tilted her chin at the fruit he now held.

Hades folded his arms and fixed her with a look that went on for several breaths. Aphrodite didn't flinch.

"You came all the way to my realm in person to tell me this?" he said at last.

Dark red brows tipped up in amusement. "Do you think I want word of my involvement in this getting back to Demeter? I've learned to trust only myself when I require secrecy." That smile, he suspected, was one her unfortunate husband had seen a great many times. "Shall I find the Guardian again to show me the way out?"

"No need for that," he said, setting the pomegranate at his feet. "Kerberos prevents the escape of *mortal* souls from my realm. There are quicker ways back to Olympos."

He pulled off his iron ring and drew it out between his palms. At the end of the sweeping motion, the weight of his bident rested in his grip.

Aphrodite *tsked*, teasing. "So *godly*. Have you done that little trick for Persephone? I'm sure she'd be impressed to see your 'weapon' grow."

Hades ignored her and stabbed the iron tines into the æther. With a swift downward slash, he tore a gate to the upper realm. Blazing sunlight carved a swath onto the floor of his cavern and the goddess blinked against the glare.

"Your cautions have been noted, Goddess of Lust." He presented the ephemeral gateway with an open palm. "Should you find your way into my realm again, might I suggest you come bearing good news? My patience has limits."

She stepped to the glowing threshold and painted him with a sideways grin. "Indeed, my Lord." In a flutter of yellow fabric, Aphrodite slipped through to Olympos. Hades closed the rift behind her with a twisting motion of fingers and wrist.

The orchard was silent. He nudged the discarded pomegranate with a sandaled foot and condensed his bident back to its ring.

Demeter's wrath would be on them within days. He had in no way had his fill of the Daughter of Olympos who wandered his realm at this very moment. Not the give of her flesh, not the exquisite sounds she made, and certainly not the urge to spar that alternated with bouts of pure submission.

Is it possible to have your fill? Of her?

But his goal had never been to find a bride. The Lord of the Underworld had want of no such thing.

I approve of thiss mmatch, Lord Hades. You havve made a wise choice.

Hekate's words nagged him. The Goddess of the Crossroads had been the first to use the word 'consort'. What could she see, from those thrice-knowing eyes of hers?

"Are you listening to me, Polydegmon?"

Kerberos interrupted his thoughts, the three-headed beast approaching again along a flanking aisle of trees.

"My mind is elsewhere, Guardian. You were saying?" It would never do to remain so unfocused.

"Any other immortal visitors you expect lurking on the banks of the Styx I should know about?"

Hades shook his head. He hadn't expected this one. "Let us hope not."

"That female of yours is in heat, yes? I feel your mind on the rut."

He sighed under a grimace of irritation. The keen eyes of his fearsome colleague were, as always, the only set to see the truth of his moods.

The Goddess of Growing Things *did* have his attention.

By her own admission, she was a breaker of rules. Her adventures on the mortal plane were evidence enough. Yet, here she obeyed with only minimal prodding, and he was sure even *that* bare token of resistance stemmed from fear of the unknown more than any real aim at defiance.

What guise had she worn when she'd seduced the Sons of Man? Had she chosen some nondescript mortal face? Sought to keep her dalliances inconspicuous? Or had she wooed with a full complement of earthly beauty? Surely nothing like the perfection of her true, immortal form. She would never have kept her secret that way.

It was almost a shame necessity kept their unexpected tryst confined to his domain. For all he had shown her thus far, his curiosity burned to see the Green One in her own element. Would blossoms burst in her wake? Forests surge up at her command?

Aphrodite had come with her demands, and Hades had gone to their fulfillment with little enthusiasm. After the fall, the sight and scent of the goddess in his arms, he'd set aside indifference for the oft-ignored call of lust. But now …

Now Persephone confronted him with unknowns.

He had called out her name. Forced it out at those moments of pleasure, spun silk-fine but strong as steel. The Lord of the Dead did not dignify playthings with the calling of names.

Because she is not a plaything.

Submission had been his goal from the moment he'd laid her in his chariot, but their every exchange showed such ends to be laughably simplistic. He could force submission. He could threaten and command.

But when Hekate had appeared on the bridge and Persephone had stepped without thought into the protection of his arms …

Hades shivered.

What he wanted now, he would have to earn.

What is she doing to me?

She was driving him to distraction.

"I'm sorry, Kerberos, what was that?"

The hound snorted hot air from all six of his flaring nostrils and lashed an irritated tail.

"*You are useless this moment for hearing reports. As always, I have our borders under control, whether I am thanked or not. You should find and mount that bitch of yours. Clear the fog from between your ears. And your legs.*"

Hades glared. He *should* have been paying attention, but the Guardian's familiarity of late signaled a need for a return to order.

"You serve the Underworld well, *as always*, Guardian. Be grateful you were given wardship of a kingdom whose ruler tolerates your tongues. I assure you, either of my brothers would not."

Kerberos shook himself, the vigor of threshing pelt and ears retort enough as he reared on hind legs. With a rude whipping of his tail, the beast turned and prowled away among the trees. *"Insufferable gods"*, the dog thought back at him, disappearing into the cavern.

The Guardian was right, though. He did need to clear his head. And he knew who would help him do it.

Hades knelt to retrieve the discarded pomegranate. The fruit filled his palm, a lusty pink rind with a little crown bursting from one end.

… a more permanent way of binding her to your side.

A small, ancient voice at the back of his head suggested this was not the way.

He ignored it.

✦

The palace of Helios stood as far to the east as it was possible to go, on the banks of the river Okeanos. Around it glowed the land of the Hesperides, though the Nymphs of Evening and their hundred-headed Drakon were nowhere in sight.

The many windows of the House of the Sun painted a mosaic of golden light across the deepening purples of night, and Demeter, reserves of energy exhausted, passed over its gilded threshold alone.

The day's trek had pushed her to the edge of her abilities, but Helios was close. She scouted a path to the throne room, guided by nothing more than heat, and soon laughter.

The halls of the palace were a blazing excess of immortal ostentation: surfaces leafed in gold and teeming with precious stones. Columns, friezes, pediments, all adorned with every conceivable metal and mineral chosen from the finest riches of the earth. Donated by Hades, no doubt—a bribe to keep Helios out of the Underworld. Why anyone would need extra incentive to avoid the Lord of the Dead, the goddess didn't know.

She did not have to search for long. A beam of light blared with frightening intensity from a pair of immense gilded doors. It was as if a thousand—ten thousand!—war horns sounded their fearful news all at once.

Demeter passed under a lintel high enough to admit sailing ships and squinted against the violence of the light. Her forearm snapped up to shade her eyes in an attempt to make out anything at all. The giggling trickled to a halt and there might have been the outline of moving bodies some distance into the space, but her impaired vision played tricks and she couldn't be sure.

"This meeting will be much easier, Goddess, if you face the other way." The good-natured, booming voice came from where she thought she'd seen the silhouettes.

Demeter turned as suggested and discovered instant, if only partial, relief. The wall surrounding the door soothed the eye in polished obsidian. It must have been the only dark object in the entire palace, and the titan had to have imbued it with some additional properties to absorb the bulk of the glare.

Behind her, she could now see the reflection of Helios lounging on his throne. One of the Hesperides lay draped over his lap. Was it Aigle? Erytheis? She could hardly tell them apart. Either way, the golden head rested on one arm of the titan's seat, and lustrous knees folded over the other. Helios played with her hair, and another of the nymphs leaned against the high back of the throne, smirking. Where the third sister was, Demeter couldn't imagine. Perhaps still with the dragon, guarding the infamous golden apples.

"My apologies," he said, the smile always present in his words. "This is just about the only way I can greet a guest. Believe me, I grow tired of speaking to the backs of heads myself." The Titan's easy laugh echoed around the room. Looking directly at even his reflection made her wince, but at least she was no longer blind.

He is far older than you. More powerful. Tread with care.

"Forgive this intrusion during your hours of rest, All Seeing One. I have journeyed far this day seeking answers only you may be able to give."

"Peace, Goddess," he said, "there is nothing to forgive." Despite the grandeur of his palace, Helios paid no mind to formalities. "I saw your travels. I was expecting you."

"Of course." Demeter gave him a respectful tilt of her head.

She should have known. There was no surprising an immortal who saw literally everything under the sun. He *was* the sun. It was the very reason for her presence within his walls.

Helios leaned back in possibly the gaudiest throne Demeter ever had the misfortune of seeing: an amalgamation of gold and gems so layered and ornate one could hardly recognize it as a chair. The *real* treasures of the earth, of course, were sheaves of grain and fat cattle, not jewels and other shiny bits of rock.

Best to keep thoughts like those to yourself. Especially when you come seeking favors.

"What knowledge do you seek, Fruitful One? Ask and we shall see what I know." His fingertips played along the profile of the nymph in his lap, stroking her nose, the bow of her upper lip like the petals of an exotic flower. The Hesperides, it seemed, were accustomed to such imploring visitors. They paid Demeter little mind.

"You are most generous, Helios." It could only help to fan his pride. "My daughter Persephone has gone missing. Do you know where she is?" Had it sounded too much like a demand? She resisted the urge to wring her hands.

"How long ago was this?"

"I believe you have crossed the skies four times, maybe five, since she disappeared. I sent her to Nysa for a day of leisure and she never returned. Artemis and Athena were with her and claim ignorance. They speak of earthquakes, but the shape of the land disagrees. Nor does that tell me about my daughter. I do not trust their words."

"Four days ... Nysa ..." The titan's focus dissipated while he thought. The nymph took two of his luminous fingers into her mouth, and Helios smiled at the resulting glow that came through her cheeks. Demeter held back an irritated sigh as the demonstrative sucking went on, but Helios ended it with a bark.

"Ah yes! Nysa!" The fingers withdrew with a pop and he shook one at the ceiling in success. "Please understand, Goddess. I see such a great many things each day; it becomes a task to sift through them all."

"Then you know where she is?" Demeter clasped hopeful hands, impatient.

"I do," he said, "but I'm curious. You say Artemis and Athena claim to have seen nothing?"

Would he not come to the point?

"They tell me they saw a chasm open in the earth, only to close again moments later. They claim it was after this they noticed Persephone missing. I believe they lie to hide their half-sister."

Helios shook his head and gave the nymph a tap on the shoulder. She slid to lounge near his feet and he shifted in his chair. "The Hunter and the Warrior did not lead you false, Demeter. I can confirm the tearing of the earth they described. What Zeus's daughters did not see was your Persephone tumbling into the rift during the tremor."

Demeter's throat closed and the reflection of her eyes bugged back at her. Her mouth came open, tongue and palate working and failing to produce sound. When she found her voice at last, it broke at a wail.

"So she's *gone*? My daughter is *gone*?" Her hands were at her face, a barricade to the sanity that might escape through her mouth.

"No! Not gone at all." Helios rose and stepped in her direction, one bright hand raised in reassurance. "I saw her fall to its end from my chariot. The rift opened æther as well as earth. Lord Hades was there to catch her. I assure you, Goddess, I saw her unharmed."

Her lungs tried to collapse. Demeter whirled on the titan, and then hissed at the light and turned to face the obsidian, the heels of her palms rubbing her eyes.

"*Hades?*" There was horror, and then there was this. "Hades has her? For what purpose could that *stone* of a god possibly want my—" Fingers flew to her mouth as her own gasp severed her words.

"I think you may wish to have a conversation with Zeus about this," the titan said. He resumed his seat and made some oblique gesture at the two Hesperides. They gathered themselves and disappeared away behind the throne, but not before pausing to whisper in his ear. The line of his mouth was much less jolly than it had been.

"What does *Zeus* have to do with this?" Her nails bit her palms, quelling fury she could ill afford.

Helios sighed. "Just over a week before Persephone's fall, Lord Zeus spoke with Aphrodite about Hades courting a wife. This did I also see while on my course." Radiant hands spread in useless apology.

"A *wife?* And Aphrodite involved as well? Am I the *only* one who didn't know of this? Why did no one speak to me?" Demeter's voice climbed octaves and her eyebrows followed.

"And if they had spoken to you, would you have allowed such a thing?"

"No!"

All efforts to remain calm in the presence of the titan fell away like so much leaden ash.

"Demeter," his reflection said, incensing with placating tones, "what could be so terrible about a marriage between Persephone and Hades? He is just, he is cool-headed. None of us have ever known him to take lovers, and the Unseen One has gone many an age without a consort. As a husband, he has much to offer your daughter: dominion in two realms instead of one, power only matched by the Lord of Lightnings himself, all the riches under the earth." He gestured wide at the gold and precious stones covering nearly every surface in the room. "I have seen tragedy, Goddess, and it did not look like this."

Her knuckles whitened around unmollified fists at her sides. Tears stung the corners of her eyes and not from glaring at the blinding immortal at her back.

"I tried to protect her!" She could feel saliva gathering in her mouth. "Hermes and Apollo? Do you know what *they* would have done to my only daughter? And now you tell me *Hades Clymenus* has taken her instead? The mortals won't even speak his *name*, Helios! He is a monster!"

"Then here we are." Helios settled back into his throne and ran fingers through molten locks of hair. "As I said, you should speak to Zeus. I have told you what I know."

The goddess faced the image of the titan mirrored in the black stone wall, her gaze unblinking. Furious. His eyes, when she met them at last, were sunspots. Hers were a mess of scalding tears. There were no words left to say.

Demeter strode from throne room, from the halls of the House of the Sun. The night waited for her. Wrath waited for her.

The presumption. The audacity! Hades. Aphrodite. Zeus!

They would return her daughter. Or they would come to know ruin. There was no other choice.

✦

V Trust

The river of fire curved its way through the Great Cavern like an endless molten serpent. Of all the unimaginable sights Persephone had seen since her descent into the Underworld, the Phlegethôn, its destructive flow somehow death and life at once, proved so far the most worthy of her combined fear and awe.

Well. Except perhaps for that first glimpse of Lord Hades.

Both red ends of the oozing ribbon of rock disappeared into the vast black of the cavern, one ahead of her, the other at her back. In the distance, what looked like a bridge spanned the river at an impossible height, and it was toward this landmark Persephone made her steady way.

She kept, of course, a wide and respectful distance from the guttural crackle of the river even as her path followed its deadly curves.

Hades had given her leave to explore and, once she had assessed the halls of his palace as more or less barren and uninteresting, one of the famous rivers of the Unseen Realm had no trouble capturing her interest. Doubly so now that late afternoon warmed the realms above and the watery *paráthyra* had gone golden and dim.

The lakes of the mortal plane. Who knew?

So many surprises here.

Her mother wouldn't even allow her on Olympos during a crowded feast day where there would have been a hundred chaperones to shepherd her interactions. Now, here she was in the Underworld, supervised by no one at all. Allowing the Lord of the Dead to play his wicked games.

And she *had* allowed it, hadn't she?

Agreed to obey at first, yes, but when the commands came, did she not enjoy them? So few had come as outright demands.

Stand up. Come here.

There had been those, true. But the greater portion had come as requests. Suggestions insinuated hot and deep, sure as the Phlegethôn twisted its inevitable way across the cavern floor.

Will you allow me to touch you? She had.
Do I have something you want? He did.
Shall I free you?

The last one made something in her belly turn over as she neared the foot of the bridge. While Persephone could curse herself for falling into his clever trap with the *Elaionapothos*—Fates, when had she become so naïve?—she should have raged more at her blind faith in a god she barely knew who wished to restrain her. Though their first unforgettable coupling had gone astonishingly, horribly *right*, there was no way she could have foreseen such an outcome. The encounter might have been much, much worse, and there would have been nothing she could have done about it.

And yet there was something in it. Something in *him*.

Was it that voice? That dark purr that rasped at the hidden core of her being? Was it the abyss in his eyes that promised to whisper back only truths, no matter how awful?

Whatever the truth, he'd promised not to hurt her. And Persephone believed. In his own realm, where Hades held the entire advantage in power, what need would he have to lie?

Not until you ask me to.

Even with the Phlegethôn's heat shimmering the air, Persephone shivered. He had sounded so confident in her eventual arrival at such a point, but she couldn't imagine what the intervening journey might look like. Yet each new advance he made had found her willing, begging.

What would she beg for next?

The bridge loomed ahead, a wonder in pale stone, larger in every dimension than it had appeared from the other side of the cavern. Its arching deck traversed a far greater distance than the width of the river alone. Persephone could see from the violent and mutable nature of boiling rock why it would be necessary to place the bridge's uprights as far out of the path of potential destruction as possible.

The arc of the crossing rose with subtle grace from the surrounding cavern landscape, its grade easy for the passage of a cart or chariot. Persephone's curiosity, however, had taken her to the base of the nearest upright, around which a staircase spiraled for travelers on foot.

Travelers. Pff. Who would those be? The mortal dead? The unsettling Enodia?

Yet as far as she could see in any direction, there was no one. An hour's lonely trek from the palace had her humbled. With the Underworld negating her ability to will herself over the distance, and the lack of other beings busying the space around her, there had been no choice but to dwell within herself as she walked.

Whether she could accept what she found there was another story altogether.

The curving stair before her fanned out around the column of the upright, not so much hewn as grown from the surrounding structure. Complicated sprays of milky crystal glittered at every crease in the stone, the spikes exceeding the length of her limbs or, here and there, her entire body. Their beauty bristled with chaos, but beneath that, the goddess felt art. Lit from below with the ruddy light of the river, the tower dazzled as surely as did the surface of Poseidon's seas or the snow-covered slopes of Zeus's mount.

Persephone had never met a stair she didn't want to climb, and this far-flung wonder was no different. It only took one sandal on the bottom step.

She was rising, circling the upright. Crystal points glinted along her path like so many lovely, dangerous teeth. The only sounds in this remote part of the cavern were the crackling grind of the Phlegethôn and the hardened leather under her feet saluting every step.

Up and up she went, the ascent continuing for what felt like hours, though the light from the *paráthyra* told her it could have been no such length of time. Persephone began to worry she'd made a horrible mistake when her steps brought her the last bend around the upright to lead out onto the bridge itself.

Flaming creation, it's about time.

She turned to survey the way she'd come and marveled.

The cavern domed roughly away in every direction, concealed in shadow except for a few, scattered lights. The spare patchwork of mortal lakes overhead, the minimal illumination Hades kept near the entrances and walkways of the now distant palace, and of course, the Phlegethôn.

The River of Fire stretched into a narrower band under the terrible height of the bridge. Though the distance made the churning breadth seem less, the heat, rising past where she stood, was more.

Her fingertips traced along the stone of the railing as she moved out toward the highest part of the arch. Far above, a small *paráthyro* let in enough wavering daylight to show her the curving roadway. Without it, the bridge's path would have been no more than a black void bisecting the bright line of the river.

The cavern, its reach vast and limits questionable, swallowed the sound of her footsteps on the high span of stone. When she made it to the center of the structure, Persephone settled against the railing and let go of her focus.

It was a weight lifted to simply steep in the enormity of it. The rising heat loosening her limbs, the glowing brand of the river on the shadows of the cavern floor. The brush of red linen over her hips. Stone under her palms that felt like a temple's steps warmed under the sun.

A glance down at her hands proved the only disruption. There was Polyxene's ring, a dim glow, reminding her of choices unmade.

The Lord of the Dead, in all his seductive Underworld glory, would be an unreachable memory once her mother found and dragged her home. Entertaining ideas of 'perhaps' alongside the ruler of the Unseen Realm would be a foolish mistake. When her days returned to their prior normalcy, as was inevitable, the ring offered a chance of escape.

But is this not also an escape?

It was, and one such as she couldn't have imagined, but, damn the Fates, it wouldn't last. Those eyes, that voice, the delicious trill of fear when he made those demands. He wanted her to walk blind toward every outcome, the potential for disaster looming, but each time had ended with her calling out for—

"The River of Fire suits you."

Hades.

She peeled her heart from the roof of her mouth as the strolling god approached. Whether he'd willed himself atop the bridge or moved with such care the daze of her thoughts had concealed the sound of his steps, it took her a handful of deep breaths to calm the speed of her pulse.

"How so?" Her best efforts not to appear startled were laughable as Hades came to her side at the railing.

"It is a live thing in a dead realm," he said, hands folded behind his back. "It inspires a healthy fear."

Persephone snorted. "No one down here is afraid of me."

"Aren't they?" The river lit him red and orange along his left side. Bottomless eyes glinted.

What does he mean by that?

"How did you find me here?" she said. "Did you send someone to track me through the shadows?"

"Why?" The corner of his mouth twitched, the beginnings of a smile. "Were you trying to run?"

"No." An indignant hand came to her hip and her eyes raked him from brow to waist. A further curve of his lips showed what he thought of her attempts at derision.

"I can smell you."

"What?"

"What else in the Underworld smells of green outside my orchards? You are simple enough to find."

"But … this far?"

He shrugged. "It is not for nothing I remain Lord of this realm."

Persephone frowned.

"You scowl, Daughter of Olympos," he said, placing his own palms on the rail, eyes cast out over the river. "When we parted last, I had the impression we'd done much to remedy your distaste for my realm. Or at the least my presence in it."

The corners of his eyes wrinkled in a mirth that didn't reach his lips. Was he teasing her?

"I still do not understand."

"Understand what?" His shoulders rotated in her direction just enough.

"Anything. The reasons I'm here. This realm. *You*." He'd made his agreement with Aphrodite plain enough, but the way Hades continued to interact with her was hardly in line with the behavior of someone knuckling under to a blackmail demand.

Now he did smile. Teeth flashed in the ruddy light, tightening her stomach. *Predator*.

"Well we can't have that." He faced her more fully, leaning one elbow on the stone. "Go on, Persephone. Ask your questions. Ask something personal. Something *rude*."

The curling innuendo licked straight between her thighs and she had to shore herself against collapse. *Fates, he'll have me on my knees, and I'll have asked for it.*

Something rude. Her eyes darted to the nearest possibilities. The river. The bridge. Hades.

"Your arms," she blurted with a curt nod. "None of the other gods have those markings. Were you born of Kronos that way?"

He tilted a brow and smirked. "Original," he said, "but maybe not as rude as I was expecting." He stood straight again. "Do you see this river, Green One?"

"I see it." Her arms folded over her chest of their own accord. Why did he irritate her so?

Hades slid to her side and then halfway behind her back, the dark forearms in question caging her at the railing on either side.

Because he was toying, of course. That's what kept her on edge. A cat playing with a mouse before the kill. It wasn't in his nature to find mercy and simply give her what she wanted.

And what is it you want, Persephone?

It was too humiliating to admit, but why?

"There are rivers in my realm," he said just above her ear now. "Three rivers and two lakes. The Akherôn is the River of Woe, the first from which the mortal dead drink. With a taste, they grieve for all whom they left on the living plane."

His voice came in a soothing hum at her back. Tension began to seep from her shoulders. The Lord of the Dead continued.

"The Kôkytos is Lamentation, and by its bitter waters, they know every misdeed of the life they left behind. It causes them to reflect and admit."

The pad of his thumb brushed over the knuckles of her right hand and she couldn't help but draw a breath.

Toying with you.

"I don't understand what this has to do with the color of your skin," she said, sounding less formidable than she would have liked.

Lips pressed to her temple and the god shifted behind her. "Patience, little flower. Do I not keep my word?"

Persephone swallowed. The railing pressed below her ribs.

"Now the Lethe is Oblivion," he went on. "If the dead wish to live anew, they must drink of it to forget."

"Forget what?"

"Their former lives. How would it do for a mortal babe to awaken squalling in her mother's arms, remembering everything that had come before?"

"I see." The breathy acknowledgement was all she could give with the sensation of nails now grazing along her wrist. "And what of the Styx? And this one?"

"You do know some of them by reputation, don't you?" His warm approval made her both swell and grimace at the same time. Why should she care what he thought of her? The void of the cavern stared back at the lesson in progress, ancient and observing.

"The Styx is my border. Kharon ferries those mortal dead who pay the toll across, and Kerberos prevents them from acting on any wild notions of returning to the living plane before their time."

"But there are other ways in and out," she said. "Aren't there."

"For immortals, yes." His lack of elaboration glared, conspicuous.

"And the last?"

"The Phlegethôn," he said, "is another boundary, of sorts. Have you noticed the silence in this part of the cavern?"

She nodded, mesmerized by the boiling flow of earth far beneath them, the liquid cadence of his words in her ear.

"All but a very few of the mortal dead avoid this river," he said, his tone dropping lower, still. "It is the Unmaking."

Something about this made her shiver, despite the heat.

"Should a mortal choose never to be born again, they may cross its fires and know the truest of ends. Their soul will cease to be."

"That sounds terrible," she whispered.

"For some, perhaps. For others, it is a release. They must choose, but I prevent them from choosing rashly. It is rare."

Persephone stood with this in the circle of his arms for a time. Her own release, embodied in mortal jewels, sat heavy on her finger.

"Your hands," she said, grasping the connection.

"Yes." Those hands slid up over her forearms before returning to flank hers at the rail. "When I accepted rulership of this realm, I would have stood right alongside the Children of Olympos, at least in appearance.

"But I am the only being who may immerse himself in the Underworld rivers and lakes unaffected. Someone must control them, and it must be me, though after age upon age, even *my* flesh cannot withstand their ravages entirely."

"But their purposes serve mortals. Why should *you* need to …" She gestured at the winding line of destruction oozing between the uprights of the bridge.

"Mortals are not always known for making wise choices." Black humor tinted his words. "I've had to fish countless poor fools out of harm's way over the æons. Attempting to drink from or cross the wrong waters at the wrong times. Almost always under the control of some wild emotion."

"But … you? Personally?"

"The care of the mortal dead is my task. I will not avoid it for my own comforts. Even if it does mean the Olympians shrink in horror at the sight of me." His final assessment curled in the shape of a smile.

Just above audible, Persephone replied: "I'm not shrinking."

"Not yet."

He pressed her against the rail with the length of his body and her jaw went tight. Fingers trailed along the back of her hand, stopping when they came to metal.

"This is an unusual jewel," he said, thumbing Polyxene's ring. "It hums with life."

Fates! Could he ask about anything else?

"It was a gift." There. Vague enough.

"From your mother?"

She cleared her throat, nerves twisting. Somehow, she knew he would spot a lie. "From a mortal."

"A *mortal* came by a gem like this? Do you remember a long-lost lover, Persephone?" She could feel the taunt rubbing her raw, exposing needs unsated.

I am not going to tell him about my promise to Polyxene.

"Did you seek me out on this bridge just to speak of my jewels?" she said, lashing irritation like a whip.

He chuckled behind her, the sound all shadows and coiling smoke. "No, I did not."

Fingertips came to the far side of her jaw. A glint of light in black eyes. That mouth on hers. Again.

Finally.

Stolen kisses on the mortal plane had been one thing. Here, however, crushed between Hades and solid stone, mere architecture holding her back from oblivion, Persephone knew kisses of another kind. A kind she could only have from the Lord of the Dead, where he took and she gave, where he pushed and she lay back, unprotesting but afraid.

It was the fear. With his tongue searing against hers, the fingers of his right hand circling her throat, the goddess knew fear to be that nagging, undiscoverable *lack* that had kept her unfulfilled in the arms of men. The one dark something she didn't want to confess, even to herself.

Fear was the reason she could feel her thighs slide, wet beneath her chiton. When he let her breathe at last, grip still firm above her collarbones, his forearm crossing over her breast, Persephone could do no better than stare.

An ebbing song of heartbeats had to pass before she could speak. Hades waited, a naked hunger painting the lines of his face where dour levity had gone before. Breathlessness did nothing for her pride, yet this was not the first time he'd cornered her against a precipitous drop, was it?

"You seem to enjoy this," she said.

"Mm? Enjoy what?" Fingers skimmed her ribs, moving toward her waist.

"Pinning me at the precipice."

A hand was on her hip, pulling her against him. "I do," he said. "Though I admit it's a rather unscrupulous way of getting what I want."

"Oh? And what's that?"

Both hands held her fast.

"Fear."

The railing disintegrated. Livid red stone churned far below, and Persephone's heels scrabbled on the edge of the bridge.

"Hades!"

Her hands flew to clutch his restraining arm, the wool of his chiton at his thigh.

"Yes?" The god was as calm as a windless sea while every frantic muscle in her body squeezed back against his body like water seeking the lowest point.

"Move back." Oh, how she hated the tremble in her voice. Hades only tightened his hold, and a sound of amusement came near her ear.

"Have we reached your limit, Green One?"

The river crackled. Hungry. Eternal. Pockets of stone lifted enough to cool into islands only for the patient devastation of the current to fold them back again into the earth's molten womb.

She wanted his touch. Wanted *him*, but fantasy was harmless, wasn't it? Reality yawned all around her now, its maw dire with consequence. No sooner had she owned her inexplicable appetite for those feelings of fear, than he'd been confessing aloud his desire to provoke them. Could he know? Could he feel it in her limbs?

Had they come one step too far?

"Please." Her mouth was the only part of her to move. Her two feet arched on tiptoe at the glittering edge of stone. Where her thighs met, a now-familiar hum began to well.

His grip was iron, but so much of her remained exposed, a dare to the Fates. At her back, another danger: male arousal twitched against her curves.

"Can you feel it?" Hard cock held the promise of more trouble to come. Persephone made a noise somewhere between gasp and whimper. "Your panic," he said, "excites me."

Fates, I can't take it.

"The speed of your pulse, the way you cling."

That voice could charm a snake, and the tension in her limbs coiled tight. Should she melt to his words for one moment … Could anyone but Hades survive the Phlegethôn?

"I will cling to you without the danger, my Lord." She dared to wriggle backward, urgent and shameless in her begging. "Please."

"But never with such beautiful desperation." Fingers hooked over her hip, cradling bone and sending need coursing between her thighs. "Tell me." It was a command. "Tell me why you're afraid."

She *wanted* to obey. To please him. That was another new wrinkle. Her impulse to balk, just for the sake of pride, had all but disappeared. Those dark murmurs of approval made her reel with want, with achievement, but the drop …

"I'll fall," she said, allowing him his prize. "The river …"

A thumb brushed her throat. Heat rose to lick her toes, her ankles.

"Persephone."

How could he make her name into a velvet caress, every single time? How could it stroke her like a tongue, in secret places, and bind her as sure as any tether?

"Have I taken you yet where you did not wish to go?"

The truth of it laid her open, swept her clean. "No."

"I would *never* let you fall," he said. "Never." The silence of the cavern built around them. Even the surreal sounds of the river faded back to a purr. "Do you trust me?"

The question weighed more than even his first: *'Will you obey?'* But that didn't change her answer.

She nodded.

"Tell me." Squeezing hands insisted, hinting at the fire of his own needs. Her breast rose and fell beneath the god's protecting arm. She closed her eyes.

"I trust you, Hades."

"Then let go."

Against all reason, Persephone did. Clutching fingers released his arm, the pointless hold on his chiton. He nuzzled her temple with his jaw. "Go on."

It took her several fortifying breaths before she could give him what he wanted. With each lungful, Persephone banished tension. With each heartbeat, she promised herself this would not be a mistake.

She let her sandal give up the edge. Then the other.

The goddess trusted the Lord of the Dead to hold her, feet dangling over the River of Fire.

Hades hissed with his own restrained approval. "Perfection," he said. "Your confidence should not go without reward."

The hand at her hip slipped to the open side of her chiton. Discovered flesh. Descended.

"My Lord."

He found her, wet, ready to leap out of her skin. His other supporting arm firmed its grip, and Hades went about complicating her world.

Those fingers knew her weaknesses. Their prior encounters had taught him where and how to purchase response. Only now, as he explored and teased, her urges to squirm and buck came with a heart-stopping price.

She had to remain limp as the circling touch found and ignited every nerve. She had to hang, all outward calm, as he caught up that sensitive pearl and worried it between his fingers, lest all the writhing she wanted to do somehow made him lose his grip.

The angle was shallow, but he managed to stretch her entrance with just the tips of two fingers. The meat of his palm ground out a breath-hitching friction over that most swollen, aching part of her sex.

Linen abraded her nipples where his clasping arm pulled it tight over her breast. His mouth played havoc on the soft parts of her ear, her neck. She could feel the slick of her own lust painting her thighs, his busy hand. The threat of the fall, much like the binding of the *Elaionapothos*, had her lost for how to hold back the flood. Sensation came washing in, helpless sounds came pouring out.

Was he saying something? Fates, her senses were everywhere.

"There is more to it," he said, jerking the cup of his hand against her mound, "isn't there?" Persephone let out a whine that might have been an agreement. She couldn't think. "Everything sharper," he went on. "Every scent you inhale, every taste on your tongue. More."

His fingers retreated, but only enough to move their devotion to that bead that made her see stars.

"Oh please!"

Bliss wrapping her up, a fiery end threatening from below: it *was* more. More than she could take in at once.

"Do you understand it, my love?" Circling fingertips increased their pace.

"Terror heightens the senses." That growl had her dripping.

Oh yes, it does.

"Restraint heightens the senses." He shored up his grip, thumb and forefinger clamping down on her throat to a point no mortal would have been able to tolerate.

Sweet Creation, yes!

"Surrender heightens the senses."

Blue and purple lights began to flare at the edge of her vision. Persephone dripped from his arms, a stilled pendulum over eternity, allowing the Lord of the Dead to bring her to perfect torment over the promise of a fateful drop.

The keening in her ears was her own.

"Surrender."

Every muscle under her ribs condensed. It was so close. *So* close. His strokes reached an impossible plateau.

"Hades!"

"Trust me. Surrender."

Persephone abandoned her limits.

For the first thudding heartbeat, she fell in black silence. Then her senses caught up to her and her own feral noises flooded in to fill the space. Her body yielded up surging totality around Hades's tireless hand.

She called his name and swore and gave up trying to be still because she *knew* he would hold her safe.

An ankle hooked back around his calf and she writhed on his fingers, tilting her head, demanding his mouth, which he gave.

Something faraway told her he was backing onto the bridge, but Persephone was still shuddering, seizing under his touch. She felt his body bend, felt her own feet touching stone, her knees folding as the last violence of her orgasm shook her.

Black eyes met hers, upside down, while slowing fingers smeared echoes of delirious heat. Her head lay on his kneeling thigh and male arousal throbbed under wool, just out of sight.

He saw to your pleasure, and none for himself.

She raised a limp hand, brushing knuckles over his length. "Hades ..." Her voice came at a rasp.

"Another time." He lifted her fingers away; brought them to his mouth in a string of soft, incongruous kisses.

She looked up at him, spent. Altered. The first dozen thoughts were too complicated to condense with her tongue. The thirteenth was absurd.

"Will we have to walk all the way back?"

His laugh was a drug.

"No love," he said. "We will not."

◆

Hades attempted to retain at least some respectable amount of focus on his duties, but this was proving no small feat with the goddess walking at his side.

His regular visit to Menoites and his herd of glossy black oxen was behind them, the rolling Underworld fields dwindling in the light of the *paráthyra* at their backs. The path through the cavern ahead was smooth from millennia of use, and he kept to it now instead of rushing to his next destination by means of the æther. It gave him an excuse to linger in the presence of Persephone without any irritating distractions.

The day after their encounter on the bridge, she'd expressed an interest in accompanying him on his rounds rather than meandering about his realm on her own.

And how could he refuse?

The collected elegance she wore like a mantle now as they strolled belied nothing of the raw abandon he'd witnessed over the River of Fire. She was a fine match for the unvarying peace of the Underworld landscape surrounding them today, but there, on the bridge ...

Suspended over the Phlegethôn, she'd freed herself to the savagery of trust. The Daughter of Olympos—who had no business being in his realm, truth be told—had allowed him that exquisite gift of surrender. She had blossomed in his arms, feral and dangerous in her acceptance.

Dangerous to *him*, was the problem.

This entire affair should have been a transaction. Instead, the Goddess of Growing Things was a Fates-damned *drug*. He wanted her and nothing but her, every waking moment. For the love of creation, he had responsibilities to attend!

"Hades."

"Mm?"

Attention here and now, immortal.

"I said, this is not something I'm accustomed to seeing in the upper realms."

"What's that?" Her half smile had him wanting to do terrible things.

"When my mother still permitted my presence on Olympos, I can hardly recall Zeus making such a diligent circuit of his domain."

Hades let out an uncharacteristic snort. "Well. The Lord of the Skies has a far larger population of immortals in his third of the rulership. No need to oversee everything himself, I suppose." He caught her quizzical eye and added, with careful enunciation: "A far simpler matter to be fruitful when one is well-liked."

And since when do you lapse into self-pity, Polydegmon?

"I see." The goddess returned her eyes to their path and, for once, Hades felt the tang of regret on the back of his tongue for airing such bitterness aloud. He didn't care for how his chest felt when her smile disappeared.

"Regardless," he said, trying to salvage her good humor, "it behooves a ruler to make his own observ—"

The air roiled hot in their path and he and Persephone balked.

Twin red orbs swelled to hovering life and Hekate poured out of the æther.

"Hades, mmy lord." Her three voices slipped and slid. "*Enodia*."

At his side, Persephone looked less ashen than their last encounter with the Goddess of the Crossroads, but Hades could see white knuckles where her hands were clasped.

"Kharon iss in nneed of you," the tri-form goddess said. "It iss *mosst* urgent."

"Well what does he wa—"

Hekate and her torches were already gone.

Hades closed his eyes and swore to himself. He opened them to find Persephone waiting, the tilt of her brows expectant. His sigh was audible. Intimate conversation would have to wait.

His bident cut through the air as he brought it to form with the long familiar gesture. He held out his other hand to Persephone.

"We will not walk this time."

✦

The æther of the Underworld was no better or worse to pass through than that of the upper realms, but Persephone tasted something … *other* in it as Hades pulled them through the connective essence of the plane. Something earthy perhaps; more condensed.

She raised no objections at all to the necessity of clinging to his side as they went, but the grim line of his mouth at *Enodia's* sudden departure had her tense for whatever their destination would bring.

As they regained their physical forms, the Lord of the Dead released her to stand on a beach.

A beach?

A shore, to be more accurate. Black sand stretched away in either direction along a calm, but steadily flowing river. Low-hanging mist obscured the opposite bank, but the water stretched for quite a breadth before it disappeared into the cloud. None of the watery *paráthyra* appeared in this place, but Hades's favored sourceless light kept the land around the riverbank visible like the grey time before dawn in the realms above.

Upstream from where they stood, a stone pier pointed out into the water like a bony finger, lanterns made from the thinnest alabaster glowing at intervals down its length. Docked at the end was a boat of such ancient and somber purpose its mere presence cooled Persephone to her immortal bones.

The ferryman's boat.

This was the Styx.

"Kharon."

The first word out of Hades against the near silent shushing of the river made her start. The gnarled immortal was already making his way across the sand to where they stood, his staff marking out a trail of holes as he went.

"My lord," Kharon said as they drew near, "we have a *hero*." The ferryman mouthed the word with the same tone one might discuss vermin.

The roll of Hades's eyes drifted sideways into irritation. "You couldn't have sent the Guardian to handle this? Or could he not spare a moment from his eternal complaining?"

"That is the very trouble, my lord." Kharon looked as though he wanted to wring his weathered hands, and Persephone suspected any sort of trepidation like this in front of his ruler was rare. "There was not merely the one."

"Oh?" Hades took a step forward, and she saw his eyes take a darting survey of the area.

"There were three more, and Kerberos gave chase." A knobby hand gestured down the shore in the direction of the pier. "I believe they were to serve as a distraction. The other has escaped to the inner realm."

"Fools." The god spat the word with a heat that threatened to fuse the sand at their feet into glass. "They waste everyone's time, including their own." He was already discarding his chlamys.

"I don't understand," said Persephone.

"Oh, every now and again some idiot mortal believes he can sneak into my realm and spirit his deceased loved one back to the planes of the living." The Lord of the Dead drew his bident out to its full, intimidating length.

"I have docked the ferry until the matter is resolved, my lord. No one in or out while the hunt is on." Kharon inclined his head and Hades grunted approval.

"I will return with our 'guest' once I track him down."

His decisive momentum had Persephone stammering, lost for what to do on the banks of the Styx.

"My—my lord," she said, stepping in his direction with a hand lifting to slow his departure, "will you go alone? May I—may I not continue to accompany—"

"You will not be able to match my pace, Green One." He strode to her side, hauling her to him with an arm around her waist. The breath flew out of her as he crushed them together with no little force. "You are not of this realm. Your abilities are suppressed, and you would need them to keep up. I will need you to wait here with Kharon."

And how long would that be?

The disappointment must have shown on her face, because the entire set of his pale features melted from brusque into something else. Those black eyes went deep, devouring.

Ravenous.

"Would you like to see me hunt, little flower?"

That voice of his had dropped to a stony grind and his arm clutched her with a fierce possession. The offer, like so many before it, held some dark potential that had her humming with want. Her lips had parted as she looked up at him. She gave a tiny nod, and his smile was a thing of deadly promise.

"Very well."

He held her eyes with a knee-weakening intensity but, on her periphery, she saw him press the pad of his thumb down onto one of the tines of his bident. When he brought it between them, a bead of golden ichor swelled from charcoal flesh where he'd pierced the skin. Without pause, he drew the thumb along her lower lip, and then descended upon her with a savage kiss.

The honeyed tang of immortal blood filled her mouth as Hades's tongue painted her confusion with the purpling colors of need.

Persephone reeled as he pulled away, but the god had already whirled to face the ferryman. The Lord of the Dead wielded his bident with a flourish and it tore the æther once more.

"See that *Enodia* finds Hypnos and has him here by the time I return," he said.

Kharon gave another nod. "My lord."

When Hades disappeared into the space between, Persephone's vision swam. She crashed to her knees in the damp, black sand, and fought the dizziness and whirling light.

Again, she tasted blood and her world went black.

Then ... she felt everything.

✦

There was no time to regret allowing her to experience him in this state. Hades had a mere heartbeat before the majority of his rational thought left him. It was just long enough to marvel at the beginnings of his arousal when she'd admitted to wanting to watch.

When the æther bore him forth some distance from the Styx, The Lord of the Dead was one with his realm.

He did not think, nor reason, so much as he felt and *knew* the Underworld around him. He had shed the need to exist in such complex states.

Dim landscapes flashed and leapt by on all sides. The chaos of his search defied any sort of method or plan. Only the burgeoning throb demanding he seek—find!—mortal life where there should be none filled his base senses to their limits.

The only difference today was a delicate new presence, hovering, it felt, just at the perimeter of his awareness. It clung, terrified but determined as he streaked along, and some essential part of him knew the goddess shared in the sensations. Pure and raw, the Unseen Realm distilled; she would feel it all.

There.

Approaching the Lethe. Mortal blood pulsing. Breathing lungs that didn't belong.

Hades could feel the impermanence of a living man.

He surged forward. Descended.

The man had just enough time to scream.

◆

Persephone sat back on the heels of her palms in the sand, panting when Hades returned.

He stepped into being again, the reality of the Underworld rippling around him in a way that made her queasy, even after she regained complete control of her senses.

This time he bore a mortal before him, dark hand fisted in the back of the man's filthy chiton, scruffing him like a cat. He propelled the man forward and the trespasser stumbled, falling to hands and knees on the shore of the Styx.

She blinked, trying to expand her awareness again after …

After what? What—*where* had he taken her?

You said you wanted to watch. Well?

The banks of the river were more crowded than when her mind had left with their lord.

Enodia churned her own dark space nearby, hands— how many?—folded at her waist, twin orbs bobbing above her shoulders with reddish light.

Kharon leaned on his staff looking as bored as an immortal could, weathered fingers drumming through the wait.

The mortal man cowered and Hades stood, arms folded over his chest, his disapproval plain.

Grey mist swirled further down the shore, and the head of a beast appeared. Then another. And another.

Kerberos.

So this was the infamous Guardian.

Each of the towering dog's three heads held a terrified man in its mouth. When the beast closed the distance to the gathering of immortals, he dumped his three charges without ceremony to the sand.

"The rest, Polydegmon."

Persephone swallowed at the new sensation of hearing the Guardian's words in her head. The dog sat on his great haunches like a sentinel, tail lashing and red eyes judging, she suspected, everyone in his sight.

The mortals ran to each other to huddle for comfort, tripping and flailing along the way. They had a mess of bruises and scrapes to share among them, and Persephone didn't envy the ride between the Guardian's jaws one bit.

"Where is Hypnos?" Hades said. His black eyes went to Hekate. "I thought I told you to—"

The æther wavered in a dizzying way at *Enodia's* side. Another god stepped forth, sweeping a fluid gesture with a hand as he came.

"Hello, naughty children."

The God of Sleep sauntered toward them, smiling in a way that said he made his own rules. He looked almost as out of place as she did in the Underworld, with tanned skin and a chiton floating about him in a subdued purple-grey. Long silver hair fell in a mane around his shoulders and pale eyes glinted with some unspoken jest.

"They're to remember nothing," said Hades.

The men stood in a rough line, facing the god with fear-wide eyes. Hypnos strolled along behind them, brushing idle fingertips over one set of shoulders after another.

"Wicked little boys," he said as though the words tasted like wine in his mouth. "The Underworld is no place for you. At least not yet."

As he passed, each mortal's eyes rolled back at his touch, their bodies slumping to the sand as their knees gave way.

"Not that one." Hades indicated the man he'd brought himself.

Hypnos stepped around the last one and his eyes lit on Persephone instead. "And I see the rumors are true." Her face flamed from the appreciative once-over as the god circled her before coming to stand aside again with a languid hand on a hip. "You may have waited around for an age or two, *Clymenus*, but I can certainly see why."

"Enough." The Lord of the Dead uncrossed his arms. Hypnos cut her a lascivious wink, but stayed silent. Soft snores came from at least one of the mortal men now deep in the grip of sleep on the beach.

"Tell us the story, hero, but do not waste our time."

The trembling man, though fit and likely in the prime of his limited life, blanched at the sight of so many immortals facing him down in a realm where he didn't belong.

I'm surprised he hasn't voided his bowels already, right here on the shores of the Styx.

A rumbling noise welled in the Guardian's chest.

"You delay the ferry, human. Speak."

The man let out an abrupt, high-pitched noise at Kerberos's words in his head, but—possibly to avoid anything more terrifying still—began to sputter out his tale.

Again, Hades met her with the unexpected.

After the violent urgency she'd experienced sharing a mind during his hunt, it seemed only natural now for him to deliver some swift and brutal justice to an interloper in his realm. The muscles in her limbs were tense, ready to have her turn away the moment the horrific punishment came.

But, no. He stood there, cool and impassive, as the man spun words of woe about a sister swallowed up by death on the eve of her betrothal. There had been an accident. A fall. It wasn't fair. It wasn't *right*.

"And so you thought to make your way into my domain and retrieve her?" The god's features remained neutral.

"My-my lord ..." The man tripped over his own words, at a loss.

"Hekate."

The tri-form goddess stepped forward at her lord's command. There was no point in Hades avoiding her true name, Persephone supposed, if she already stood in their midst.

"Fetch this one's sister." He laid each word down, quiet and distinct, the bonds of his gaze never leaving the mortal quailing in their grip.

Enodia and her torches vanished. They all waited on the beach in uncomfortable silence, the gentle waves of the Styx lapping the shore the only sound.

Well. Almost all of them.

Hypnos leaned in and spoke to her under his breath. "Has he spoken to you of making the vows?"

She blinked at him, mouth gaping like a fish. "Wh-what?" Persephone cleared her throat as quietly as she could, but Hades appeared to be paying little mind. "I do not believe vows are a part of his plans."

And what was that twinge in her chest when she admitted as much?

The god hummed discreet amusement. "I wouldn't go saying that in front of *Enodia*."

"She called me his Consort," Persephone said, more to herself as she tried to take the measure of things, than to the smirking immortal at her side.

"Our lord is impossible to please," he said, "and yet here you stand. I don't believe he's made a blood union with anyone *ever*."

The blood union. Yes. The savagery she'd experienced as he tore through the Underworld. She had known such a thing was possible, but until today, none of her kind had trusted her enough to share in it. And if she were to believe the God of Sleep, Hades might have offered her another of his firsts.

Feeling every sensation of his, knowing his every thought ... His words on the bridge over the River of Fire had shown her a truth: fear *did* excite her. But trust? There was something altogether more potent.

The æther parted in a smoky dance, and *Enodia* was with them again. This time a young mortal woman walked in her stead, ever so slightly insubstantial in the way of human shades.

"Iokaste!" the man cried, and ran to embrace his sister.

"Alexios?" Her wonder didn't cease at the clasp of her brother's arms. "You are here? And not ... not ...?"

Persephone could see the man fighting the urge to recoil. He mustered the control to draw away at a measured rate, but contact between souls on opposite sides of the cycle of life could not have been anything the poor mortal was ready to experience.

"No," Hades said, "your brother has not yet breathed his last. He imagined he would enter this realm and 'save' you from the horrors of death."

"Oh, Alexi ..." A familial sympathy melted the woman's graceful features.

"Tell him," said Hades. "He does not understand."

Iokaste brought a hand to her brother's shoulder and drew him near. She began speaking in a low hush meant for his ears alone.

The knot between his brows loosened. The tension went out of his stance. His eyes shone wet and within moments he was dropping to his knees. His sister went with him, arms around his shoulders, and the mortal man shook with grief. Iokaste remained serene and patient.

When their arms untangled at last, Alexios red and sniffling, the Lord of the Dead spoke again.

"Do you see now?"

The man gave a limp nod, climbing to his feet. His sister stood at his side.

"What do you see?" Hades said.

"I see"—he swallowed, wiping at his eyes with the back of a hand—"my sister dwells in the house apportioned to her by the Fates. She is at peace."

"And so must you be," said Iokaste, smoothing fingertips down his arm.

He continued his nodding. It would be a weary acceptance, but the misdirected fire for 'justice' had burnt out.

"You will return to your lives," Hades pronounced, gesturing with his bident at Alexios and his men. "You will forget the means by which you entered my domain. You will mourn your kin and be at peace." He took a step forward, looming tall and fearsome.

"And you will *never* attempt such a misguided feat again. My mercy has limits, and I assure you, mortal, you do not wish to see them. Do you understand?"

The man, who had shrunk down to a knee again during the god's admonition, nodded his head. "My Lord Hades, I do."

"Hypnos?"

A grey and purple swirl flourished away from Persephone's side.

Iokaste stepped near her brother again and ran ephemeral fingers through his hair. The siblings smiled at one another just before the God of Sleep had the man wilting to the sand, his memories dissipating like a cloud.

Hades nodded his approval at this and began to issue commands.

"Hekate, if you would see these mortals returned to their proper plane."

"Indeed, *Polydegmon*." The glow from *Enodia's* torches expanded, bigger and brighter to encompass the unconscious men. When the red lights winked out, the goddess and her charges were gone.

"Kharon, we will delay you no longer."

"My lord." The ferryman dipped his ancient chin before heading back to his craft.

Kerberos made some low noise Persephone could only feel in her chest, and Hades turned to acknowledge the beast. "Well done, as always, Guardian." The sound turned to something like appeasement and the massive dog turned and padded off into the mist. She tried not to start at his voice in her head, which came in time with the vanishing of his tail.

"We all serve the Unseen Realm, Mate of my Lord. If you wish to dwell among us, you must choose a way to do so."

Hades had a tongue for seduction, but Kerberos was blunt as a millstone, and twice as heavy.

"If you require nothing else, Rich One?" Hypnos raised silver brows, waiting for his lord's dismissal.

"You have done what is needed, Bringer of Dreams. Take your leave as you will."

"Don't I always?" White teeth flashed and pale eyes turned to Persephone. "Try not to dismantle him too completely, will you? We've grown rather fond of our Lord of the Dead."

In an eddy of purple linen, the God of Sleep passed into the æther. His knowing grin was the last thing Persephone saw.

The shore was empty save she and Hades, but the god spared them no time for reflection.

"I have business in the Hall of Judgments," he said. "Do you still wish to accompany me, or have you seen enough for one day?"

It was no question at all, really. She moved to his side, her sandals making prints in the sand. Rather than wait for his offered hand, as had been their pattern for the day thus far, Persephone slipped her arms around his waist and tilted her head back to meet his eyes.

"I will come."

The hand not holding his bident slipped up along her neck and into her hair. When he bent to sample a kiss, the new normalcy of such a thing rendered her mute. Simple affection from the ruler of the Underworld had become a matter of course. Not that it was any less potent, if the hum between her thighs was any measure.

"Hypnos is wrong, you know." He brushed the words against her lips. "I'm not impossible to please."

The æther swallowed them once more.

◆

The Hall of Judgments was no more a hall than *Enodia's* 'torches' were truly torches. Like an iceberg the size of a small island in deep grey basalt, the top surface leveled to provide an arena for the proceedings, the 'hall' hovered far above the River Lethe. What unseen force held it suspended there, Persephone didn't know.

There were neither stairs nor ramps nor any other physical means of ascending to its plateau, but mortal shades continued to materialize and vanish atop its polished expanse as their summons or business there required. The majority kept to the perimeter of the space, where Persephone had elected to remain. Here, in this place of ultimate truth, they saw her for the immortal she was, and most left her a wide berth.

At one extreme edge of the circular 'hall', a trio of granite benches stood raised on a set of three steps. Here sat the judges: Minos, Rhadamanthys, and Aiakos. Hades's sigil all but shone from the center of the floor, inlaid in white onyx, at least four times the height of the deceased mortal man standing at its center.

Behind the judges, the Lord of the Dead stood and observed, only inserting his own opinions on rare occasion.

Persephone had vague memories of Minos from his time as a ruler of mortal men, but that had been ages ago, and she could only recall his reputation as just, which she supposed led to his eventual appointment in the realm of the Dead. He and Rhadamanthys were brothers, both sons of Zeus, though she had long ago given over the idea of attempting to acquaint herself with every single one of her half-siblings. Of Aiakos, she'd heard only rumor, but, as with the others, she suspected Hades knew his mind when he chose them as servants of his realm.

We all serve the Unseen Realm, Mate of my Lord.

Kerberos's words echoed back to her. They'd sounded so matter-of-fact, yet a central tone in them resonated with a sliver of something growing at the back of her throat.

What was it? Disgust?

For whom?

Hades had designed her fall into the Underworld, certainly, but after the initial indignity at such an arrival wore off, how had she not used the situation to her own advantage? Out from under the purview of anyone who could enforce her mother's edict, she had amazed even herself with the speed at which she had accepted the god's offer.

Perhaps she hadn't foreseen every detail, but the intent behind his demand for obedience had been obvious enough. And while fear had often been a factor, there could be no question of her arousal—her undeniable attraction—at their every interaction.

She was enjoying this. She was allowing it to continue. Allowing him to provide her with new pleasures, literally spreading herself wide for what Hades could give. On the bench in that first bedchamber, atop the *Elaionapothos*, high above the Phlegethôn where she dangled and shuddered under his touch.

Every time she had wallowed in new sensation, yet he had attended to his own gratification only once.

And the way he called out your name as it happened …

If he glanced her way now, would he see the color in her cheeks?

Was this who she had allowed herself to become? This passive figure, lying in wait for others to offer up satisfaction? Which of them had been giving thus far, and which had been happy to receive?

She had no right to lament injustices when she hadn't been behaving in an equitable manner, herself.

From the other side of the hall, Hades caught her eye. One of his half-smiles trifled with the speed of her pulse. A silent thunderclap of truth cleared away all other thought.

If Persephone wanted fulfillment in this existence, she was going to have to be an active participant.

If her affairs on the mortal plain had taught her nothing else, it was that no one partner could ever complete the circle. The Lord of the Dead had come as close as any had ever done, but an element was missing.

Her.

She would not remain passive. She would serve. She would *give*.

I am not impossible to please.

Images of just how she might do so washed over her in a delicate shudder.

"Goddess?"

Persephone inhaled and her eyes snapped to the left. At the sight of the mortal man who dared an approach, they opened wider.

"Iacob?"

"Yes, *Karporphoros*." He averted his eyes and clasped his hands together, but did not seem at all startled to hear her address him by name. "I believe my wife owes you many thanks, as do I."

The shade of Polyxene's husband stood as near as he could brave, and Persephone was at a loss for words. Each time she had visited the woman, had they not met in private? How would he recognize her here? The statues and mosaics the Sons of Man created in her image rarely bore her much resemblance, and here in the Underworld, there was no wake of leafy growth following in a trail at her feet to make her identity plain.

She tilted her head. Narrowed her eyes. "Your beloved gave her word not to speak of my visits."

"She kept it Green One, I swear." His brow creased in protest, but he kept his gaze on the floor. "I returned to our home early one evening and caught sight through our window."

"And you chose not to enter your own house?"

"Goddess, I did not wish to risk any favor you might have bestowed on my dear Polyxene. I was certain you appeared in secret for a reason. No. I found reason to pay my brother a visit. It seemed the wiser choice."

"You never told your wife?"

"She never knew."

Persephone's shoulders eased. "There is no need for you to stare at the stones," she said. "It is not I before whom you should humble yourself in this realm, in any event." She tilted a quick nod in Hades's direction.

The shade cast an uncertain glance around before daring to meet her eyes. "Thank you, Goddess," he said. "May I … that is, might I be able …"

"Speak. You have nothing to fear from me."

He approached the question with caution, as though its answer might bite. "It has been many years, I think. How … how is she?"

Persephone smiled at this. "She is well, Iacob. I've seen her within the last month. There are perhaps more white hairs on her head, but she still laughs. The house you made together does not want. She speaks of you each time we meet."

The man's eyes shone, and he sniffed. Were shades able to weep? "That is ... to hear that makes me full."

The goddess felt a lump of emotion welling in her own throat. "I am glad to hear it."

Fates!

She made discreet use of her thumb to rotate Polyxene's ring so the stone faced her palm. For him to see it now ...

"Do you ... believe you will visit her again?"

"Unless I am prevented."

But how long will you be in the Underworld? Mortal time whirls like a chariot wheel.

"*Karporphoros*," he said, bowing his head, "will you tell her I think of her, as well? That I wait for her here?"

Damn this man, but he was drowning her in sentiment!

"I will tell her," she said.

"What will you tell?"

The Lord of the Dead appeared at her side, black eyes appraising the mortal shade. Now Iacob did shrink, and did go to one knee.

"My—my lord!"

"I have seen what I need of the hall today," he said, circling her shoulders with a charcoal arm. "Come."

"I will tell her, Iacob," Persephone said again to the wide-eyed kneeling man. "I will."

Hades pulled them into the æther.

✦

The space they arrived in was rectangular and deep, flooded with that nebulous light he preferred throughout his somber halls. This was another formal venue, like the Hall of Judgments, only enclosed on all sides, as she remembered from Olympos. Here were twisting columns, running parallel to the outer walls, a finished ceiling vaulting high overhead, and massive doors guarding an entrance behind her.

Should I not have been speaking to Iacob?

Ahead was what could only be his throne. Lords of realms had thrones. This one was serious and black, intimidating between two soaring stalagmites glossy with life in a dead land.

Persephone swallowed.

"So," he said, meandering in the direction of the seat meant for him and him alone, "who was your 'friend'?"

Between them, above a medallion in the shape of his sigil in the stone floor, a misty likeness of Iacob materialized and hovered.

Creation take me, is he jealous?

"A mortal I know. Knew. During his last lifetime."

Hades turned, lips curling into the beginnings of a smile. "How well did you 'know' him, Persephone?"

Her nervous laugh brought her an internal grimace. As if this god had any authority or right to an opinion over her activities on the mortal plane. He'd admitted to such indulgences, himself. "I knew of him through his wife. I was surprised he recognized me, as I was sure I'd never appeared before him in my true form. He claims to have seen me one evening when his wife and I imagined we were alone."

"More intriguing by the moment." Hades lowered himself onto the bench of his throne and crossed one dark ankle over the opposite knee. "And why show your true form to this woman of his?"

"She was … I was something of a—a matron of hers, I suppose." Why did everything sound so foolish when she had to say it in front of him? Probably those black eyes flustering her now, as they followed her every movement.

He let out an amused huff. "Interesting. Why bother? It can only last for so short a time, with their little lives. Come."

The Lord of the Dead held out a beckoning hand, and she fought the flush in her cheeks when her mind leapt at once to the last two times he'd told her to come.

You're in an awful lot of trouble, you know that, Persephone.

Iacob's likeness dissipated into the light of the throne room as the goddess made her way past to join Hades on the dais. When she took his outstretched hand, he gave a subtle tug.

"Sit."

There was room enough for one, of course, and here she was again, on his lap. No, not again. The bench in that first chamber had left room for her to sit on the stone in front of him. Now, Persephone had to perch on a thigh.

She was able to abandon at least some of her tension, though, as his questions had taken a casual turn, rather than the interrogation she'd been dreading. An arm slipped around her waist, pulling her right side against his chest.

And he expects me to think, this way.

"I suppose," she said, "if I were a mortal, I would choose to be like this woman. Polyxene."

"Was it she who gave you the ring?"

Persephone felt fingers come up and brush her hair away from her neck. Knuckles grazed along the top of her spine.

"She is."

"And what is it that places this Polyxene ahead of so many others? That a goddess would trouble herself to emulate her."

His leg shifted beneath her and the subtle movement had blood rushing in Persephone's veins. How did he do it? How did he keep her in this state, without even appearing to try?

Her mouth and body were having two different conversations. The latter grew warm, wet, impatient, while the former answered his mundane questions.

"She does something useful." Her eyes were on the dip between his collarbones. "Something good. She is helping others, improving their lives."

She has known love.

"You do not imagine yourself this way already?"

Persephone frowned. Arrogance and seduction were far easier tones to handle coming from the Lord of the Dead than the hint of concern she heard from him now.

"You are useful by your very *being*." His thumb brushed her lower lip, muddying her impulses further. "You are an invaluable force in perpetuating the mortal cycles. We both are. I collect life as it collapses, and you push it forth as it renews."

"But what am I doing with *intention* for anyone?" she asked, waving him off with a hand. "Nothing. I am without purpose."

Hades caught up her dismissive fingers, lacing them with his own, a study in light and dark. He brought her knuckles to his lips and pressed them there, black eyes intense when she met them at last.

I will give. I will please him.

"You have at least one purpose in my realm, Persephone." By their linked hands, he hauled her close; close enough to make her breath hitch and his next words fell in place of a kiss over her open mouth.

"Would you like me to show you?"

◆

VI Service

Slow down. Slow down. Slow down.
Did his chest heave visibly as the æther gave them up into his private rooms again? Hades hadn't even bothered to stand. Persephone still sat on his thigh, and he'd willed himself to arrive sitting, the resting *Elaionapothos* taking the place of his throne.

He needed to gain control of himself, but how with his senses drowning in green? The shift in venue hadn't given the goddess pause any more than it had him. Alone with her at last in the Great Hall, he'd fought down a fever and lost. The heat of her mouth on his told him it was catching.

Kissing! He could have laughed if he wasn't busy trying to devour her whole. A goddess of the upper realms, squirming in his lap, delicate fingers at the side of his face, lapping up kisses from Hades *Nekrodegmôn* with abandon. Had Aphrodite promised any such impossibility in the first place, he would have banished her from his halls on the spot.

The Fair One had been cautious enough to make only the vague prediction that Persephone would be 'quite suited' to his 'proclivities'. He'd been so dismissive.

He had to make a fist in her hair to break the thrall of their kiss. Green eyes stayed trained on him, her lips swollen and parted. His free hand cupped around the knee she bent closest to him, lewd fingers dipping in suggestion into the press between the back of her thigh and calf.

"Shall we play a different game?"

She nodded, eyes locked on his.

Selfish. She confesses her woes and you bend them to suit your own ends?

But he would go mad as Dionysos if he waited. Perhaps the effects of the blood union lingered, to have him wrestling with impulse this way. It didn't matter.

He stood, bringing her to her feet with him.

The goddess's waiting posture spoke her apprehensions. What would he demand of her today? Would he stoke her fears again? Challenge the limits of her trust?

No. His needs were baser today. The hunt still sang in his veins. He'd shown that mortal a mercy on the shores of the Styx, a beast that had caught but not killed. A call to claim victory hung unanswered.

Persephone could fill this void for him.

In rapid succession, he yanked one fibula after the other from the shoulders of her chiton. "You won't be needing this." Red linen rippled to the floor and she did not hide herself.

She stood there, challenging him with the nudity he'd wrought, tension in her stance, as though she might leap at his next word.

"The rest," he said, eyes flicking down to the sandal straps binding her calves.

The goddess sank to a knee and pulled loose leather lacing, refusing to surrender her hold on his eyes as she did it.

She knew.

Perhaps not all of it, but enough. She saw his barely checked restraint, the way his gaze raked her curves while she knelt and he stood. While she was vulnerable and he was not.

Aren't you?

As she rose to her now bare feet, he twitched a nod to the *Elaionapothos*. "Up here."

A series of deft movements saw her kneeling atop the black gloss of the platform, petal pale flesh in the most perfect contrast to the dark surface. She sat on her heels, palms atop her thighs, and waited.

No objections. No questions.

No idea how the blood rushed in his veins at this new, ready obedience. He'd announced no detail of his intentions, but the candid lines of her mouth, her shoulders, told him she would accept whatever he gave.

And he *would* give.

Hades came to stand at the edge of the platform.

"Closer."

A few shuffling movements on her knees and she did as he bade.

"More."

She came as near as the Oil's resting edge would allow, the wool of his chiton grazing the tops of her thighs. With both hands, he gathered the mass of her hair and piled it atop her head. "Hold this."

Her fingers laced in under his to secure the flowing burden, and Hades bit the inside of his cheek. Arms poised above her head, breasts raised and presented, throat exposed: she was going to destroy him, and it would be his own doing.

He removed the iron ring and called forth his bident. Its tines touched the ground at his side and a sound like falling sand whispered into the silence.

Persephone's chest rose and fell at the sight of a glittering black flow rising with a purpose along the weapon's haft. When it reached a suitable height, Hades drew the material off into the air.

To her credit, the goddess held her position fast and didn't balk when the black ribbon followed his gestures to settle around the stem of her neck. Her breath was audible, however, when she felt it solidify into the form he intended.

He drew the malleable fruit of his realm through deliberate fingers, the essence hardening as he went. The line swung in a satisfying clatter while he spent a last gesture forming another of his desires into stone.

The finished implement lay in his hand. Like the collar circling her throat, and the black chain spanning the distance, an obsidian hook a handspan wide gleamed at her from his palm. Hades smiled.

"Is that not fine?"

Her eyes moved along the chain to where it disappeared out of sight beneath her chin. To watch understanding slacken her jaw made his cock stir.

"You can let go your hair."

Olympian fingers descended to the ring of Underworld stone. She made a tentative exploration for a closure, but there was none to find.

"You will have freedom at my pleasure," he said, gathering more of the chain back into his grip.

"Do you expect me to run?" Her question came at a gentle tease. "Or am I being punished for speaking to that mortal?"

Hades doubled the chain around his fist. Hauled her to her knees.

"I expect you to submit," he said, "because that is my pleasure, as well."

Green eyes searched his and he jerked the goddess closer, still, earning a quiet gasp.

"You will stand for me." He fed her the words.

"You will kneel for me." And she swallowed them down.

"You will *beg* for me," he said, "and you will begin now." He lowered his fist and her collar with it.

"Hands and knees."

And so she went.

Her movements were smooth, accepting of his commands. In a breath, she was on all fours, the curve of her spine presenting that perfect immortal shape to such advantage that Hades wanted to dismantle her piece by piece and absorb every mote of what she was into himself.

Instead, and with deliberate care, he followed her down, sitting on his heels beside the *Elaionapothos* to look his goddess in the eye.

"Because I trust your obedience *so* much," he said, holding the hook up to illustrate between them, "I will leave this here and not sunk into the Oil to hold you in place."

Her eyes followed the movement of his hand as far as she could as he reached over her shoulders to lay the hook and its wicked promise flat in the center of her back.

"And Persephone"—he stood, trailing a fingertip along her throat, under her chin—"if this were a punishment? You would know it."

Her gaze followed his ascent, waiting. The bident he'd been leaning on collapsed back to its ring form at his will, and Hades slipped it onto a finger. He brushed a thumb over her lower lip.

"Do *not* move."

The goddess did not.

The Oil gave under his weight just enough to prevent discomfort as he mounted the platform behind her. His demands had exposed her secrets and there was no stopping the call of her flesh, at least not at first.

Round cheeks filled his palms. He kneaded, indulging, and she hissed through her teeth when he spread her to add to the lewd display. Every impulse cried out for him to cover her—now! To rut her like a beast and own her screams, whatever form they took.

It will please you for mere moments. What will it buy you in the end?

His higher thoughts ran true, fighting to be heard as they were with the storm of want battering him from all sides.

Later.

As a parting promise to himself, he stung her bottom with a slap. Persephone gasped, but did not turn her head to look back at him. A subtle mark blushed onto her skin, and there was no possibility he would not need to produce more of the same.

More, and darker. Heavier. She will make such sounds for you.

But not today.

Not yet.

Hades dipped experimental fingers between her thighs, his touch the lightest mist. He watched her toes curl in, the soles of her feet crinkling at the sensation. She was hot. Slick. Not a single gamble he'd taken had done anything to cool her.

He ducked down low, ready to stoke the fires of her want some more.

At the first long lap of his tongue, Persephone moaned. The sound came straight from her very bones, and the Lord of the Dead went hard as the obsidian around her throat to hear it.

He would consume her.

The goddess dropped her head between her shoulders as Hades set to work. With every slip of his tongue, every pull of his lips, he could hear the soft labor of her breath. And the taste of her!

Karporphoros. Bringer of Fruit. Her epithet served here, as well. Persephone was a sweet glory, glossing his chin, fogging his senses.

Lips, tongue, and teeth; he brought them both to torment. Wet flesh and the scent of her arousal were close on all sides, and Hades burrowed deep, unable to find the limits of his fervor.

He paused to breathe, to draw away and look upon all that was lovely and pink, swollen under his efforts. The goddess felt the lack and leaned her weight back onto her knees, tilting her hips, spreading for him. Pleading.

Every hidden place she has will beg for you.

Hades lowered his attention to something new and earned a raw noise of surprise from Persephone. Puckered flesh quivered under the rasp of his tongue, and he would remind her again that here, with him, no one could forbid her *anything.*

The goddess writhed on his mouth. Whimpered as he explored, as he tested the give of that tight ring. Would she surrender this to him, as well? How deep? How deep could he take her into those places that darkened his dreams?

Not today. You have not seen all you wish to see.

He reached and found the chain where it lay along her back, sliding it through his fingers until he held the hook again.

The weight in his hand returned a measure of his focus. He hefted the obsidian hook and traced it between her shoulder blades. Down the curve of her spine while he teased her with his tongue.

The black stone slid along the cleft between her cheeks and he drew himself away to make space for it. When the cool, blunt tip settled against the first entrance it found, the goddess exhaled. Hades introduced the smooth curve with a subtle pressure, his immortal blood boiling as he worked it inside, watching it sink past her defenses.

Only when the hook came to rest, snug in her tightest channel, did he sit back to admire his handiwork. The black chain glittered like a scorpion's tail, taut between the obsidian that claimed her ass and circled her throat. Whenever she moved, the collar would tug at the chain, and the chain would tug at the curving stone shaft.

Her breathing had already grown short, and Hades couldn't resist the call of torment.

He brought up an experimental thumb and drew it over the sensitive pearl between her lips, exposed now in her arousal. She cried out and he did it again. And again. Her lust leaked out over his knuckles, and if he continued in this way, Hades knew she would have her release.

And he would not allow it. Not today. Today she would know want. She would teeter on the edge for him, and if she could withstand this …

Hades abandoned his position. Her sides heaved as the platform shifted under his weight, the movements of his departure.

She twisted to watch his return to the edge of the Oil, still on her hands and knees, cheeks now beautifully flushed.

She hasn't moved. She obeys you still.

"What's wrong?"

"Not a single thing." He drew the tip of a nail down over the bridge of her nose, her parted lips. "Your pleasure belongs to me now, Daughter of Olympos. You will have it when I allow."

The tilt of her brows at this, the way pupils dilated in spring green eyes and her back bowed in defeat, gave him understanding, hate, and love, all at once. Persephone was a chorus singing the hymns of his every need.

Then take what you need. She will give it.

With a tug and flourish of his free hand, he had his chiton over his head, baring himself as the wool fell to the floor.

His cock stood out from his body, marble hard and looming level with her kneeling line of sight. She watched it bob, and caught her lower lip in her teeth.

"Persephone."

She surged forward and he disappeared into her mouth.

Hades swore.

The goddess brought fingers to circle him at the root, and began to feed herself with a will. She'd warned him of her adventures among the cities of men, but now her experience became plain.

You didn't even have to ask her.

She worked him with an angry mouth, a vent to her frustrations. It was a backward means of retaliation for the way he'd left her, but the goddess aimed to see him just as helpless under the yoke of sensation.

With her hand, she stroked and pulled. With her open mouth, she bobbed over his length. The heavy crown popped back and forth over a taut lip. Her tongue danced along the sensitive ridge of flesh that descended from the plump head.

When he shifted his weight to steady himself, her grip held him fast. She made her lips into a tight entrance, and made a show of pushing him through it with all the speed of a sunset. His eyes rolled back and she drew him out and did it again, knowing full well the picture she painted.

It was only when she aimed him upward with a slick fist and bent to take the loose skin of his scrotum into her mouth, pulling in one of his testicles after it, that he came close to losing control.

Keep your wits, immortal. You can have it soon, but not just yet.

Hades leaned over her body and the full press of his cock had her stilling her motions, breathing just to accommodate the depth. His hands traced her spine on both sides of the chain until he reached the hook and took hold. When he began to help the polished stone in and out, a new, wet mewling welled around the flesh filling her mouth.

He wanted to throw his head back as she sucked, as she *writhed* in the trap he'd set, but he forced himself not to let go. Not yet.

Look at her. Look what she has become for you.

Persephone worshipped at his altar, submitted to his whims. A low noise in her throat vibrated up over his cock, just as a flicker of movement caught his eye. The surface of the *Elaionapothos* moved in a ripple.

As he watched, the Oil began to lap over calves, the backs of her knees. As she swallowed his length, the black gloss of it spiraled in twin ribbons, climbing her parted thighs. There was only one possible destination, but it made no sense.

The Oil formed to *his* desires, and Hades had left her quivering on the cusp by specific intent.

Yet their first time in this room ... The frenzied growth, the formation of stone.

Impossible.

But was it?

The *Elaionapothos* arrived from both sides to cover her other wet mouth.

Consort of my Lord.

Hekate's words returned, heavy with portent.

His realm could respond to the whims of another, but only if …

A deep thrum arose within the Oil—he could feel it against his shins. If Hades was not mistaken, the *Elaionapothos* had risen at her desire to flutter against her most sensitive flesh.

He was too astonished to deny her now.

She screamed around his cock as her body found the shining path. A hand rose to his flexing backside and he felt her urging him further into her mouth. When he saw what she wanted, there was no hesitation.

Hades plunged to the back of her throat and laced his fingers through her hair. His hips snapped in a fury and he rode, reckless, parting that jaw, increasing the pitch of her urgent sounds.

Persephone knelt before the Lord of the Dead, yielding at every entrance to the stone of his realm, the demands of his flesh. When the rabid cries began to sing out around his plunging girth, he knew he would have mere moments.

He slammed home and the breach sent her eyes wide. The goddess sputtered and wailed and Hades lost himself with a roar.

She swallowed him down, throat working in greed, her own sounds primal as she came.

Even as they shuddered and drew their first breaths in the aftermath, Hades knew his games were at an end.

It was too perfect. Too right.

He had never gone looking for this.

A match? After all this time? And if such a thing could be true, there was only one question.

What was he prepared to do about it?

✦

For the first time that day, Persephone did not insist on accompanying the Lord of the Underworld. Somewhere in the haze that followed the events atop the *Elaionapothos*, where they'd lain, entwined and exhausted, he'd murmured something about the rest of his duties and risen to depart.

Her limbs were too limp, her thoughts drunken and sliding. She made no objection.

The silence of his chamber cooled her. Distilled the chaos between her ears. She lay on the platform still, purchasing new ideas with each slowing heartbeat.

Her choice to give, to serve and please with intention, had torn open a rift. Like that bident of his, ripping the æther, it had revealed another realm. The possibilities were vast.

There was a release she'd never imagined in riding the current of another's want. *His* want.

You will beg for me.

And oh, those things for which she might beg. He'd only hinted at a few. The crack of his hand over her backside. That hook, burrowing as she took his cock. They were but a taste. A summer storm on the horizon, roiling with the dark potential of all she could surrender, still.

The question had become not how much would he take from her, but rather, how much could she give.

Your pleasure belongs to me, now.

His words had unlocked a new understanding, but that didn't explain the *Elaionapothos*. He wanted her unsatisfied, hungering on the brink after the wicked efforts of his tongue. She'd recognized his game and accepted it; rolled on a sea of exquisite suffering, just as intended.

Why change his mind and will the Oil to work for her release? When it had come to circle her thighs, to overwhelm the thirst for completion between them …

But had he? Changed his mind?

The Oil responds to his *desires first, he said so himself.*

And if it hadn't? If the only other possibility were true … what could that mean?

As sleep folded her back into its arms, a sibilant voice sang a threefold song, laying open the gateway to dreams.

The Underworld ansswerss to Underworld gods.
Aren't you home? Aren't you home?
Aren't you
aren't you
aren't you home?

◆

Hades returned to the goddess in his chamber some hours later, only to find Persephone sprawled across the surface of the *Elaionapothos*. The ambient light was as dim as he'd left it, and the tide of sleep had rolled her down to the depths.

She lay on her side, top leg bent at the knee, the crimson fabric of her chiton draped over her as a blanket. Her breathing was deep and regular, but at his approach, she stirred. Made some tiny noise of … what was that? Frustration?

He made himself still. Any sound might disturb her and, in this moment, Hades would see her unguarded again, just as she'd been after her fall into his domain.

How long did he stand there in that silent trance? Long enough to lose awareness of the boundaries of the space around him, the stalagmites receding to the edge of his perception, the ceiling and floor fading back to mere shades of reality. He and his goddess were alone in the heart of the Unseen Realm. They were the only two who needed to be.

Then, her hips shifted. She exhaled a murmur, unintelligible over the Oil.

She dreams.

Intrigue seized him and he padded closer, rolling his steps in a bid for silence. He leaned low, ready to catch the next sound she made.

There was nothing, but he waited.

Waited. He—

Lids fluttered. Her breath hitched.

Fates! He could tear his hair. What did she see, on the other side of sleep?

Hypnos could tell him. The Bringer of Dreams saw as much in his own intangible domain as Helios did of the skies.

And you will what? Summon him here? To this *room?*

He ground his teeth as reason thwarted his wants. No. The complications expanded with each successive immortal to become aware of the *Elaionapothos*. Aphrodite had been trouble enough. And Persephone …

The goddess made a soft sound, and he bit the inside of his lip. Her hand dusted along the curve of a hip.

"Hadesss …"

His nails gouged his palms at the unconscious slur of his name.

"… please I wnn …"

Her grip on him coiled tighter.

By the three realms! Wake her! Wake her now and make her yours!

Perfect lips parted and exhaled. Dark brows furrowed and delicate fingers clutched at something that wasn't there.

"… need … love me …"

Love me.

His vision swam and a black fire roared to life on some other plane of endings and beginnings.

He wanted to destroy worlds. To burn it all. Burn until the æther itself became ash. The feeling was too, too …

The Lord of the Dead backed away from the dreaming answer to his many, many questions.

Persephone slept and he needed to be anywhere else. Where control of the self failed, regret would soon follow, and he could not trust himself in the violent grip of such impossibility.

For ages, there had been certainty, and now there was none.

The memory of Aphrodite's smile mocked him, pomegranate flashing between her fingers.

A more permanent way …

He drew out his bident, snarling in the silence.

You will not.

Tore open a jagged rift.

But the vows. The vows! She will never …

And fled into the æther.

✦

VII Pain

Leaves fell from trees in Athenai.
Fields withered in Kornithos.

At Delphoi and Argos and Pella, fruit rotted on the vine as though it had sat on the ground for weeks.

Demeter's wrath knew neither bounds nor precedent.

The sons and daughters of Man wailed and pled at her temples, but the goddess had abandoned mercy. For where had been the mercy of Zeus when he'd sentenced their daughter to the advances of the Lord of the Dead?

The well of her abilities ran deep, and Demeter drew from it as she hadn't since the war, all those many sprawling ages ago.

Granaries writhed with weevils; stores of wine spoiled in hours. As her chariot rode in ruin over mount and vale, the Daughter of Kronos reached down into the marrow of the earth that was hers to nourish, and closed a vengeful grip around the source of its lifeblood.

Plows crumbled to dust. Cattle, goats, and fowl alike knew sickness and demise. Such a blight on the world of men she wrought as hadn't been seen in ages.

If they have no way to eat, they have no way to live.

And the gods of Olympos needed *live* mortals to worship them. Altars would lay bare of offerings and songs of praise would be extinguished.

They will beg. Before it is all over, they will beg me. And I will have my price.

◆

Persephone was lost.

Not from any additional overwhelming displays from Hades, but because she had no idea where she was.

Upon awakening, she'd found herself alone. After waiting and waiting, with neither *Elaionapothos*, nor paired empty chairs, nor darkened fireplace providing any sort of company, she'd decided to leave.

Her first goal had been to seek him out, but that had proven fruitless. She knew how to get to the bridge over the Phlegethôn, but that was some distance from his palace and she didn't imagine him having any reason to be there. What she didn't know was how to get almost anywhere else in his realm.

Of course, he had taken his time strolling with her through some of the more interesting parts of his domain, but more often their travels had taken them through the æther. Such means of movement left her with no sense of direction at all, not with her abilities suppressed and him the guiding will behind their journey.

For a time, she'd hovered on the smaller bridge where her unintentional summoning of *Enodia* had driven her into his arms. She'd stared out into the Great Cavern, her gaze going unfocused over the scattered *paráthyra* and the meandering red line of the River of Fire.

The Underworld answers to Underworld gods.

This realm had a dark, still sort of beauty to it, but Persephone was not an Underworld goddess. She belonged at the new green edge of Spring under a morning-bright sky, but the words kept singing along in her head, regardless. How had they gotten there?

In her resolve to either find Hades or find anything else of interest within his spare and silent palace, she'd quit the bridge for the tangle of hallways. At each crossing where there had been a choice, she'd turned left in an effort to remember her path back to his rooms, should she give up her pursuit.

Once she *did* give up her pursuit, however, the return was not so simple. Having found nothing and no one of value after what felt like more than an hour wandering corridors, trying doors, and surveying the sparse contents of otherwise empty rooms, Persephone doubled back only to find her path not matching up to the one she remembered taking in the first place.

Had there been a gallery she'd walked through that faced this side of the cavern? There had been stairs, yes, but so many? And with a landing in the middle?

She rubbed her forehead with a frustrated hand and made another right turn. This hallway was more rough-hewn than the last, and her mouth went into a thin line.

You're probably getting further away from the heart of the palace with every step.

The only thing keeping her from the true heat of irritation with herself was the knowledge that no matter how turned around she got, the Lord of the Dead would be able to find her. And after the escalation of events over the last few days, she had little doubt he would come looking.

Some dim sense of familiarity began to tickle here at this outcropping of stone, at that pair of alcoves. Ahead, on the wall, there was something …

His sigil angled into view as she approached. Curves and lines spanned the stone in the same dull iron as that bident he wielded with such violent grace. Her fingers rose to the embedded glyph and traced along its edge. The shape brought to mind the sound of his name on her lips. An exhalation at first, a hiss at the end. She sampled it there in the hall.

"Hades."

"Goddess."

She gasped and whirled. There he stood, a pace away, the faintest hint of a smile on that mouth of his. Had she summoned him, as she might Hekate, just by saying his name? Impossible.

"How long?" she demanded.

"Moments," he said, stepping forward. "I do enjoy hearing you speak my name."

Persephone felt her cheeks go hot, but he was already crowding her against the wall, the iron symbol at her back. How did he continue to bring her, without a word, to that place of quavering heat in an instant?

"With what frequency"—he braced a hand on the stone beside her, black eyes on her mouth—"are you willing to tolerate my attentions?"

The space was all but gone between them, and the strange new calm in his words made her heart speed.

He's wasting no time on preamble today, is he?

But this was different. There was no command. Only a question.

"Are you … are you asking me if …"

"If I have pushed you too far, and too often."

Fates, not far enough.

"No," she said as he leaned down, "and no."

There was a kiss, and it was slow. Deliberate. Her palms drifted up to his chest. When they parted, more of his smile had returned, but it was calculating. She swallowed.

"I thought perhaps you sought darkness again," he said, "to return to this place."

"This place?" He still had her pressed to the stone, but she turned her head to the side glancing at the corridor walls.

"You don't recognize it?"

Persephone shook her head and mischief flashed in his eyes. The stone at her back chose to be elsewhere.

He had to catch her at the waist to keep her from falling backward into the empty space. As soon as he was sure of her balance, Hades turned her by the shoulders to face a room that hadn't been there a moment ago. Or, it *had* been there, closed away by a wall of basalt and the will of a god.

There was the platform and its array of cushions. The granite bench. The rugs, many of which were now conspicuously absent.

He stepped up behind her and circled her waist with a now familiar arm.

"In truth, my Lord, I did not seek this place at all," she said. "I was quite lost."

"But now I've found you." The words fell at her ear, shadowed with meaning upon meaning.

"You have."

Fingers trailed down her right arm and laced together with hers. She let her shoulders settle against his warmth.

"I did not want this," he said, deceptively conversational. "When Aphrodite demanded I bring you to my realm?" She felt a little shake of his head. "I wanted nothing to do with it. Or you."

His free hand slid up to cover the front of her throat while they faced the chamber where she'd spent her first three days in the Underworld.

"And then I sat here in this place," he went on, "in the darkness, as I preferred it. With you. I heard your voice. I felt your fear, but little flower, I felt the first stirrings of your lust. And I knew." She shifted against his chest, the press of his hips. "I knew," he said, "I was wrong. That I wanted you very, *very* much."

The last he punctuated with a roll of his firming erection at her backside. A comparable buzz of arousal was building between her thighs.

"I could lay you down, Persephone." His voice had dropped an octave. It had her ready to turn and kneel. To shift his chiton and worship him with her mouth again. But Hades was not finished.

"Right there." He allowed his smallest finger to make a tighter circle around her neck. "Those soft cushions? I could part your legs." The second finger joined in the firmer grip. "I will make it as sweet as nectar, if that is what you want."

The words were genuine but saccharine. Somehow, she couldn't respond. It didn't seem right. She shifted her weight, her touch coming to rest on his knuckles, just above her collarbone.

"Or"—his middle finger closed with the other two—"we could go elsewhere." And finally the first finger, his hold on her throat complete. "If gentle and virtuous isn't the sort of immortal you're looking for, my love."

And there he was. Fresh dew wept down the inside of her thigh. There was the dark god who'd helped her answer so many questions she'd had about herself. She couldn't help the escape of a low noise of want, and it hummed against the fingers possessing her neck.

"Here?" he asked. "Or in my rooms?"

Her eyes flicked to the cushioned platform. She had awakened there, scared and confused, a lifetime of discovery ago. Memories of uncertainty lay on every surface. It was not the place for today.

"Your rooms."

"Very well."

The æther swallowed them whole.

◆

Persephone could feel it. Whatever she'd agreed to with the choice of Hades's rooms, it was beyond mere physical desire. There was something larger, more consequential at play.

There was also an imbalance.

You have come on his cock, but have you looked him in the eye?

Never at the same time, it was true. Despite the show of extracting a promise of obedience from her, the Lord of the Dead had asked permission, in his own way, to take every new step on their path. But had he surrendered control even once?

Never.

And as much as she wanted every depraved thing he still might have to offer, he didn't appear to be surrendering it now, either.

"Wider." He rapped at her bare ankle with his sandaled foot.

Imbalance. Ask him. But not now.

Now she stood, bereft of her chiton, at the center of the open floor, well away from the *Elaionapothos*. She slid her feet farther apart on the stone. Hades tipped a fraction of a nod.

His steps took him in a slow circle, the tip of an idle nail carving out gooseflesh at her waist as he went. When he stood at her back, both hands rose to her ribcage and then slid up under her arms.

Wool brushed her shoulders as he leaned in with his next instruction.

"Arms up."

They were such simple commands. Yet they made things inside her tighten. They brought that coveted new tingle of fear. Anything. He might do anything.

Persephone raised her arms. They were parallel to the floor and he moved his palms up, coaxing her elbows higher to show he'd meant her hands to be over her head. He brought her wrists together and held them aloft with circling fingers.

A rumbling sound from above tripped a snare of the familiar. She tilted her head back, curious, and her breath caught.

From the limestone ceiling overhead, a stalactite flowed to life. With that crackling liquid motion that defied all explanation, the stone descended in a queasy parody of a growing thing. Just like the bridge over the River of Fire, the bones of the Underworld came at his call.

You've come at his call a time or two, as well.

Hades stretched her arms up to meet the living rock. Higher. *Higher.* She stood on the balls of her feet.

"Be still for me." And she was.

Fluid stone coursed around her wrists and trapped them together in place of his hand, hardening again as though it had never moved at all. Persephone flexed her hands. Twisted her arms against the restraint. It was solid like no other.

Imbalance.

He traced his palm over the taut muscles along her spine before stepping around to face her again.

"Villain."

She meant it as both curse and jest, but it was hard not to sound breathy with her raised arms stretching her lungs.

Hades closed the distance between them and took her jaw between thumb and forefinger. "And?" He raised a challenging brow. "You love it." The accompanying smile was cruel and everything she needed. It was the last thing she saw before he claimed a rough kiss.

Black eyes bored straight through to the truth of her when they parted from the kiss, and she knew her troubles had only begun. His hand withdrew from the folds of his chiton, coal-dark fingers curled into a fist.

"There is no jewel capable," he said, "of refining the perfection you are."

He turned his wrist and let go the trap of his fingers. Glittering on the open palm were three tiny golden bells, each was attached to … something. Hades took one up between his fingers.

"But they may serve to augment"—and here he came, whisper close again—"those states which have brought us to understand one another."

Her lack of power had her pulse flying. He wasn't making any sense.

"My Lord, I don't—*oh!*"

Her eyes flew to the bite. The smallest of gold clamps latched onto pink flesh, and her left nipple thrilled under the intense, unabating pinch. One of the bells dangled from the source of her shock by a delicate chain, swinging against the lower curve of her breast.

"Pain," he said when she looked up at him, open-mouthed. The clamp's twin caught her other side and she let out a helpless yip. "Pleasure."

The bells tinkled with the increased rise and fall of her chest.

"When you make those sounds for me, Goddess"—he tugged on both chains at once and she gasped—"your beauty becomes almost too much to bear."

She could do nothing but watch him and suck in air. Twin blossoms of unavoidable sensation radiated from her nipples. It hurt, but there was something else.

And then she remembered the third bell.

Hades already sat on his heels. Her parted legs hid nothing. The kneeling god found what he wanted. She closed her eyes. Bit her lower lip.

Tiny jaws nipped into place and the Daughter of Olympos swore. The sensitive pearl at the peak of her sex cried out for relief, and there was none.

Persephone was on fire. Three condensed points of pressure funneled her awareness down to an intense focus. The pain subsided after a moment, but only until she realized she'd forgotten to take a breath.

He gave the dangling bell a flick as he stood, and the goddess rose even higher on her toes.

She met his eyes, both sure and not. *Was* he unpredictable? Or did she already know?

Without looking away, he slipped off his clothing and sandals. A naked foot pushed them out of the way, and the Lord of the Underworld stood bare and powerful, like the shameless god he was. Nothing marred his glory save the thin leather strap that had belted his chiton, now doubled in his fist.

She could not keep her mouth closed.

He stepped to close the gap. Drew the folded leather down between her breasts. Over her belly. She tried to repress a shiver and failed. The golden bells sounded at the movement.

"This is not a punishment," he said. "Do you know why?"

She blinked wide eyes at him. A polarity of bitter delight and delicious torment throbbed in time with her pulse at each of the clamps he'd placed with such intent.

Here. This was the place to which she'd never believed she would come. His words from their first time atop the *Elaionapothos* haunted her, and Persephone *did* know.

This is not a punishment.

Part of her stood by in awe as the impossible words left her mouth.

"Because I'm going to ask you for it."

She watched *his* chest expand now, as her admission quickened his need, but he said nothing. Did nothing.

Except raise a single brow.

He wants to hear it.

"Hades, I"—she swallowed, preparing to hear it, herself—"I want you to …"

Such patience as he waited for her to come to it.

"I want you to hurt me."

His eyes closed for a moment, and she saw his jaw flex. Knuckles tightened around leather. He sealed it with a single, slow nod.

Fates, what have I done?

As Hades slipped around her, he laid the most dangerous words in a whisper at her ear: "Feel. Everything."

The curve of the belt licked a slow caress between her legs. Her heart thudded away in her chest. He slid a palm in lazy, smoothing strokes over the backs of her thighs, her defenseless cheeks.

Then: nothing. Cool air on her skin. Silence in the room.

What is he do—

THWACK!

The leather snapped a line of nettles across her backside. She jerked forward on her toes with a yelp, and the infernal bells danced. His hand returned, the soothing motion a mockery where it burned across the path of the belt.

THWACK!

Persephone cried out again, but his hands were at her waist. She could feel the weight they supported as he knelt.

And then there was his mouth, following in place of the leather, smoldering over the signature of his cruelty. He stole a stray lick between her thighs, and she whimpered, unable to cope.

"Persephone." A command.

"Hades?" Were those tears wetting the corners of her eyes?

"Beg."

The word choked her, but not more than that thrice-damned voice of his. The one that vibrated through to her core and made her into a senseless creature. She knew she would do it the moment it left his mouth.

Persephone leaned her head back, blinking. He would not see her weep. Not yet. Her eyes traveled the restraining column of stone down to the twinning of her captured wrists. He possessed her entirely now.

She could feel him rise to his feet again at her back.

"Beg for what you want, Goddess of Mine," he said, "and I will give it to you."

She did not know who she was anymore.

"Please."

Silence stretched and there was nothing.

Not nothing.

She wanted it for herself. All of it.

"Please, Hades." Her voice wavered. "I want to feel it. I want to hurt for you."

There was a growl behind her and Persephone tensed, but no more than cool air kissed her flesh. And then she knew.

Your pleasure belongs to me now.

His purring words from yesterday were the truth of it. It was not about her, or what she wanted.

"My Lord, I am yours." Did the stone under her feet move? Or had she gone mad? "My pain is yours. *Please*."

"Yess. *Mine*."

The god who would court her for a wife began to paint her backside with fire.

THWACK!

He striped her cheeks and thighs in a steady rhythm.

THWACK!

And she shook under his strokes. The bells jangled and her skin blazed with every pass of the belt, and Persephone called out with abandon in a place so deep in the Underworld no one could possibly hear her screams.

No one but him.

The rain of blows went on unceasing. Her suffering, however, did not. It reached a point of such infinite density that it simply was no more. And what came flooding in after to fill the void ...

Her knees began to tremble. Her breath came hoarse.

The storm was at an end.

He cast the strap aside and moved in to press himself against her back. His skin was a hot brand on her welted flesh and she hissed in acceptance of such a claim. Her neck, shoulders, and outstretched upper arms knew the desperate scatter of new kisses.

"Persephone. So beautiful." His words were close and rough against her ear. "You wear my marks so well. I—"

He drew her against him, hand on her belly. She could feel him dancing on some blade-sharp edge of thought and action. "I'm—I'm *sorry*." Was there a catch in his voice? "I had to. I *had* to."

Contrition? *Now?*

But why?

"Hades, I *asked* for it," she said. "Did you not hear me beg?"

For a time, all he did was breathe, his face buried in the crook of her neck. Tension abated in his hold, but he made some low sound of warning. Of a beast, awakening to Spring.

"I did," said Hades. "By the *Fates*, did I hear it."

She sniffled, floating on the last of calm waters before a fall. Dark hands flowed over her curves, cupping her breasts, making the little bells dance on their chains. Fingers dipped between her legs from behind, spreading liquid want.

The blunt, warm head of his erection settled along her furrow, and Persephone sighed. This she knew, this was familiar. She widened her stance what little she could while on tiptoe, ready to sink into the comfort of filling strokes.

Hades moved into position. Began to push.

It wasn't right.

"Mmm ... lower." She shifted guiding hips.

The softest *huff* of amusement prickled the back of her neck. "No, love."

Her eyes came open. She squirmed in her bonds.

"My Lord."

The stone hook from last night had been a slender thing, but Hades ...

"Persephone." The nudge became an insistent press, the slick of her need aiding him. "Are you mine?"

"Mmhm." She nodded, brows furrowed together, anticipation stealing her words.

"Then let me in."

Her breasts rose and fell, nipples at a dull throb as she made to relax.

His.

Hades pushed past her barrier.

Her mouth came open in an O of recognition.

He owned her.

The tight ring stretched wide. She was the eye of a needle through which someone was attempting to thread a rope.

There were soft words as he took his time. Whispered kisses and shushing while he worked himself inside. She stood on the tips of her toes, but there was no ease to be found. The Lord of the Dead claimed his ground by measures and Persephone knew every breath and pulse of their joining.

Eternity came and went before she felt the thatch of hair at her parted cheeks. She'd taken every bit of length he had to give.

There was a time of adjustment as he held them still. She could hear the rush of his hard-won restraint, steaming in and out through his nostrils. She wanted to let herself go; to attune to the way he filled her, but the brilliant ache was inescapable. No matter how long she stood there, trying to drain herself into a state of surrender while he waited, there was nothing for it. The way his cock held her open felt endlessly precarious, a lifetime teetering at the edge of a cliff.

He began to move, and it was slow. Excruciating.

The length of him drew all the way out, before he labored once more at pushing it home. New sensation threatened to drown her, and Persephone gasped for air.

His fingers dug into her hips and she felt the tight grip he had on his own reins. Everything was the opposite of comfortable; she wanted to writhe and shift. Her hands bound in stone. The unrelenting fullness wedged into her bottom. The hungry vacancy where his cock should have been. The wicked insistence of the clamps and cool air teasing the wet havoc between her legs.

Every sensation thrilled and clamored at once, and Persephone hovered in a giddy heightened awareness. His tentative movements were a path toward madness for them both.

This cannot be what he wants. To hold back?

No.

"Hades."

"Mm?" Concentration curbed his words.

"I'm not a doll."

He came out of it. "What?"

"You're not going to break me."

He stilled, pulsing within her, and set his forehead against the back of her neck. His warning came ground between teeth. "You do not understand what you ask."

"I do."

"You do *not*."

"I do!" she said, jerking with the force of her protest. "I want what you have to give."

The god was quiet, but she knew he listened.

"Give me your pain, Hades *Clymenus*. And I will hurt for you."

His nails were carving half-moons into her skin. She decided to be more direct.

"Fuck me."

Silence behind her, heated throbbing below.

"Hades!"

"Forgive me," he whispered and drove himself home.

He was not gentle. He was not kind. He was the rough god she needed him to be.

His cock speared at her, unrepentant, and charcoal hands hauled her back at the hip. Her feet came off the ground.

Persephone called out his name again and again, arms stretched far overhead, to the furious tune of jangling bells. With each violent thrust, he shed another layer of remorse, and relief throbbed, just out of reach.

"Please! H-Hades!" The cry came choking out as she bounced on an erection hard as the stone imprisoning her hands.

And he knew. The dark god knew and had mercy.

He let her feet touch the floor.

With only the slightest pause in the urgent siege of his hips, he fumbled a hand around to the jouncing golden bell between her legs. The jaws of the clamp came open and he sent it tinkling across the floor. Stinging heat flowed into the vacancy left by pressure, and all sensation narrowed to a blue-white focus even as he resumed his assault.

And then Hades brought his fingers down to massage at her swollen nub.

It was too much.

He was everywhere, making her sing, making her hurt. She painted the chamber with feral sound and went flying over the edge.

Between cursing and shuddering, she could no more than ride the current. Her muscles flexed. Pulled taut. That immortal cock never ceased to punish and reward.

"Hades! *Sýzygos!* Yes!"

Whether it was the impact of the name or he was already there, Hades erupted with her.

He planted himself deep. Completion spilled inside her, pulse after hot pulse, to disastrous perfection. He remained, emptying it all in a scalding purge, his breath hissing in and out through his teeth.

They stood there, joined, filling their lungs in the silence. Perspiration beaded her brow and the small of her back and her mind floated in blessed emptiness.

The withdrawal came as a shock, slippery and wrong, luscious and horribly right. The stalactite retreated into itself, leaving her arms to fall at her sides. Hades caught her up in an instant, lowering them both to the floor where she could crumple against his chest, head lolling, extremities limp.

One at a time, he removed the two remaining clamps and their dangling bells and tossed them aside with the third. The blood returned to the aching tips with a vengeance, and his thumbs stroked to soothe, though that was a torture in itself. She wanted to swear, but the best she could manage was a raw groan.

The dark hands collected her now, massaging, petting, smoothing. Bringing damp hair away from her temples, returning feeling to her hands.

"Persephone." He said her name like a vow. "Goddess."

She turned her face and brushed his lips in a ghost of a kiss, his fine features blurred through the fringe of her drooping lashes.

"What do you need, love?"

Imbalance. Now you can ask.

"I want control," she said, fighting the dreamy slur in her words.

"You what?" He, on the other hand, sounded quite sober.

Persephone shifted and wet her throat with a swallow. She needed at a grip on her faculties, or at least the appearance.

"I want to lead," she said. "I want to choose how we play. See your face. When we come."

Hades blinked at her and it was clear this was the very last request he'd expected to come out of her mouth. For a time, he only continued to cradle her against him, eyes distant, considering.

Perhaps you've crossed a line.

When he met her gaze again, she could see a walling off had taken place, though the lines of his face held no hint of anger.

"Fair enough, my little flower." A single, dark-nailed finger trailed down over her breastbone. "You can take the lead tomorrow if you answer one question. A riddle, if you will."

She watched. Waited. It could be another of his traps.

And which of his traps have you hated yet?

"Tell me one secret about myself," he said, at last. "Something I've confessed to no one. Answer me that and the night is yours."

◆

Demeter's hair stirred in the ever-shifting winds of Olympos, along with her simmering temper. The dome of the sky overhead was blue as the heart of flame, and

Helios, who'd shared information she both wanted and didn't, rode high overhead in his blinding chariot.

There were many immortal palaces on the slopes of the mount of legend, but it was toward the grandest, the topmost, the seat of the Sky Realm's throne, that Demeter made her way.

She picked a path through manicured gardens and obscene fountains, excessive colonnades and grandiose fields of white marble. The Lord of the Skies had summoned her, but the goddess would arrive in her time, as did the seasons she governed.

How many of them came crying to you, Zeus? Did the Fair One pout when her pool of acolytes dwindled? Did Ares rage when his armies lost the strength to shift their spears?

She wore a frightening grin at the thought of the inevitable confrontation.

Her display of wrath had served its purpose: she had his attention. Helios had suggested she 'discuss' the matter, but to do so upon no foundation would have been pointless. The Lord of Lightnings did not, in her experience, listen to talk and reason. He respected only one thing: power.

She'd given him a reminder.

Her daughter would not languish away in the Underworld if there was anything Demeter had to say about it.

The halls of the palace of Zeus stood open to the sky with soaring white columns bounding the rectangular structure on all sides. The breeze caught the drape of her chiton and plastered the linen to her limbs as she mounted the last of the wide stairs to the throne room. When she reached the top, she swore to herself.

Faithless god.

There he was, seated on his throne, Hermes at his side, bending his immortal ear. None of the others were present, and the pair broke off their exchange mid-sentence at Demeter's approach.

Zeus sat larger than life, as he always did, a bold orange chiton draped around his knees and his gilded crown of oak leaves resting atop the silver-white curls. Broad shoulders and muscled calves were a superfluous reminder of might, as he lounged against the throne of thrones.

Seven steps, each in a different type of stone, rose to the platform where he had placed his seat above all those of the other gods. Each of the Olympians—herself included—had a seat in this place, but none so grand as Lord Zeus. The golden likeness of an eagle, a gift from Hephaistos, sprouted from the right arm of the throne, an array of lightning bolts crafted from tin clutched in its talons; a symbol of the power wielded by the king of the gods.

I loved him for a time. And I was a fool.

"Lord of Thunder." She made his name an insult and approached at an unhurried pace.

You will remain calm, or this will not work.

"Goddess of the *Fruitful* Earth," he said. "You know why I've called you here. What is it you imagine you're doing, *Hôrêphoros*?"

Bringer of the Seasons. She smirked as he twisted home his point.

"Well"—she strolled now to one side of the hall—"things have been taken from me of late. It is only right I should take back."

He scowled and Hermes glanced between them both.

"Did you think I would not find out about Persephone?" she said, before leaning a shoulder against one of the columns. She crossed one ankle over the other and her arms over her chest.

"Our daughter is not a 'thing' which someone might take," said Zeus. "She's a goddess in her own right. You cannot keep her from a marriage." He sat back, hands resting on the arms of his throne. His protective reaction was unexpected, but irrelevant.

"And you can *sell* her into one?"

She pushed away from the stone supporting her and advanced on the Lord of the Skies. Hermes shifted his weight from one leg to another, silent for once in the growing heat of their exchange.

"I sold no one, Demeter." The bluest of eyes flashed a stormy warning. "I merely approved the suggestion of a courtship. All I receive in return is the slim possibility of a contented brother. Whatever he thinks of me, I do not wish him ill."

"Ugh!" She wanted to tear her hair, but settled for the poison of sarcasm. " *'Your brother.'* I can't imagine. You need to have her plucked from that pit of his and brought back to me, *Basileus*," she said pointing a demanding finger, "and without any of your usual delays."

"Demeter." His tone was patient. Infuriating. "She'll be with him a week tomorrow. Lord Hades has no tolerance for anyone or anything he deems unsuitable for his realm. I do not believe a potential consort would be different. That he hasn't put her out of his domain entirely by now should tell you they've —"

"Filth!" she spat. "I won't hear it! I refuse to even imagine what horrors that … that *beast* of a brother of yours has forced her to submit to down there." Her arms were across her chest again in firm denial. Zeus only raised a silver brow.

"He's your brother, too, Daughter of Kronos." Thunder rumbled in the distance.

So much for calm.

They faced off in electric silence, anger arcing from eye to Olympian eye. Hermes attempted to look anywhere else, taking up a sudden and intense interest in the cleanliness of his fingernails.

Zeus ran a knuckle over the bridge of his nose, closing blue eyes in fatigue. She couldn't help feeling the resentful thrill of achievement.

"Do you know how long it will take," he said, "between my rain and Helios's light before we can return the land to its bounty?" She made no reply, waiting. "*Months*, Demeter. It will be months at least."

And now let him understand.

"It will be far longer than that, Gatherer of Clouds. Do you think I will allow the earth to be restored while Persephone is prisoner beneath it?" Her volume grew as she spoke. "*Nothing* will grow. The land will not yield a single kernel of nourishment while the lot of you conspire to deny me my daughter. This, I promise."

When he drummed impatient fingers, she began to ascend the steps to his throne. "You think I've exhausted my ability at a day's worth of famine?" she said. "The losses of today will seem like the buzzing of a gnat compared to the swarm of deprivation I will bring. The children of men will crumble to the Earth until there is not one beating heart left to worship at your altars."

A flurry of reddened leaves flew in on the constant wind, a harbinger of the winter to come.

"Demeter, be reasonable," he said. "What's done is done. I cannot simply insist he give up his consort, it—"

"You *WILL!*" Her fury echoed across the hall and beyond its columns. "You will return her, Zeus, or I will undo us all, myself included."

The Lord of the Skies sighed and leaned to press his fingers against the grim new line of his lips, his elbow resting on the arm of the throne. He gave a slow shake of his head.

"Hermes."

The Messenger snapped to attention, as though he hadn't been a fly on the wall for their thorny exchange.

"My Lord?"

"You know your way into my brother's kingdom. Go and explain to him"—his eyes never left Demeter—"that although he has been promised the opportunity to court an immortal *wife*"—he stabbed the word home—"and has no doubt already grown *fond of her*, that now he must give her up again to her worrying mother." The god finished off his instructions with a note of disgust.

"I leave tonight, my Lord."

Hermes bobbed a nod and, turning on a winged heel, all but fled from the hall of thrones, no doubt to gossip about what he'd just heard to every immortal ear along the way.

Good. Let them hear.

"Satisfied?" said Zeus.

"I will be," Demeter said, "once Persephone is returned."

✦

VIII Submission

The ferry receded into the hanging mist with a haste not often found on the crawling waters of the Styx. Kharon poled the barge of the dead with an irritable vigor, back toward the outer shore where the mortal shades had been amassing at a concerning rate since Demeter had begun her assault on the good will of her fellow immortals.

Hades paced along the sandy bank, arms clasped behind his back, head down, frowning.

It will not be long now.

He'd been ready to return to Persephone, but after hearing the ferryman's report, the Lord of the Dead needed some brief measure of solitude to gather his thoughts. His intentions.

How many more days like this would he have? Their number, limited, would fall away again to the drone of his routines. The predictability of his realm would return. Why was he clenching his teeth?

Why was he allowing the game to continue? There were ways. Torturing himself was unnecessary.

Because you, Polydegmon, are a beast of the lowest order.

And for that, he owed her. At least this once, all bargains aside.

He should have worshipped her. Any suitor in his right mind would have. The way she'd stretched from the descending stone, exquisite. Helpless.

But who. Who was helpless?

Was he not the one who could not keep hold of reason? When the mere sight of her had his depravity welling up, obliterating all sense? When her flesh called out for his marks, when her body jumped at his licks?

Hades shivered.

There was no need for any of it, and yet he could not stop. And when she'd begged him …

"Please, Hades. I want to hurt for you."

He hissed at the sound of her voice in his head, seared by a longing he couldn't relieve. Wavelets from the river lapped at the bank, ineffectual in their soothing.

When Persephone had begged for the pain he had loved her. And not just any pain had she asked for. *His* pain. His! He came to her with his corruption and, with her eyes, her limbs, her tongue, she said, 'Purify yourself upon me.'

He could have imagined no greater gift until she'd cried out at the height of their passion. That single word, that impossible jolt.

Sýzygos!

Beloved. When had the Lord of the Dead been anyone's beloved?

It was a thing decided.

He could not let her go.

And he could not keep her.

You can. And you already know it.

The fingers of his right hand curled into a fist. Persephone was … different? No. 'Different' was not a large enough word. There *weren't* large enough words.

He had fed his darkness in the past; sadistic games stringing together a trail of forgettable mortal women. They had been playthings, to a one. The Goddess of Growing Things was everything but.

He still wanted her cries, though they sank like a hook beneath his ribs. He still wanted her fear, though it clutched at his lust the way no Daughter of Man could have ever achieved with her temporary whimpers. But now, he …

He cared. Enough to ask her permission. Enough to wait until, impossibly, she crumbled in want of the cruelty he had to give.

He cared enough to cede her at least one opportunity. He took so much, surely, he could grant a request.

You didn't outright give it to her, Clymenus.

It was true. The riddle he'd put to her was nothing more than a failsafe. She would never answer it and he would enjoy the self-righteous feeling of having offered her a reasonable bargain. Utter nonsense, of course, but when had Hades *Nekrodegmôn* ever allowed anyone to face him with even odds?

In a smooth gesture, he brought forth the bident from the ring on his hand, slashing it through the æther above the shore of the River Styx. He could travel the spaces between without the use of the weapon—it was his domain, after all—but the action had a satisfying decisiveness about it, and that was what Hades needed now. To decide.

He stepped through the rift and into the corridor just outside the doors to his chambers. Persephone was inside. He could feel her heartbeat when he allowed himself to settle into the silence of the hallway.

What methods she'd used to find her way back today, he wasn't sure, but the goddess had requested the night and half the next day to contemplate his question while she roamed his realm undisturbed. She'd promised to meet him here at the end of that time. Perhaps she hadn't left at all. It didn't matter.

Hades schooled his features to the stony calm that had served him so well over the ages and pushed open the double doors.

There she sat, regal and expressionless in one of the heavy walnut chairs as he closed the doors behind him. Her legs were crossed under her chiton and graceful wrists dangled from the arms of the chair.

He clasped one wrist in the opposite hand at his back and moved into the room at an unhurried pace. She hadn't twitched a muscle since his entrance, and it was clear her eyes had been on the door, waiting.

There was something on the air. Some premonitory tang that made the back of his neck prickle.

"You are afraid."

It was as if she'd inherited the lightning and struck him.

"What?"

"Again and again you have demanded it of me. 'What is it you fear, Persephone? Tell me why you're afraid.' " She leaned forward in the seat. "And each time I have given you truth. And each time I have felt your satisfaction, to be able to claim those vulnerable pieces of me. Because it is an obsession. Your own fear is an obsession, and you can't control it, but you *can* control mine, and it grants you a feeling of security to do so."

She assaulted his foundations in blow after ruinous blow, but he managed to keep it from his face. His heart thudded in his chest, and somehow he twisted it into a smirk.

"And what is it I'm afraid of," he said, "if you're so sure that's the case?"

"You need control."

The smirk shifted. She uncrossed her legs to place both bare feet on the floor.

"That is your secret, 'confessed to no one', I believe your words were? Hades, Lord of the Dead, has to maintain control of every situation, at all times, because if he doesn't, he fears someone will gain a single toehold and take from him that which he has carved out for himself."

She ... she cannot.

"You are *very* afraid"—she slid to the edge of the seat—"someone will uncover your secrets and use that knowledge to ruin you." The goddess tipped a nod at the *Elaionapothos*, but a new shadow on her words told him 'secrets' extended beyond just the Oil.

"That is why you chose this question," she said. "You believe you've hidden yourself with such skill, *Unseen One*, that you never bothered to prepare for an outcome in which I *might* come up with an answer."

Was his mouth open?

"I have, haven't I." Green eyes blazed. "I've found one of your secrets."

"I ... I suppose you have." Hades swallowed to wet his throat, and she was already rising to her feet. "Persephone, last night I ... I need to explai—"

"Irrelevant." Her hand cut the air in a negating line. "Do you give over control, or not?"

"Yes, of course"—familiar territory rushed away at the speed of panic—"but I wanted to tell you ..." He fumbled for words like he never had. "There are things you need to understand, Pers—"

"Hades."

There wouldn't have been a larger reverberation had the Hall of Judgments come crashing to the cavern floor.

"I already told you," she said, stepping in his direction, "I *asked* for what you gave. All of it. Again and again, you have cautioned me to speak if I've reached my limits, and I tell you I have not. I begged, Hades, because I wanted those words you whispered in my ear. I wanted to feel everything."

Her reassurances rolled over him like a balm. He thought to pull her to him, his hands already reaching out. "Persephone, I—"

"Enough." A halting hand came up, fierce now instead of delicate. "Enough with your words. That voice of yours in my head. I can't *function*. You will not twist this day back under your thumb, lord of this realm or no. If you wish to earn the rest of my trust, you will keep your word. I've answered your challenge. Today is mine."

Persephone's cheeks flared hot with color, eyes glinting a warning: if he wanted to save this, he was not to provoke her further.

She closed the distance between them and splayed her hand in the center of his chest, green eyes locked on his, intense, and began herding him backward with decisive steps. He came to a stop when the backs of his knees bumped against the platform of the *Elaionapothos*. The goddess gave him a push.

"Sit."

Hades sat, but searched her eyes for some sign of what was to come. An unfamiliar tension knotted his gut. Nerves? Is that what this was?

Is this what she feels? When you corner her?

She came to stand between his knees, so like their first encounter on the bench the day after he'd revealed himself. Today, however, her features were cool and detached instead of warring between panic and affront. Her eyes moved over him like a problem she needed to solve.

Persephone brought her hand to his temple and combed her fingers back through his hair, nails grazing the scalp. When he couldn't repress the entire resulting shudder, the bow of her lips grew into half a smile. A fist at the back of his head took a handful of hair and tilted his face up to hers.

She stared at him. Whatever she read in his eyes, it went unrevealed, but the pull of the connection deepened as her hold went on and on for unblinking moments. When the surrounding chamber seemed to have disappeared, the goddess reached out to pluck at the taut thread between them.

Her lips lowered to brush his, not quite a kiss, and his heart thundered in the silence.

"This is how it feels, you know." Her whispered explanation came against his mouth, provoking feelings he couldn't quite name. "To have your heart wrenched in anticipation. Uncertainty." Persephone flicked the tip of her tongue between his lips, just as he'd done with that first kiss he'd stolen from her.

She pulled away, a satisfied glint in her eye as he twisted on her line. Some objection began forming in his mind, but, before he could give it voice, she bent again to melt her mouth against his. That sweet tongue sought entry and Hades gave it to her, the first kind of submission he could ever remember offering. The sheer novelty had immortal blood rushing to swell his cock.

Every slow lap of her tongue was excruciating. It was everything he could do not to seize her by the arms and throw her to the platform behind him.

She's obeyed your every monstrous demand. She has kept to her word. Now you keep to yours, fiend.

He gripped the edge of the platform.

Be still.

Her hold on his hair changed hands and Persephone moved her kisses under his jaw and down his throat. One of her knees came to rest on the platform alongside his thigh so she could crowd him. Claim him. Her mouth burned at the muscles of his shoulder, his collarbone.

She inhaled at his hairline, just behind his ear.

"You smell like wet stone after it rains." Her words curled warm with her breath. "Do you know I can't get enough?" The fingers in his hair tightened. "Do you?"

Hades had never given a moment's thought to what he might smell like. She, on the other hand, had been clawing away at his sanity since the day he'd trapped her in his realm.

"And you," he said, "You are the dew at sunrise. Green leaves in the Spring. Do you know I had nearly forgot what those were like?" She was everything he could not have, every possibility the Fates had never seen fit to afford him.

And what do they afford you now?

Persephone drew back, searching him, and whatever she sought she must have found because the kisses came again, wet and ardent. His hands moved to the backs of her thighs, sliding his touch higher as he went.

"No."

He blinked at her. Where had her mouth gone?

She took his wrists in a gentle grip and placed his hands back on the Oil.

"I will tell you when you are allowed to touch."

Fates!

Persephone's fingers went to the fibula at his shoulder and worked it loose. The dark wool fell away from his chest, exposing him to whatever purpose the goddess intended.

She took her own, unendurable time, fingertips marking out what seemed hours along the lines of his shoulders, the hollow at the center of his throat. He inhaled through his nose when her thumbs grazed his nipples. Had anyone ever bothered? If they had, it was beyond memory.

Her light touch tightened to a pinch and Hades grunted. Before he could contrive any sort of rude remark to misdirect from his shock, the goddess was kneeling between his thighs. A hot mouth replaced her fingers, and his erection twitched in eager response beneath the drape of his chiton.

She brought her teeth into it, and he made some sound. Some noise no other being outside this room ever needed to hear him make. There was a smoky little chuckle and she shifted to mirror her actions on his other side, letting him lean back on his arms to absorb the new sensations a second time.

The gossip of her lips and tongue traveled lower across his belly, and then her hands were working at his belt. By the time he managed to open his eyes, the goddess had him bared, his garment laid open beneath him.

His cock stood out, bobbing and vulgar before the divinity of her features, but Persephone's gaze held a covetous focus. What could she see beyond impatient male lust?

It didn't matter because she was taking him in hand and the warmth had his eyes rolling back.

No! Look at her!

And he did.

She drew the head across the silken skin of her cheek, and her smile warned of mischief. A crystal bead had grown at the swollen tip and a pink flash of tongue stole out to clear it away just before she rose to her feet.

She creates a balance. She gives just enough to make you squirm, but not enough to satisfy.

Just as he had done to her.

Images came flickering back from their previous encounters. Persephone with the collar and hook, writhing for release in this same place, atop the same Oil, and him letting her suffer from want. And then he remembered his clothing, undone around him.

The strap.

Would she expect …?

No.

No? How much balance would she want?

Not content with his silent struggles, Persephone had the blood red of her own chiton rippling to the stone at her feet.

Here she was again, a picture of everything he wanted to consume. Long and graceful, tight and round, cream pale and blush pink, and so full of life as nothing in the Unseen Realm truly ever could be.

Hades met the green eyes and what he saw there had him cursing to himself.

"Kneel."

The Lord of the Dead, who did not kneel for anyone, felt himself slide from the edge of the platform. Felt his knees bend and support his weight on the limestone.

He knelt for Persephone.

She came to stand before him with a roll of her hips made to incite oath breaking or madness or both. One naked foot rose to the edge of the Oil beside them, and the goddess splayed herself at eye level, glistening and perfect.

"Worship."

It was as if the earth had buckled beneath him.

He fell on her, rabid to obey as he'd never been, her pleasure his only goal.

Hades worshipped. He consumed. He buried his face and his tongue painted her with truth.

Consort.

She made no objection to the touch of his hand now. His fingers parted her, midnight dark alongside dewy rose, so he might taste her every hidden delight.

Persephone bathed him in low noises of encouragement and put a steadying hand on his shoulder. He lapped and she moaned, sucked and she whined. Her unbent knee began to have trouble in its support.

The fist was back in his hair, in silent, vigorous approval, and his cock throbbed along with a rush of unexpected pride. Hades *Clymenus* was capable of serving, of pleasing, another.

Not 'another'. *Her*. Persephone.

His free hand moved to his erection, stroking to purchase relief while he smothered himself in her scent, her sounds.

"No."

The slick velvet was gone.

Hades blinked up at her, open-mouthed, as the goddess stepped back and stood on two legs. She nudged his working hand away from his lust with a foot.

"Your pleasure belongs to me now, Son of Kronos." The trouble in her smile made his gut tighten, and he knew what words would come next. "You will have it when I allow."

Thrice-damned Creation!

And what were the depths of her self-control, that she could wrest herself back from completion in order to make a point?

But he had agreed. He had agreed.

She moved around him to sit on the bed—for what was the *Elaionapothos* when they were together now, if not the nest of their lovemaking?—one leg tucked under her, the other dangling to the floor.

"Bring your idle hands," she said, gesturing with a nod for him to join her.

Hades got to his feet, marveling at his own obedience, and slid onto the pliant, waiting surface.

"On your back."

The commands kept coming, and Hades followed. He shifted to stretch out, face up, on the platform beside her, his hands folded behind his head. Persephone wasted no time.

She brought her knee over his waist and sat astride his hips. When the bare flesh of her bottom brushed the standing heat of his cock, it was Hades's turn to smile.

But the goddess had other plans.

She splayed her hands over his chest. Slid them up along his biceps and past his elbows. When she found his wrists, she drew them apart and laced her fingers with his, pinning his hands on either side of his head.

She is trying to lead today, isn't she?

He chuckled at the little display and let her hold him like that as she leaned down for a kiss. Her sweet mouth was on his, tasting. The twin points of her nipples grazed his chest. His hands grew warm in her grip. Very warm.

Persephone sealed off their kiss with a hum of contentment and sat upright. Her arms stretched over her head, one hand pulling at the other wrist in exaggerated languor.

What is she hoping to—

Very warm.

She was no longer holding his hands. The *Elaionapothos* was, right where she'd sunk them.

He tried to pull free but the Oil held him. Above, Persephone smiled.

The Underworld answers to Underworld gods.

It was true, but ... where had he heard it?

Hades brushed speculation aside. The reality they shared at this place and time was simple. She wanted his restraint more than he wanted release. It must be so, and he would have to endure until it wasn't.

And how thoroughly she'd founded his fears! No sooner had someone discovered one of his secrets than they were using it against him. Not that Persephone's idea of exploiting a weakness was altogether unpleasant.

"Well done, little flower." He crooked a grin up at her. "I'm impressed."

"Shhh"—a finger was on his lips—"or I'll have that fiendish tongue of yours held in check, as well."

Could she? Was her mastery of the Oil already sufficient to form any sort of gag?

Her head bent low and his questions became irrelevant. Teeth were grazing his throat, pulling his earlobe. Her hands ... her hands were everywhere, taunting and sliding, along with the damp heat of her sex.

He needed to touch her. To grab and to pull. To possess. But the Oil held him and he had to do without.

Lower and lower she moved, until she knelt between his legs, green eyes intent on his rearing cock.

Her teeth caught her lower lip, and she tilted her head to one side, studying. After several breaths where his ribs rose and fell, she seemed to come to some decision.

Knuckles drew down over the skin of his scrotum, and Hades did nothing to repress a groan. With her thumb and forefinger, she banded the base of his sack, pulling the heavy pair away from his body in a gentle stretch.

Persephone grew something of a smile at her own handiwork, just before lowering her head. Whatever he'd been expecting, it wasn't the rasp her tongue. His throat condensed on some guttural noise and his wrists pulled against the hold of the *Elaionapothos*. Even his hips strained in her direction, pleading.

She took her time, toying with the skin she'd made tight, that laving and squirming tongue centering all its attention on the sensitive jewels in her hand. But there was more for him to feel. Far more, and she had the advantage. The goddess who had him trapped in his own bed flicked those long, dark lashes up at him and grinned.

Her tongue slid the length of him, from base to raging tip.

It was an effort to hold his head up and watch, but watch he did. Not a force in the Underworld could tear his eyes away from this.

She drew his erection over her chin and along the front of her throat, all but painting herself with it. Down between her breasts it went, as she lifted her body, pressing bosom in all around him with her hands. The soft flesh surrounding his cock had Hades rocking, shameless, hips churning in a crude imitation of the genuine act. He needed it! Now!

She chuckled at his misery and slid back down to take him in her mouth.

Persephone moved over him, lips and tongue working at his pleasure in earnest this time, rather than teasing with hints and promises. Her hands stroked while she suckled, tactics changing as soon as they might become predictable. One moment she was fanning the flames with a skilled and sliding grip, the next she was swallowing him whole.

Tension built in his thighs, his groin. If she—*Fates!*—if she didn't stop soon …

She rose to sit on her heels, lips pink and swollen from keeping him on the edge.

"Persephone."

Did his desperation show on his face? What was she *doing* to him?

"I wouldn't worry so hard, my captive lord." She brought her knees over his hips, a hint of a smirk dimpling her cheek. Her feet pushed his thighs together as she sat astride him again. "I won't make you suffer. At least not for too long."

With no warning, she came up on her knees and had him in hand. Had him sliding along that wet furrow, anointing his hungry length with a slick promise to allow him to enter her temple.

The hammering in his chest threatened to be his end. She was going to … she was going to *claim* him.

He was marble hard, and willing beyond a doubt, but there was no question: Persephone was going to take him. No one had ever. Hades had always been the one to decide. To impose his will.

Here he was now, hands held fast within the Oil, flat on his back. The submissive side of this game was foreign. Disorienting. Persephone had accepted his commands with such relative ease, and having known him for a matter of days. The Lord of the Dead became still in the dawning of a newfound appreciation for her adaptability.

Poised now above him, ready to lower herself and douse the flames of his lust—or stoke them! He could have growled—Persephone caught his chin in her hand. Green eyes mirrored his desire; she withheld from herself, as well.

"Do you want it?"

"Of course, love." He thrust upward, seeking. Was it not obvious? But she lifted her hips, denying relief.

"Beg."

Her new smile exulted in the reversal.

You are the lord of a realm. You do not beg!

But madness. Madness loomed. To be without was to be less than whole. Was to burn and burn with no respite. What choice did he have?

"Persephone, *please*."

"I think you can do better."

She flirted her sex over the tip of his erection. On the day Aphrodite made her demands, he would have laughed, but now the move was all it took to break him.

"My goddess, let me love you!" He strained to reach her, begging with his body, as well. "I need it. I *need* you! *Please, Sýzyg—unh!*"

She sank onto him in approval, all the way to the hilt.

Worth it! Worth it, pride be damned!

Persephone ground against him to their mutual sounds of relief, stilling herself for the span of several lung-filling breaths after, while he flexed, excited and helpless in that wet clutch between her thighs.

Just when he thought he'd have to start pleading again, she ducked her hips and began to roll. It was slow like the growth of the cavern. Hot like the River of Fire. Exquisite.

It could not last.

She found a rhythm. Placed a steadying palm on his chest. Took what was hers.

Yes. Admit it is so.

She rode with startling zeal, seeking her own pleasure from his body. The pace of his breath increased, working to follow her rhythm. He grunted and pushed, his efforts beneath her the best he could give, but frustration grew on her face.

The goddess bent low to savage his mouth with a kiss, and Hades nearly betrayed them both with an early end. She was too much for him. Too good for him. He couldn't take it.

But the torment didn't last. Persephone drew back, brows furrowed, and came to a halt. Something in her eyes dissected him.

"This isn't what I need," she said at last.

Her hands slid to his wrists and pulled them, one at a time, out of the mire of the *Elaionapothos*.

"Oh, love." Shock at his freedom lasted an eyeblink before he had his knees bent for leverage and his hands at her waist. Now he could make a worthy effort. He could please her.

"No."

A stilling palm was on his cheek.

Persephone leaned down and began to slide from him, her weight taking her to one side. He caught her up in his arms, insides knotting against the idea she might abandon him now. Their faces were very close, and she met him with those eyes.

"I need you on top of me."

Every last shred of him roared an affirmative. He rolled her beneath him, immortal blood singing in his veins, and plunged into his goddess with a growl.

The familiar position of power earned anew after such a trial made his head swim. Yes, *yes*, damn him, she'd asked to lead them today, but the sight of her spread below him, pulling him down as though this was her aim all along, had his inhibitions scattering like so much ash.

He tried. He tried to pace himself, to close his eyes. That perfect face was more than his endurance could bear.

Is that why you always take her from behind?

But how else would he hold onto the control she'd so astutely pointed out he needed?

"Hades!" She slapped him with his name, the wrong tone entirely. "What are you doing?"

His eyes flew open, exultation lost at what sounded like accusation. Green eyes flared in outrage and he stilled himself, the weight of his upper body held up on his arms.

"Persephone, what?"

Was he hurting her?

"Today was mine! You gave your word! Why this?" The words became sharp, but Hades was lost.

"Why *what*, my love?"

"My feet!"

He twisted his neck around to follow the line of her legs where they parted around his hips and saw her feet sunk ankle-deep into the *Elaionapothos*.

But I—

And then he knew.

Hades brought serious eyes back to hers.

"Persephone *I'm* not doing this."

"What?"

"The only thing I want is you. And I have it." She opened her mouth, but no words came. "It's the Oil," he said. "It answers to *you*."

Tension coiled in his belly when he spoke his next thought aloud.

"Little flower ... you *want* this. Don't you."

It wasn't a question.

Something like lightning arced from her eyes to his and back again. Her pupils dilated, the thunder of comprehension rolling in the aftermath.

As deliberate as the passage of time, the Daughter of Olympos beneath him fanned her arms out to the sides and over her head. Her fingertips met above the pool of her hair. His lovely Persephone's throat moved as she swallowed, her eyes demanding witness. The *Elaionapothos* swallowed her delicate fingers, accepting them inside, pinning her in place.

Hades had given her control and Persephone had chosen to surrender. To submit.

"You're right," she said, some new peace smoothing her features. "I *do* want this. I think I've always wanted this." She tilted her hips in offering. "Take what you want, Hades. I belong to you now."

The question of keeping her loomed, but yes. He had her.

Again and again, he had her.

Creation spun away from the two of them and they were all that moved and breathed on the deathless plane or any other. The god of endings and the goddess of beginnings closed the circle and were one. Hades took and Persephone gave, the maelstrom consuming itself.

In a far deeper corner of the Underworld, where power roiled sufficient to frighten gods and monsters alike, the Fates exchanged a final nod.

✦

There had hardly been time to explore the orchards of the Underworld the day Hades had dealt with the trespasses of that mortal man, but Persephone wandered among them now.

Row after row of fruitful trees stood impossibly green and healthy in the light of the *paráthyra*. Her time in this realm was approaching a ripeness as well; she could feel it swelling in her limbs. The plucking would come in the form of decisions, but they were choices Persephone found herself ill-suited to make.

What was she *doing* here?

The reasons behind her arrival in the Unseen Realm Persephone understood. And the reasons she remained— as much her complete lack of resistance to the idea as it was the will of its lord—were plain, as well.

But what was she doing with Hades? *Nekrodegmôn*, Receiver of the Dead. *Clymenus*, Notorious. What was she doing languishing in the bed of a god who turned mortals mute with fear and made even most Olympians flinch?

A few fallen leaves and a sparse carpet of grass crunched under her sandals as Persephone walked through her troubles.

She had spent the last few days in an opium dream. Hypnos would be proud. Eight days of discovery, trepidation flowering into bliss. Was she becoming something new, or had all this been a part of her all along, so many seeds waiting for a rind to burst open and birth them upon fertile ground?

Persephone, Daughter of Olympos, would have recoiled at Hades's touch; would have fought tooth and nail to retain every bit of the control she'd surrendered of her own will, just the previous night.

The Persephone who watched the Phlegethôn churn beneath her feet as she dangled in the grip of trust, however ... *That* Persephone only knew hunger. She had tasted an equal, opposing force. Where Hades sought control, this new Persephone found an inexplicable readiness to submit.

She circled the fingers of her left hand around her right wrist, recalling the grip of the Oil her own desire had forged.

By the Fates, do I want to submit.

She turned down a row of citron trees with a grimace and kept her meandering pace.

What was she to do? Wallow in euphoria, here in the Underworld, forever?

Is that what you want? Forever? After eight days?

Her cheeks grew hot even at the idea. When had she grown so impetuous? Had so much time on her back made her heart and mind shift places? Or perhaps she was drunk on immortal seed and hadn't abstained long enough to be sober.

Hades had spoken of marriage, of Zeus's approval of a courtship, but why dangle an opportunity to leave the Underworld with Hermes if only she were to obey? How did he intend to have a marriage with his consort in another realm?

Or had it all been a ruse? The tale of his bargain with Aphrodite a lie, and Persephone, another forgotten toy to cast aside as her novelty expired.

His 'consort'. Hekate's words had dug in and burrowed deep. All while her body had been thrilling in a tangle of fear and lust, some portion of her more profound than flesh had been sampling the idea. Savoring and finding it not unpalatable at all. Neither god nor man had made her feel such things, not on any plane or in any age.

When the time came for her to leave, would she find herself persuading him to let her stay? Why was it so difficult to put a finger on what she wanted? What she ought to do.

She paused to reach for a nearly-ripe citron, the oblong rind pebbly under her fingers. It was alive, there was no doubt, but she could not feel its pulse the way she could have in her own realm. Sight and scent and touch would have to suffice for her here, as though she were a mortal. Persephone left the fruit on the branch and moved on, frowning.

The Lord of the Dead carried out his duties here in the Underworld, she had seen it herself. Who, then, would be responsible for such matters as only the Goddess of Growing Things could remedy? If she remained here below the earth, her abilities unable to touch any green living thing, what then? And what of the mortals? Did they not need food and shelter?

A marriage here would upset the Balance. It could not be done.

And there was another matter.

Her thumb fumbled with the back of the silver band. She had a ring to return, and cringed to think how long eight days on the deathless plane would have been for her dear and worthy friend. The passage of time was a tricky thing between the realms of gods and m—

"Persephone."

She gasped and whirled.

Hades stood behind her, composed and somber while she swore and caught her breath.

"It is time," he said as her heartbeat slowed. He held his arms clasped behind his back, his posture upright as though he were making some pronouncement in the Hall of Judgments. The fine hairs on the back of her neck stood on end.

"Time for what?"

"I have word. Hermes comes for you tomorrow. I assume you still wish to go?" He spoke with a cold formality and she felt her brows coming down into a knot.

So. It *was* time. And she *did* need to go, but why did it feel like this? As though it were tainted somehow.

"Hades," she said, "you must understand. The Unseen Realm requires oversight. You maintain an order here. I have my own responsibilities above. The mortals depend on my gifts as surely as they do yours. I cannot abandon them."

He nodded, jaw set. "Then this is as it must be." She had seen her father brew storms less ominous. "You will do one last thing for me before you leave."

"Which is?" Their stances had become adversarial, and Persephone didn't care for it.

Hades produced a hand full of something round and dusky pink, and held it out to her at arm's length. She stepped toward him, squinting.

"A pomegranate?" She eyed him. "I don't understand."

"I want you to eat it. Before you go."

"What does it matter if I eat a p—"

Oh.

To eat the fruit of her captor was to be bound to him forever.

He had a slow single nod for her moment of realization.

Betrayal, she found, tasted more like that under-ripe citron.

"Then what is the point, my *Lord?*" She stung him with the honorific and his eyes narrowed. "Why bother to let me leave at all? Why fashion some elaborate tether when you can just keep me prisoner here?"

How in the three realms had she thought there had ever been a choice?

"Because if Hermes is coming for you," he said, gesturing with the fruit, "he does so at the command of Zeus. Unless I intend to start a war, I'll have to give you up, at least for a time."

Persephone gaped, and her arms folded over her breast. "So it was *never* my choice, was it? 'Obey and leave one day'." She looked him up and down, willing herself not to spit. "It was always your intention, yes? To force me? I trusted you, *Polydegmon*."

Her reality skewed into wrongness, and a sickness churned in her gut.

"I did not always have this plan, Persephone. Not in the beginning. I—" The famous control slipped. "I cannot lose you!"

Too many emotions slapped at her at once. Hades seized her wrist and pushed the pomegranate into her hand, trapping her fingers around it beneath his grip.

"You've obeyed me all this time, Green One. Do it once again. Eat this cursed fruit and be done with it." She tried to pull back from his grasp, but he held her and his voice was fierce. "You cannot deny what we shared last night—you know this is where you belong."

The angry crescendo, the peal of finality in his words had her eyes welling. Persephone shook her head.

"How could you do this?" Her voice broke, dismay winning out over shame. "Will you force it down my throat?"

"One of us will see it past your lips."

She was reeling. Reeling.

When your heart was free, you called him 'sýzygos'.

"All those times you called me 'love'?" The pathetic plea made her insides twist. "*This* is a courtship? This is how you treat the one you hoped to have as a wife?"

Whether her accusations stung or the villain had seen enough, he stepped back from the scene he'd wrought and left Persephone holding the pomegranate.

The Lord of the Underworld drew out his bident and painted her with a withering eye.

"Hate me or no, I expect that fruit eaten by morning, *little flower*. Or, so help me"—the æther split in two in the wake of his iron weapon—"I will feed it to you, myself."

With the threat in place, Hades stepped through, and the orchard was silent again.

It was the first time he'd called her 'little flower' and it had hurt.

This was what it was like. Her mother had warned, and she'd refused to listen.

But you don't have to suffer this. Not forever.

She turned over the pomegranate to consider Polyxene's ring.

No, indeed. Not forever at all.

✦

The Helm of Darkness was the only thing between Hades and a terrified riot of mortal shades where they gathered on the shores of the Lethe. To walk among them unseen was not a necessity, but their cowering and wailing would not help him think. By contrast, their milling procession in his unfocused line of sight helped to still him the way beings of brighter realms might be stilled by gazing at a pond of gliding fish.

If I could only drink from the river myself. Forget this entire disaster.

The souls of the dead took up the waters of the Lethe to forget all their previous incarnations. If they chose to spin from the dark womb of the grave again, to bloom on the earth anew, it was the bargain the Underworld required them to make. It was their only chance to begin again, wiped clean and innocent as a babe.

And what of *his* next life? In the past, he had divided his existence in two: the time before the War, and the time after, in which he'd ruled this domain away from the struggles and machinations of his peers.

Now, he would portion his ages another way. There was the time before Persephone ... and then there would be everything else. There was little doubt left: his actions had destroyed the 'everything else' for them both.

He had heard the sons and daughters of men in his realm describe the winding trail of the Lethe as a disorienting sight to behold. The River of Forgetting, they said, appeared to both exist and not exist, at once. To look upon it was to know the lead-grey current was present, and yet to blink and shake their heads as though they couldn't quite remember what it was they'd just seen, or why their gaze had fallen where it did.

As the realm's immortal lord, Hades had no choice but to accept the truth of their tales. Other than its contribution to the darkening of his extremities, the Lethe left him unaffected. He was as blind to its influence as he was to any number of important realities, it seemed.

Realities like tears over a cursed pomegranate.

Regret reached between his ribs again with a clawed hand. It took hold of things vital and soft, squeezing and twisting.

The betrayal on her face accused him, lovely features contorted in his mind's eye to reflect the damage he'd done.

Should he have known? *Could* he have known?

Aphrodite's veiled suggestion, once a distasteful scheme, had become a matter of unfortunate necessity, as Hades saw it.

Persephone, it turned out, did not feel the same.

His ability to read the motivations of others had yet to fail him in such a spectacular fashion. She wanted to stay with him, did she not? Or at least return after this charade with Hermes played out to its ridiculous end. He'd pictured her leaping to eat the fruit, to make certain no further Olympian schemes could part them for long. After the last time they'd made love, he'd only assumed …

Yes, made love.

He let the word roll around in his skull, just short of forming on his tongue. The Lord of the Dead had never loved anyone, possibly not even himself. Was this what it was to love? To ache in the other's absence, to covet their smiles beyond any sanity of his own?

How had he arrived at a point such as this?

There was Aphrodite blackmailing him into abducting a goddess he'd never met. There was his instant lust for Persephone that had grown into … into what? Coming to care about her pleasure and pain? *His* enjoyment of fulfilling *her* desires? What had happened to him?

When had the idea of marriage vows become anything more than lip service he'd paid to Aphrodite?

When had he begun to love her?

Does it matter, when you've destroyed it all now?

He had never attempted to force her into anything until the pomegranate. All the pageantry of asking for her obedience, his games of restraint, had been just that.

Pageantry and games; titillations meant to cater to his dark fancies—and hers, if he could believe his good fortune. Every step of the way he had sought her permission, had extracted promises she would speak if they reached her limits. She never had.

The Olympians had entrusted him with countless deaths over untold ages, but never a single life. Not until Persephone, and it had been her own. She had trusted, she had served, she had begged, and she had surrendered. All with such a naked, honest desire as Hades had never seen.

And now he had become the villain, just as she'd named him in jest the night he'd come to her with the belt. When the inevitable ties of the pomegranate—her captor's fruit—brought her back to the Underworld, Persephone would feel nothing but resentment.

If he forced her, she could not choose him. She would never share his company with the same blissful abandon she'd shown this last week.

She would not love him.

It had become the most miserable fate he could imagine, and he'd brought it upon himself. He had done everything wrong. Actions which in the past wouldn't have made him think twice now haunted him as sickening. Sickening and awful and *wrong*.

Well what are you going to do about it, Polydegmon? Wallow in self-loathing here on the shores of the Lethe?

He removed the Helm and every mortal in sight shrank back with a collective gasp. His bident drew out between his hands, and the Underworld tensed at his whim, ready.

◆

The *Elaionapothos* rested in its platform state, and Persephone sat on its edge, elbows on knees, clutching the pomegranate in grim hands.

Hours and hours staring at the fruit had seared her mind barren, like a cloudless summer sky traversed by nothing but the sun. She'd thought every thought it was possible to think, and they'd abandoned her to a stillness by turns until the space inside her head grew eerie with quiet.

Every thought save one.

"I will feed it to you, myself."

She had no doubts he could do it. Her abilities were nothing in this realm. His command of the stone, the power he had to come and go unseen? Those alone would likely be enough to accomplish his ends, and if Hades was any peer to the lords of the other two realms, then the displays she'd seen thus far were but a sliver of his entire might.

Persephone shivered.

What choice would be left to her n—

"Goddess."

The double doors to the chamber burst inward, rebounding against the walls. Persephone leapt in her seat and fumbled the pomegranate. Hades strode into the room, collapsing his bident as he came.

Her heart was in her throat.

"Hades, wai—"

"*Have* you eaten it?"

She looked him up and down in disdain.

"No."

His eyes found the red fruit, discarded on the floor. In a heartbeat, he was across the room to retrieve it, to stand in front of her, holding it out in one dark-fingered hand.

She crossed her arms over her chest, the refusal clear. Hades sighed and something loosened in his shoulders.

The god knelt at her feet.

"This is a heavy thing I have asked of you," he said, placing the object of her displeasure upon her knee but not releasing his grip.

"You didn't ask," she said. "You commanded." She made no move to touch either him or the offending pomegranate.

"Yes," he said, "and for that I am sorry." Was there sincerity in those bottomless eyes of his? Who could trust anything now? "If you will only listen, my lov—"

"Don't call me 'love'."

His head tilted down and to the side, jaw tightened, but he continued.

"Persephone, you were right." She blinked at him, forgetting to glare. "About the control, the fear. About everything. I cannot give over control of this to the Olympians. It is too important."

When the line of her mouth firmed up even more, he set the fruit on the Oil and returned the imploring hand to her knee.

"I thought," he said, meeting her eyes at last, "you would want to stay with me. I thought this—" He seemed to bite his own tongue, before trying again in a more measured fashion. "I *thought*, with the pomegranate, we could … it would give us some assurance."

"Assurance?" She could feel her brows climbing.

"That even after Hermes came for you, Demeter wouldn't be able to keep us apart. Not for long. We both know she'll have you locked away even more strictly now that this"—he gestured between them—"has happened."

"It seems you and my mother have plenty in common." She uncrossed her arms to lean forward on her hands, seething. "You both want to keep me locked up."

He inhaled, a deep, rib-expanding breath, and let it go. When he spoke again, he sounded tired. "That is not true."

Her silence challenged his denial, but Hades was not deterred.

"This," he said, taking up the pomegranate again, "can be a way, but it is not what you think." When she opened her mouth to snap at him again, he held up a hand. "If what we've shared means anything to you at all, you will hear my plan. Please."

Against her better judgment, Persephone listened.

It was ridiculous, and it answered none of the questions that burned in her chest. It was also the only way she would leave the Underworld unscathed. The weight of Polyxene's ring reminded her there were other escapes as well, provided she could get through this first, and trickiest of doors.

His words stopped and Hades stared at her, waiting for acceptance. When she said nothing, he dared to reach for her hands. To gather them up and close them around the fruit of his realm.

"Please," he said, and such a foreign word on his lips, for him to repeat with such frequency. "In the orchard. That was a mistake. That is not how I wish it to be between us."

Persephone looked at his hands over hers, a study in darkness and light. The Lord of the Dead had persuaded her before, and blinding joy had made the cost dear.

Still, the goddess saw no other way.

"Very well."

Hades nodded. Rose to his feet.

He offered her a hand, and she took it, questionable though their alliance was, and stood up after him.

"There is one more thing I must ask of you," he said, "before you leave this place."

She scowled. "Have you not asked enough?"

"Do you agree this is a complicated matter?"

Her eyes narrowed, but she tipped her head.

"Then I hope you will agree not to complicate it further by speaking to any of the others about the *Elaionapothos*. If there is one additional distraction we don't need, it's a race among immortals to lay hands on a new object of power. Not to mention if they come to realize the lord of the third realm has an advantage ..." He shook his head. "I might almost say I regret its creation, but how can I? It brought me to you."

If such a thing were possible, Persephone softened and hardened at the same time.

"Please," he said. "They cannot know."

Agree and leave. The only way.

"I will keep your secrets, Hades," she said, brandishing the pomegranate like a weapon, "but you will not break my trust again."

✦

Hermes stood before the Throne of Tears, the bearer of ruinous, if expected, news. The Lord of the Dead faced him from the seat of his rulership, stoic in a way he appeared to reserve for other gods. Persephone sat on his thigh, the picture of a lord's chosen consort, just as they'd agreed.

He'd asked her, for appearances, to arrange herself just so, but she was no longer blind to his motivations. It might be the last stretch of physical contact they had, and Hades was going to squeeze from it every last drop. She tried to convince herself, for her own sake, that she wasn't sitting there trying to do the same.

"And *Basileus* expects to simply rescind his word, not two weeks gone?" Hades looked down his nose at the Messenger. "Did he not imagine the Fair One's matchmaking would be effective?"

The arm around her waist curled tighter. The result of this meeting was inevitable, but the impression Hermes left with was not. Persephone nestled further against the planes of Hades's chest.

"My Lord, you must understand," Hermes said, with a subtle bow, "there will be nothing left for any of us if Persephone does not rejoin her mother. Demeter's wrath on the mortal plane … it's killing them. What would you have us do?"

To see the mischievous god speaking with such humble sobriety had Persephone frowning again. Just how dire had matters become up there in her absence? Had her mother lost her mind?

"The sons of men barely make offering to me *now*," said Hades, "and yet my realm flourishes as they pass across the Styx. Why should it trouble me if *Hôrêphoros* fills the Underworld with their shades in *mountains* with her petulance?"

His fingers pressed in at her hip, somehow warm against the chill in his voice. Against her better judgment, she leaned into the half-embrace.

There had been *such* joy. Is this how mortals experienced their little lives? Everything so temporary? So easily broken? The nights in his arms, in his thrall, they were all slipping away like so many clouds through her fingers.

Hermes paced the floor, a little of the Trickster she knew returning. "You claim you want Persephone for a consort, *Polydegmon*." Slate blue eyes glittered and a blond brow ticked upward. "Will you have your beloved watch her mother destroy herself along with all of us? Will you ask your bride to watch the flowers and trees she loves wither and die, and to stand aside and do nothing?"

The god spun his words with careful and clever intent, but that did not stop them from carrying a pang of truth. Her arguments with herself and with Hades centered around this very question, though the Swift One could not have heard them. She considered the Lord of the Dead from the corner of her eye, the trappings of his mad plan making her squint.

If looks could have turned another immortal to stone on the spot, the one Hades fixed the Messenger with then would have had Medusa nodding in approval. When he broke from the glare at last, it was only to nuzzle his mouth behind her ear and steal his last and lightest of kisses. It was no more than a brush of lips and Persephone had to allow it. Their audience was watching.

"The agreement remains," he whispered. She tried to keep her features neutral as the hand at her waist began slipping up her side to her shoulder.

He turned to the fleet-footed god and cleared his throat.

"Very well," he said, voice just the wrong side of too loud. "I will permit you to leave here with Persephone today, Swift One, but understand this"—his fingers came in a possessive circle over the front of her throat—"the daughter of Zeus at my side has eaten the fruit of my realm. By consuming the pomegranate, she has bound herself to me by the laws of the Fates, which even your lord on Olympos will not dispute. Have her explain this to the Lord of Lightnings, and to her mother." A thumb nudged her jaw, making her face tilt toward his. "She will return to me, whatever they demand."

The god who set her blood on fire was making no subtle display of his claims, and if fury wasn't enough of a struggle for her to contain, arousal managed to make up the difference. Were they alone, she would claw his eyes.

Right before spreading your legs. You're a disaster.

Hermes was agog. "Is this true?" he asked her. "Have you eaten the fruit?"

Hades released his hold and she straightened herself.

"He speaks the truth, Messenger. I am bound to the Underworld. To Lord Hades."

She didn't look down, but felt him capture her hand and lace their fingers together into a squeeze. Now his trust in her would have to begin. With the secret of the *Elaionapothos*, with so many things.

"But Persephone, this"—he made some ineffectual gesture at the pair on the throne—"this—"

"This what?" she said, standing. "Do they not believe me capable of making my own choices on Olympos?" She hoped her words were a jab for Hades, as well.

Hermes tried to swallow the new development, no doubt reworking at a frantic pace the way he would report it to Zeus. He looked from her to Hades and back again, and it was the Lord of the Dead who broke the silence.

"Be off with you then," he said. "Fulfill the letter of your lord's command, and have him see the truth with his own eyes. But you will respect my consort, Messenger." Hades stood now, radiating menace so the hall seemed to shrink around him. "I expect Persephone to return unmolested. The consequences for failing me in this will only *begin* with a permanent expulsion from my realm. They will end somewhere you do not wish to contemplate. Do I make myself clear?"

"Indeed." Another quick bow and Hermes took a step away from the throne. It was the only time Persephone had seen him cowed.

Their audience had concluded with far less debate than she'd anticipated. Something rushed away from her that she could not control or grasp with her hands, so many waves retreating from a shore.

The goddess stepped down from the dais in a daze, the pomegranate looming large in her thoughts.

It's over. Done.

And when her father found out? Well ... she was not able, at that moment, to distinguish relief from lament.

"Lord Hades." Hermes accompanied his curt goodbye with a nod and turned to the throne room doors. "Goddess?" Neither of them could travel the æther unaided in this realm. They would have to depart by less efficient means.

Persephone let out the breath she'd been holding and moved to follow. When her foot touched the bottom step, an iron grip came around her upper arm.

"Persephone."

Hades stood over her when she turned, everything that moved her and killed her at once. Those black eyes consumed and made promises. The heat of his touch branded her with the most bitter reminder of the depths to which they'd descended in a matter of only days.

"The equinox," she said. "Our agreement stands."

At her hushed words, he pulled her close, made her hands collide with his chest. The Lord of the Dead laid his final caution on her lips, riding with it that blade edge of danger and affection as their every interaction had done.

"Beloved, you will have my mercy. The others," he said, "will not."

She couldn't help a tremble at the endearment, but he released her and stepped back before joining them in any sort of embrace.

Every choice she made would have consequences. For him. For her. For countless others oblivious to the affairs of the gods.

When she turned at the double doors, Hades had not released her from that throat-tightening stare.

You must do this. You must.

She set her jaw and followed Hermes out of the palace.

◆

The light of day dazzled anew after Persephone's time in the Underworld. The subdued light of the Unseen Realm had taught her to see with less.

Tall, dry grass swished around her ankles, and she squinted ahead as she walked, doing her best to ignore the incessant chatter of her escort.

Hermes trotted along beside her, his questions buzzing like gnats. He walked backward to face her since she wouldn't stop for him, and Persephone wore a grim internal smile at the way she was forcing the Swift One to curtail his normal pace. This must have felt like the trickling of sap to him.

"Is it true?" he said. "The ground tore open and you *fell?*" She eyed him and made a face, but he went on, incredulous. "*No one* can enter the Underworld that way. How did you survive the drop?"

"Lord Hades caught me."

Another short answer, but her patience wore thin. And how formally she referred to the god with whom she'd shared such intimacy this last week. Now that she was out of his sight, Hades seemed so very far away.

"Ugh! With those black claws of his?" Hermes grimaced. "How perfectly wretched for you."

Did he think to commiserate? What would his face look like if he knew she didn't share his revulsion? The dark hands of Hades fading to grey at the elbow and then marble white by the shoulder … and the way those fingers looked when they pressed into her flesh …

This is helping in no way. Stop.

The Swift One barreled forward in his line of thought, eyes wide with speculation. "Persephone!" he said. "You were down there for over a week. And Hades means to have you as a consort? Did he try to—I mean, did the two of you—"

"I don't see how that concerns you, *Messenger*." She marched on, refusing to look at him.

He gasped in scandalized glee. "You *did!* Oh how *awful* for you! Is his touch as cold as it looks? Did he have to truss you up so you wouldn't run away?"

The rude questions made her face burn. He *had* trussed her up a bit.

But you didn't want to run. Not unless it meant he might chase you down.

The very idea called up memories of the blood union. Of seeing, of *feeling* him hunt that mortal. But Hermes only saw her cheeks coloring. The god all but cavorted under the late morning sun.

"Persephone, you *liked* it, didn't you? Fates! Wait until your mother sees you in such a state." He untangled his pipes from his belt and brought them to his lips, playing out a mischievous series of notes.

She shot him a glare, but didn't stop walking. "Enough, Hermes. I will go to Olympos with you as my father bade. I will *not* listen to nonsense the entire way. Wag your tongue for someone who cares to hear it—it isn't me."

How had she ever seen this frivolous god as anything but the shallow reflecting pool he was?

And then he was standing in her path, making her jerk to a halt before they collided.

"What *now*?" Her hands came to her hips.

An impish grin turned the corner of his mouth, and his hand rose to grip her shoulder. Then he was tracing a thumb over her collarbone, blue eyes traveling her flesh anew.

"You are maiden no longer, Daughter of Zeus." The thumb tickled her throat. "Perhaps you'd care to sample a lover a bit less ... *grave?*" He managed the audacity of a smirk at his own word play.

"Did you hear nothing in that throne room, *Trickster?*" She swatted the hand away and stepped out of his reach. "I am bound to Lord Hades as surely as Hera is bound to my father. I've no room for any of ... *this*." She gestured at him with a nod of disgust.

"And yet Zeus has tasted many sweets outside his marriage bed," he said, advancing on her again. "Your own mother being one of them. You're not in his kingdom anymore, Persephone. The Lord of the Dead needn't know a thing."

Not in his kingdom. Yes.

"You're right," she said, growing a cruel little grin. "I'm not in his realm. I'm in *mine*."

Power she hadn't tasted in days flooded her veins in a twisting rush. The soil burst at Hermes's feet. Before he could finish swearing, dark, damp roots as thick as an arm coiled around those swiftest of feet and began surging up calves and thighs. She only halted the ravenous growth at his waist, but Hermes stood trapped on the spot, all the same.

Still, mockery curled his features.

"What will you do?" he said. "Leave me here and run off to tell your mother? Or Zeus, if you think he'd listen?"

She stepped close now, scalding him with a look. "It is not Demeter you should be afraid of, God of Thieves." The roots began to constrict, making an awful stretching, snapping sound. "It is me."

She halted the squeezing growth at his first grunt of pain and crossed her arms over her chest.

"I know the way to Olympos," she said, "I have no particular need for your guidance. If you wish to be silent, you can accompany me the rest of the way. If not?" She shrugged. "Well. I'm sure someone will happen along who might find a way to free you."

Hermes spread his hands wide, all smiles and paper innocence. "I was only trying to broaden your horizons, Goddess. You've shown me how the wind blows."

"My horizons are broad enough," she said. "Which will it be?"

"Not another word from my lips, I swear it."

She wanted to slap the insolence from his face, but it would be one more thing wasting her time. Instead she cast her will over the roots and pulled them back down into the earth.

Her escort stood dusting his chiton while she shouldered past him toward the inevitable. Olympos waited. Her parents waited.

Decisions … waited.

The nimble god skipped after her, mute as promised, but trilling away on his infernal pipes.

♦

IX Limits

"What do you mean, 'she's eaten his fruit'?" Demeter's outrage furled among the columns of the throne room. The Lord of Lightnings raised a silver brow and Hermes cringed.

"It is as the Messenger says, Mother." Persephone maintained straight shoulders and a cool façade as best she knew how. "Lord Hades bid me eat of the pomegranate and I did so. I am bound to him now. You know what will happen if I do not return."

"But *why*?" Demeter clawed at the air, as if she could drag away answers. "Why have you done this thing? You know the laws of the Fates."

"I had no choice."

"You had no *choice*?" The heads of wheat crowning her mother's brow bristled with ire. "There is always a choice," she said. "Choose now. Refuse him. Remain on Olympos. He has no power in this realm to come and claim you—what can he do?"

Persephone felt the color in her cheeks and lifted her chin, defiant. "What would you have me do? Stay in the upper realms until I grow weak and wither away? Never seeking the communion as the bond now requires? You would have me a husk of myself rather than bend your will on this single matter?"

Demeter's eyes widened and she inhaled what must have been all the air on the mount. But it wasn't her daughter on whom she rounded.

"*Zeus.*" She was halfway up the stairs to his throne, a thing that was not done without invitation. Rancor seethed from her pores. "*You* approved this nightmare in the first place. You will extract her from it." The goddess stabbed a finger at him, and Hermes made himself smaller still on the fringes of the confrontation.

"You heard her," Demeter said. "He didn't give her a choice. He might as well be attempting to force the vows. Speak to the Fates. They can't bind her to your brother forever over a faulty premise."

"Have you forgotten in whose realm the Fates dwell? Shall I venture to a place where *I* am without power? Where I now have quarrel with its ruler?" Zeus's smile glittered as he leaned forward in his seat. "You know the laws, *Hôrêphoros*. We don't trifle with the workings of the *Moirai*. The only thing we can do is return her to his halls before the bond saps her completely."

Demeter never released him from her glare, but made demands of Persephone. "Tell him," she said. "Tell your father how that fiend stole you from the fields of Nysa when my back was turned."

Persephone looked at the floor and said nothing. There was no point in adding to the crackling tension in the hall.

"Leave us," said Zeus. She jumped, as his voice had dropped an octave in command. "I wish to speak to my daughter alone."

"I will do nothing of the sort," Demeter said. "I will remain on this very step until you pull your head out of your Olympian a—"

"Do not test me, Goddess." Thunder growled from far away, and a heartbeat later, not so far. "I have very little patience for such wailings as all of these. You will wait in your palace or I will have you wait elsewhere."

Demeter's mouth opened for another retort, but it was Persephone who spoke.

"For every breath we waste here, Mother, your blight pours more dead mortals onto the shores of the Styx. The Underworld and its ruler swell with power as we stand here and debate. Is this your aim?"

Whatever flashed in her mother's eyes then could be described by none of the four seasons over which the goddess ruled. Demeter set her jaw. Stepped back down the stairs with shoulders back and an arched brow of warning.

"Consider carefully before the two of you insist upon your way," she said, holding each of their gazes in turn.

Demeter touched the wreath on her head and it leapt into her hands in the form of her scythe. Much the way Hades would do in the Unseen Realm, she sliced the æther and whirled herself from the hall. Hermes flew from the room in her wake, streaking away on foot at his usual quicksilver speed.

Persephone found herself staring at Zeus. Had she ever stood alone in his presence? In some respects, it was like standing before Hades. In others, it most certainly was not.

Do not think of that now. You'll be bright red in a heartbeat.

The Lord of Lightnings stood and interlaced his fingers in front of him, inverted his palms, and stretched massive arms away from his chest. Then he descended to the second step from the marble floor and sat.

"Sit with me, daughter." He thumped the stone beside him with a palm.

What else was there to do? She sat, and folded her arms around her knees. More than any other immortal, her father made her feel tiny. It did not help that she hadn't seen him in ages.

Zeus turned blue eyes on her and the air in the throne room shimmered. Something inside her chest felt like it was curling open, white waxy petals at dawn. The feeling peeled up through her throat and her tongue grew heavy, then light, just before the words spilled of their own accord.

"I didn't eat the fruit."

Fates! Why?

But she knew why, didn't she? Her father's ability to compel truth was well known in the upper realms, but Persephone had never experienced it firsthand. It was … oddly freeing, once a body got past the sensation of something opening the core of their being like a fish.

He had a slow nod for her blurted revelation, his gaze turning out over the hall, considering. His elbows were on his knees, his fingers laced together out in front of him.

"And yet Hermes believes you did." It was not a harsh accusation. He tried to solve a puzzle, not shame her for lies.

"We—Lord Hades and I—decided, well …" *You shouldn't be telling him any of this.* "If my mother were to think I had eaten of the pomegranate, she would see my return to him as the only possibility. If she believes I still have a choice, she will never let me alone again."

Persephone shrank in on herself, ready for the tirade to come. She'd deceived Hermes, deceived her mother. Deceived the Lord of Olympos, if only for a time.

The outrage came in the form of a smile.

"Hades is wise in this plan," he said. "He is right about your mother."

She had to make an effort to close her mouth. He was … accusing her of being *right?* She sat there in rudderless silence, but after a time, Zeus had more questions.

"Persephone, do you know why I approved this courtship?"

"I don't," she said. "Not when you knew Mother had such fierce protections on my innocence."

He tilted his head and glanced over from under knowing eyelids. "Helios sees all, Daughter. Even such happenings as we might attempt to confine to the mortal plane."

The mortal pl—oh!

"You do not understand, Father. I went to the m—"

"I *do* understand," he said, "but that isn't the reason for the courtship."

She shook her head, but Zeus found her right hand and took it in his. Fingers squeezed with affection.

"You deserve more than I was able to give your mother," he said. "Hades is ... well ..." Air huffed out through his nose. "Hades is many things. The Unseen Realm is not like ours. Mortals fear him because they do not understand death. *Immortals* keep their distance because they do not understand his ways. He is from a time before the War. As am I. As is your mother. But Persephone," he said, "he will be a fair and loyal husband, should you choose to make the vows."

Her brows came down, perhaps trying to dip into a place of hope. "How can you know this? Mother is sure he will leave me in disgrace."

"She does not see many examples on this plane to establish her confidence otherwise. So many of our kind"—he let go her hand to gesture—"grow restless and bored over the æons. Our attention wanders. Aphrodite should be faithful to Hephaistos, Poseidon should have eyes for none but Amphitrite, and I ... well, I'm sure your mother has regaled you to no end about what sort of creature I am." A rueful chuckle accompanied a shake of his head.

She gave him a look, but Zeus only shrugged.

"I do not deny it. We are what we are. All of us." He turned an unfocused gaze back to her, blue eyes serious now. "It is for this reason I can make such judgments. Hades has ruled below all these many ages without choosing a consort. What would have stopped him from doing as so many of us have done? From speaking the vows out of passion, and then forsaking them when he grew tired?"

"I ... don't know?"

"Whatever it is he seeks in a consort, the Lord of the Dead has waited for it. He has a patience none of us can match. He will stay true, Daughter, and this is what you deserve. So much better than what Hermes would have given you, or Apollo."

Loyalty. Who knew? It had been her father's concern, just the same as her mother. And yet *his* assessment, of at least one immortal, differed from Demeter's as the night from the day.

Hades's attentions had swept all other concerns out of existence. It wasn't until the end of her time in the Underworld that Persephone had begun to consider practicalities. She hadn't been able to catch her breath—or stay on her feet!—long enough around the god to even worry about a marriage, let alone whether he would remain faithful.

Her father bounced her palm in his. "You spent a week in the Underworld, daughter of mine. I'm sure it wasn't to sit alone in the dark." Now he wore half a smile, and her face went hot in an instant.

The gentle teasing was like nothing her mother would have to say on the matter. How had her parents tolerated each other long enough to produce her?

"Do you love him?"

Persephone almost choked, but the question should have come as no surprise. Zeus was about as subtle as the lightning he commanded. Still, after settling herself, she nodded. "I believe I do."

There. Her father compelled truth, even when he wasn't trying.

"Will you go back to him then?"

"If only it were that simple."

Both brows climbed now, a series of lines furrowed above them. "I see." The two words speculated and judged, but also kept a surprising respectful distance.

He stood from the step, straightening his chiton as he went. "Well," he said, reaching a hand down to help her up, "we won't tell Demeter otherwise, will we? I don't know how much peace it will afford you, but it should continue to buy you time."

When she joined him on her feet, her father caught her in a warm embrace, thumping her back with a massive palm. "Don't make him wait long, Persephone." The words brushed the top of her hair, "If you're not going back, you should tell him before it hurts too much."

◆

It was beginning to hurt too much.

Hades stirred atop the platform of the *Elaionapothos*. There was comfort in no position, rest after no amount of silence. The stalactites above pointed at him in accusation while their counterparts rising from the floor all stood by to witness.

It was his very own Hall of Judgments, right here in his private rooms.

He lay on his back, fist clutching what remained of the torn chiton Persephone had worn the day she fell into his domain. As he'd done dozens of times already, Hades brought the grey cloth to his face and inhaled the fading memory of her scent. An angry erection refused to leave him be.

How had he let Hermes walk out of his palace with her, unopposed? He could have had the Trickster bound in stone. He could have seen that thrice-damned pomegranate down her throat any number of ways. Who could have stopped him?

No one.

But you wanted her to choose. Her presence here must be her own idea, or it will be meaningless.

The *Elaionapothos* moved under his free hand where it lay on the flattened surface. He rolled on his side and the Oil responded further in a boiling of slick curves. Again, the twitch of his need was in hand. Again, he began the pointless strokes.

It had happened twice already, in the time since Persephone had left him. Though a deathless god had no need of sleep, he'd resorted to its attempt for the sake of escape alone. But solace refused him its mercy.

Closing his eyes had become a cruelty as it never had. She waited for him there; the scent of spring and petal-pale curves for him to ruin with his lust. The music of that voice, calling his name. Green eyes holding his, permitting, accepting.

Those eccentricities of his desire nature, which had him forgoing a consort these many ages, had met their match in Persephone. Against all reason, she'd understood his sickness, if that's what it was, and had offered herself as a remedy. He'd grown to believe no immortal lover would tolerate his urges and yet, each time they'd welled up and Hades thought he'd go mad, she'd opened herself and said, 'Take'.

She was the only immortal to have given freely to him without asking anything in return. And the more savage he became in the taking, the more zeal she poured into her surrender.

Persephone was his every desire and the *Elaionapothos* existed for one purpose alone: to give those desires a shape.

And so it had, after a fashion.

He ran a palm over the shifting black form at his side. If he closed his eyes, its surface felt all too real. He palmed a counterfeit breast and it was warm and soft with the proper weight and give. A nipple tempted his tongue, but he knew the salt and sweet of his little flower was beyond reach. The Oil would offer back a tasteless nothing.

When he opened his eyes, some nameless horror rippled along his spine and up through his throat. Here was the forgery of his love, wrought by his wishes and an object of power. The glossy black curves pretending to be his Persephone repelled with the chill of the uncanny. Sightless eyes stared out into a void, and they were not hers.

Not hers.

Hades levered himself away from the *Elaionapothos*, his own growl of disgust propelling his limbs. The false

Persephone melted back into the slick platform while he stood back several paces, breath coming ragged with the violence of need.

The flames of indignation stoked him and the fury vented through his hands. He pulled at his cock, a punishment and relief at once.

When was the last time his passions had driven him to this? He couldn't say. Before Aphrodite's bargain, his ages below the earth had served to subdue his fervor. But no longer. Persephone's gifts had ruined him, and his fist pumped over his ache in a poor imitation of her perfect embrace.

You had it. You had it and you lost it!

Completion tore from his throat in a roar. The sum of his fury slicked his pumping fist, drops of bitter seed, of useless temper, splattered the limestone floor. Hades's vision blurred to scarlet as he stood, laboring for his breath.

Everything was out of his hands. His rulership meant nothing, would buy him *nothing*. What purpose did it serve? Even as he would draw the time near, the equinox retreated from his grasp.

And if she doesn't return? If you are not her choice?

He staggered down to one knee, knuckles to the floor, and swore an oath no other god would dare repeat. On the mortal plane, there were tremblings in the earth, and the Sons of Man fled to their altars with offerings and fear.

Persephone, it turned out, had been right: Hades needed control. He needed *her*. And for all his power and reach, the Lord of the Dead had neither.

The act of gathering sandals and chiton again, of clothing himself and raking the wrath of his fingers back through his hair, had to suffice as an avenue to composure. He had eternity, but it was useless.

In a flickering of will, the columns of his throne room took the place of stalactites around him, and light shuddered, baleful and violet at the edges, from his sigil in the floor.

Hades assumed the seat of his power and tapped the veins of the Unseen Realm with a word.

"Hekate."

✦

Persephone ground her teeth at the newest disruption to her peace. Helios was only beginning his climb from the east, and she'd spent the time before dawn watching the stars dim over the fields of Nysa. A return to the birthplace of her troubles, a suitable cradle for thought in these days since she'd returned to the upper realms, and then the rift had opened in the æther.

Now Demeter stood over her shoulder, glowering into the sunrise as Persephone sat, arms around her knees wearing a matching scowl.

After a building storm of silence, the goddess spoke over the dawn, her voice low and dark. "I spent ages protecting you," she said. "You repay my efforts this way?"

Persephone controlled the breath she let out through her nose. From the corner of her eye, she could see her mother's chiton rippling in a breeze that affected none of the grasses around it.

"You speak as though it were my choice to tumble into the abyss," she replied through a tightened jaw. "I did nothing to invite this."

"You could have refused him."

There would be no peace. No peace here.

"Oh?" She tilted her eyes up to her mother at last, her brows rising with them. "With what power? Or do you believe the Lord of the Dead tolerates refusals in his own domain?"

Now the elder goddess deigned to fix her with a look. "And the pomegranate?" Her lip curled, hand coming to her hip. "Was it the only seed of his you couldn't refuse?"

Persephone made a face, and her arms unfolded so she could brace her weight on her palms and lean back for a better look at what her mother had become.

"You've let him ruin you," Demeter said.

Persephone looked her up and down, incredulous. "Are *you* ruined?" she asked. "After your time with my father?"

The immortal mouth turned down as though it harbored something sour. "My mistakes were yours to learn from, Daughter."

"Ah"—she pushed herself to her feet—"so I'm a mistake." Demeter opened her mouth, but Persephone swept her response aside, along with leaves and dirt from her chiton. "Let me banish any false notions you may have had, *Mother*. I ruined *myself* on the staves of Man ages ago. Many, *many* times over." She pressed home the emphasis with a deliberate enunciation, relishing at last the way her mother's face condensed in denial.

"You did nothing of the sort." A wind began bending heads of grass, rustling tree boughs at the edge of the field.

"Oh, but I *did*." She couldn't help a flash of teeth as she stepped around the goddess, orchids bursting around her feet as she went, their petals lurid and suggestive. "You wasted your worry for Hermes and Apollo, but I knew mortal flesh across oceans and empires and time. Consider well the reasons Lord Hades came to know this before you did."

"Willful child." The force of rushing air grew, carrying dying plant matter with it in whirling eddies. "You will listen to the wisdom of no one. And now you will what?" She stepped toward her daughter. "Abandon your duties to the call of immortal cock?"

The scattering of orchids withered to black as the goddess advanced, but the building violence of Persephone's emotion had the field writhing with spontaneous life. Ivy zig-zagged across the ground like lightning. Tree ferns exploded from the earth. A forest of sundews shot up in the wake of her retreat, higher than her head and bristling wet, poison to match her words.

"And my 'duties' require me to exist alone?" she said, raking the air with clawed fingers. "To never know love?" Low-lying flytraps snapped shut.

Demeter's scythe appeared in her hands and the mother goddess began to shear through rampant plant-life. "You have known my love since your birth," she said, eyes the color of a storm as she carved her way toward her daughter.

Willows lumbered full-grown from the soil on all sides, massive and whipping their branches in what was now a howling, aggressive wind.

"Ah yes," Persephone shouted over the gale, "the two are entirely the same. Why ever did I not think of this before?"

Out of a cloudless morning sky, the air flurried with snow. Withering cold crisped their breath and Demeter came at her, relentless. Tree limbs popped and shattered under ice and the same was on her mother's tongue.

"What you haven't thought of, Persephone, is your reason for being." Split trunks crumbled to ash as she curled her fingers into a fist. "Each of us is born into a purpose." She came forward, freezing, as her daughter seethed to a boil. "How will you fulfill yours from the Underworld? Hm? You said it yourself. With what power?" Drifts began to pile up against the carnage of growth and destruction. "The mortals will suffer under your need for 'love'," she said with a sneer. "Will you place your wants above those who rely on your gifts?"

The words hit Persephone like a fist in the gut, and brambles erupted from the earth around her, thick as sea serpents and snarling to her defense.

"I could ask you the same question, Goddess of the Seasons." Thorns stabbed outward in every direction, woody and coiling with spite. "Or have you forgotten the deluge of shades you sent to the Third Realm in your fury to have your way?"

A hum welled beneath Persephone's feet, and she teetered on the blade edge of refusing it all. Something familiar and yet unfamiliar began to crackle and grind along her extremities. She tasted iron.

Demeter was shearing past the brambles with arc after arc of her scythe, some nadir of threat dilating her pupils as she came. Her voice groaned now, ancient and deep. "You do not belong there, *Karporphoros*. No more than some cowering mortal belongs *here*."

Persephone's bones were the bones of the earth. Some dormant portion of her will sounded to a terrifying depth in a single choking heartbeat, and brought back the only answer it could.

Stalagmites thrust up from the ground in a maw, gnashing a barrier between her own choices and everyone else.

"*You* do not decide where I belong anymore, Mother." The scythe swung. "I decide." Chinked against stone and stopped. "*I* do."

The Goddess of Growing Things stood white with fury, while Demeter stared open-mouthed at Underworld stone negating Olympian power. Right there. In the upper realms, right out in the open.

And Persephone ... Persephone *had* decided.

She'd decided everything was too much. Every desire, every responsibility, every sacrifice. All of it. She could please no one, and so she *would* please no one.

The æther rippled and she melted through it, away from her mother's dumbfounded face.

At least no one on this plane.

✦

Blackness furled above the throne room floor and twin torches smoldered into being. *Enodia* was with him.

"My Lord." The goddess folded two and six hands at her waist; blinked one and three pair of eyes. Hades shored himself as he must against her shifting, tri-fold presence. He gripped the arms of his throne.

"I will wait no longer," he said. "I must know what she does."

Hekate hovered with her usual cryptic serenity, the possibilities of her being too nebulous to stand on a floor in any defined place or time. "You agreed to alllow herr wwill to prevail, *Polydegmon*."

"She will have her choice," Hades said, tightening his jaw, "but I will know what it is." He slid forward to the edge of his seat, voice lowering with his need. "You have dominion over every crossroads, Hekate. You will find her at her time of choosing, at the forking of her path, and you will learn her mind for me."

The layers of her voice shushed together, a friction of discarded snake skins. "I cannott agree on the wissdomm of ssuch a disscovery."

Light dimmed in the columned space, flickering with the hold on his patience. "I do not ask for agreement."

The ruddy orbs began to bob in orbit around their mistress, lazy at first but picking up speed. The goddess closed a number of eyes and let her arms fall to her sides, her focus moving between planes. "But perhapss you assk for knowledge to abate yourr mmisery," said Hekate, even as she acquiesced and settled into her element. "I can promise nno ssuch—my *Lord*." There were frowns. She made several faces at once. "Do you tesst me, Hades?"

"What is it?" He was leaning forward now, ready to leap out of his seat. *Enodia's* torches whirled faster, making their way toward a blur.

"The Green One toils withinn the confflux as we sspeak," she said. "Did you know thisss?"

"What do you mean?" He felt his knuckles strain. His nails began to etch granite. "How would I know anything?"

More than one of her heads tilted back as she sank, events on another plane enfolding her sight. "Her decisionn iss imminent." Silence from within the ring of red light. A fluttering of so many eyelids. "She battless her mmother."

"What?"

The one word echoed at a low boom among columns of stone, but Hekate was elsewhere, seeing events he couldn't.

"Demeter remindss her daughter of her obligations to the mmortalss," the goddess said, "annd it painss her."

Hades began to slide the iron ring from his finger, the line of his mouth turning grim. "They were not to interfere."

Terrifying smiles warped the scrying faces. "Perssephone is clever," she said, some thread of pride entering her voice. "Shhe gainss in power, she—"

Enodia gasped, a chorus of shock, and the torches flared to a halt, all but winking out at the disruption. Hades was on his feet, bident in hand.

"By the thrice-damned Fates, what do you see?"

Only Hekate *Perseis*, Destroyer and Lady of Shades could stand before the raised voice of Hades, unflinching.

"It ..." She searched for something. "My Lord it matters nnot. She ..."

He gripped his weapon.

"She. What."

"She hass chosenn."

Some searing thing clawed from inside his chest. He knew, but needed to punish himself. His steps flowed from the dais, sending him to loom and hiss over the immortal dashing his hopes.

"What did you see?"

Enodia folded her hands again and faced him with manifold eyes. "Your goddess hass called the Underworld," she said. "Ourr rrealm has answsered."

The mere beginnings of Hades's fury looked like the culmination of others'. The tines of his bident boiled to a livid amber, the very teeth going white as though he'd pulled them from the Phlegethôn. The doors to the hall burst open under a howl of sourceless wind.

"It was to be her choice," he said. "*Hers!* They were not to interfere!"

Hekate stepped out of his way.

◆

The mortal plane weighed heavy on her limbs, but it was the ring on her finger that pulled her. Persephone descended into Smyrna from where she'd emerged on the mount, south of the city proper.

Dawn saw the markets beginning to swarm, the Sons of Man abuzz in furious trade, even before Helios had cleared the line of staggered rooftops. Only the slimmest of her efforts kept her mortal guise in place; her strides ate up the crowded streets between her and the fate of her choosing.

The door to Polyxene's home was under her knuckles, their particular rap coming from long memory. As soon as she heard movement on the other side, Persephone flew right past the exchange of their normal safeguarding phrases.

"Good Mother, I have come."

A young woman who stood under an awning two doors away looked up from the linen she wrung of water and cocked her head at the stranger. Stepping through the æther directly into Polyxene's dwelling might have been less conspicuous, but terrifying the woman with such a sudden appearance would do no good at all. Nor could she know whether the healer would be alone.

At the dull sounds of a latch, the door swung inward and Persephone faced the wide eyes of an unprepared mortal.

A mortal with far more white in her hair than the goddess had seen on her last visit. The woman gaped at her, and Persephone struggled to keep herself from doing the same in return.

"May I enter your home, Polyxene?"

The woman rattled a nod and stepped out of the way, holding the door wide, and then closing it after her.

"My goddess!" The incredulous greeting came even before Persephone released her hold on her guise. No one else addressed her as 'Good Mother' or tapped on her door, just so. Still, Persephone shed her false appearance and stood as herself.

"Polyxene, I've come as I promised."

"Goddess, it has been"—the woman's eyes darted around the room and she made some helpless gesture—"it has been *so* long. I believed you would never return."

Only now was Persephone seeing the darkness to the lines on Polyxene's face, the slightness of her frame more pronounced than she remembered. As she stepped backward into the space, her focus expanded to her surroundings. The shelves were less heavy with containers, the surfaces less crowded by baskets and drying greens.

She dragged her gaze back to the ominous portent of silver hair. "My friend, how long has it been?"

"Eight ... eight years, Goddess." Polyxene ducked her head, as though such a revelation might anger her matron.

Eight *years*? Did time skew so awfully between the Underworld and the mortal plane? But Hades had said as much, hadn't he? *"The mortal and deathless realms come together in odd ways."*

Fates! What have you done to her?

"I am so, *so* sorry," she said, stepping forward, hands coming up in supplication that only set her mortal friend bowing. "I didn't know, Polyxene. I didn't *know*."

"Please." The woman was shaking her head, eyes still on the floor. "*Please*, Goddess, you cannot apologize. Not to me." The hand wringing began, and Persephone had to bite her tongue. "It is a gift for *any* mortal to have been visited by a deathless god once in their lifetime. And you have returned here, again and again. I am not worthy. I am *not*." In her distress, Polyxene had sunk to her knees, and the sight squeezed at something in Persephone's chest.

"But this is why I've come to you now." Persephone went to her friend and placed fingertips on her shoulder, a bid for the woman to meet her eyes. "To return your ring. Please," she said, as Polyxene braved another look.

"I have come to give you this gift, as I said I would." She had the ring off her finger and the green gem caught the light as she offered it to the healer. "Take it, my friend, you will have back your lost years and so many more. So many more!"

Brown eyes dropped, aghast, and the sight of immortality trapped within stone made her retch just as it had the first time. Polyxene wiped at her mouth with the back of a hand and coughed against the condensed distortion of time. The cough devolved into great, racking sobs, and the woman fell forward onto her hands.

"What is it?" Persephone dropped to kneel beside her. "Are you well?"

Polyxene smeared tears from her eye sockets with the heel of a palm, her mouth contorted, unable to cope. "My Goddess," she said, "I ... *Kings* wage wars over such gifts. There are stories. Heroes, I"—dark eyes snapped up to immortal green—"*how* can you offer this? To *me*. Who am I?"

The goddess's heart poured out onto the ground for this woman. "You are my *friend*," she said, her hand still resting on the mortal shoulder. "You are the most worthy being I know."

Defeated sniffling accompanied the placement of Polyxene's hands, palms upturned, in her own lap. "I ... I have a grandchild now, I—what will I do?" Her voice had gone soft and her eyes pleaded, wet and unprotected. "Live and live to watch my son grow old and die? To watch my granddaughter do the same?"

"But you will heal so many. I have watched you." The logic Persephone had carried into this house kept tumbling from her lips, even as she felt the Fates begin to pluck at it, threads unraveling. "You will use it in a way I am failing to do. It will be *you* about whom they write stories."

"But I do not *want* stories!" Now the passion was back. "I want ... I want ..." Her hands fluttered like doves.

Persephone's voice came down to a hush. "What do you want?"

The mortal risked another glance at the ring, but the vertigo sent her eyes back to the floor.

"I miss my love," she said. "I miss Iacob. If I accept this gift, my Goddess, I will never meet him in the Underworld. If I alone of my loved ones cannot die ..."

Persephone blinked at her several times and then her chest swelled.

What are you doing?

She felt the lump come in her throat.

Selfish immortal, what do you ask of her?

This was not a way. Not a way to escape, not by handing her troubles to this Daughter of Man. She could call it a gift; it would alter nothing. Persephone was trying to avoid pain. That's what this was.

She sat back on her heels, then on her tailbone, one knee bent and one leg falling straight out in a distressing array for any mortal in the presence of a deathless one. The side of her hand came to her eyes, which were hot and stung. She bit her lip, working to keep it at bay.

"*Karporphoros?*" The voice came meek as a mouse, but it called down her tears like the ruin of a dam. "It is the most generous offer I could ever hope to receive," Polyxene said. "I am ungrateful, I have upset you."

"No." She swallowed, trying to contain it. "No, you are right. This will not be a blessing for you. I am selfish. I only see what I want for myself."

A long silence ensued, broken only by small, wet noises of grief.

"And what is it"—Polyxene dared to scoot closer—"Goddess, what is it you want for yourself?"

"Not to decide!" The gentle words were too much. Her true mother had never spoken so, and the genuine concern broke her. "My choices are the same as yours!" she wailed. "Abandon the care I owe humanity and return to the Unseen Realm to seek my love, or dance in eternal springtime. Alone." Persephone knew her face would be red and wet when she raised it to look at the healer again. "I want both," she said. "I want neither! But this is not a matter for which you should suffer so I might escape my pains."

Polyxene's mouth came open, at a loss for how to respond. Here was an immortal, collapsed, weeping and undignified, so very much *not* like the statues of gods in the temples.

You've done enough here.

The ring slid from her finger, her opposite hand gripping it even as Persephone righted herself. She felt the mortal scuttle back from the thing as though the infinite might be catching.

It had been a push, the first time. Now, as Persephone narrowed her focus, it was a draw. Something in the very humming core of her reached out, sought and took hold; a vast taproot sucking deep and eager at the well of life in the borrowed stone.

Her hands warmed before going hot. There was no gradual rise toward the event this time. It rushed to join her, like seeking like, unstoppable. The light and life of Olympos filled the goddess until it seemed it must burst from her temples in streams, each toenail, each eyelash, violent with the blaze of eternity.

Persephone shuddered, head lolling on her shoulder in the clanging silence of the aftermath. Long heartbeats passed before she opened her eyes.

Polyxene gaped, but the goddess was uncurling a fist from around the ring. The stone sat black and glossy in the dim light, a gift from her husband and nothing more. The goddess offered the jewel between fingers abuzz with her birthright once more.

There was hesitation, even fear, in the woman's eyes, but she reached out and took the ring, no sooner clutching it to her bosom than the profusion of thanks began bubbling from her lips. Persephone gathered herself and stood, composure returning with the surge of godhood in her veins.

"There is one gift I *can* give you," she said, "though you may only keep it for a few moments."

Polyxene stared up at her while slipping on the ring, too dumbstruck to respond. Persephone gave her a tired smile.

"You'll want to close your eyes. That ring was bad enough."

When the woman did as her goddess suggested, Persephone found that place. It was the same new source that had been there when she'd fought her own mother at Nysa. The cool inevitability of shadow and stone. She drew her voice along it like a bow when she spoke the word.

"Hekate."

Even with her eyes shut tight, Polyxene gasped at the name. The air in the room condensed and, though she could both believe it and not, twin red orbs of light preceded their mistress into being.

"Chosen of mmy Lord," the three tongues greeted her even as their body coalesced into shape. "How may I sserve?"

She ... she came!

It was enough to collect her own tongue in the presence of the tri-form goddess. "I would ask a favor," she said. "An assurance for this woman, who is my friend."

"Indeed." At least two smiles curled *Enodia's* face at once.

"Is there an earthly guise you might assume first, Goddess? I fear you may be too much for mortal eyes."

"I cannott conceal mmyself in a ssingle physical fform," said Hekate, "but I nneed not maniffesst a body on thiss plane for uss to sspeak."

Particulate darkness scattered in a whirl, leaving only the bobbing torches to confirm the additional presence.

"Doess thiss ssatisfy?"

"It does." Persephone ducked a nod, eager to proceed. "Polyxene, you can open your eyes."

Even the orbs were enough to have the woman clutching her hands to her chest when she saw. The healer knelt, jaw slack, and said nothing.

"I know you have dominion over mortal shades," Persephone said. "I would ask you to summon this woman's husband, Iacob, so she might speak to him and know peace. As you did Iokaste to the mortal Alexios on the shores of the Styx."

"Lord Hadess is nnot plleased to havve the dead wanderring outside hiss rrealm."

Polyxene had backed herself against the door to the street, but couldn't tear her eyes from the hovering torches.

"If his motives are pure," Persephone said, straightening, "he will tolerate my wishes in this."

Though there were no faces to see, she could almost feel the smiles overlapping, smug. "Vvery good, Daughter of Zeuss. I will nnot be long."

Hekate's lights winked out and the air in the room seemed to crackle. Persephone turned to the healer. "It should be moments," she said. "I have seen this. You will not have much time." She tried to soften her expression for the awestruck woman huddling in front of the door. "You should stand, my friend. He will not want to see you afraid."

Polyxene gained her feet in a daze and, as if the prospect of seeing her own husband's shade was too much to contemplate, skipped straight to another timid question:

"My Goddess ... you say your love is in the Unseen Realm. Hek"—she gulped down the name—"the Lady of the Crossroads named you 'Chosen of Her Lord'." Brown eyes searched hers. "Does that mean ... is your love, is he ...?"

"Yes."

She saw the woman blanche, but it was no more than could be expected. "He is not what you think," she said. "I have come to learn this." Who, exactly, Persephone was trying to convince, remained unclear.

Another presence coalesced and the fiery orbs were with them again, but the arrival did not end there. The shade of a mortal man, distinct but insubstantial, stepped from the æther. Polyxene's limbs trembled.

"Iacob?" She stepped forward, tentative.

He smiled and opened his arms. "Lyxe."

Whatever shock came from such contact between planes did nothing to deter Polyxene. Her grip on him was fierce and her tears free. "*Sýzygos,*" she said, "I've missed you. Every day."

Beloved. The word hammered Persephone with its demands.

"I know, love." His face was in her silver hair. "I know."

Iacob's shade began to whisper a long string of comforts at the ear of his living wife, promises from the dark side of the veil. The woman nodded and tucked her arms in between their bodies, allowing the embrace of a dead man to assure and press her home.

While the couple stole their moments of reunion, voices meant only for Persephone curled in her immortal ear.

"Theirss is nnot the only time that growss short," Hekate said. "Lord Hadess knowss of yourr quarrel withh Demeter." Persephone inhaled at this, but *Enodia* continued her warning. "The Unsseen Realmm will not containn hiss wrath. You musst decide, Green One, and eitherr wway you mmust tell him yoursself. There has been a balance ssince the War, but I ffear the planes cannot withsstand himm now."

She remembered the fury he'd shared with her through the blood union. A reservoir of power vast beyond comprehension. Her gut twisted into a knot as she watched the mortal souls, reunited for the briefest of moments before her.

Persephone had to choose, and soon. She could not bring more grief on these people. On any of them.

"It iss time," Hekate said, and not just to clinging husband and wife.

Iacob released his hold first, his understanding more complete than that of his beloved, and Polyxene looked to her goddess, eyes shining.

"Thank you, *Karporphoros*," she said. "Thank you. It is the greatest gift. The greatest."

This. This was right. This was so much better.

"You are most welcome, Good Mother," she said, "May your family bring you joy, in this life and the next."

The woman smiled through tears as her impossible guests receded to other planes. *Enodia* drew her charge back to the Underworld, and Persephone willed her being toward Olympos.

Toward the equinox.

◆

"Then where was she last seen, Messenger?"

Hades stood in front of his throne, the *Elaionapothos* hovering at his back in the form of a glossy disk an armspan wide. Though it rose, conspicuous, over his head and shoulders in a dark halo, Hermes knew nothing of its capabilities.

The swiftest of gods addressed him from the foot of the steps as Kerberos and Hypnos flanked the seat of their Lord. "Her and Demeter fought," Hermes said, back straight in an effort to present a collected front. "At Nysa."

"And then?" said Hades.

"She fled."

Kerberos growled. The Guardian had escorted Hermes this far without incident, but that was no guarantee of the beast's continued tolerance.

"To where?" Patience wore thin all around, and Hades saw Hypnos grimace at the current of threat in his tone.

He can make whatever face he wants. If this sky dweller doesn't tell me what I want to hear …

"We don't know," said Hermes, glancing from one Underworld face to the next. "Another plane?" The Oil began to change form at Hades's back. "Surely if her mother had seen," the Messenger went on, eyes darting, "she would have given chase. Their disagreement was …" He had only helpless gestures.

The *Elaionapothos* pooled on the floor.

"Was. What."

Black tendrils extended from the mass and began to slither along the stones toward the fair-haired god.

"Violent." Hermes took a step back, but it didn't matter.

"Violent?" said Hades. Glossy coils climbed Olympian limbs and circled for grip. The Oil began to slide Hermes toward the throne. Winged sandals, useless in this realm, scrabbled for purchase along the floor, and Hades descended to the bottom step. "How do you know this?"

"H-Helios!" The Messenger's eyes were wide, his gaze darting for some ally he wouldn't find. Hypnos might cringe, but the God of Sleep would not undermine his lord.

"Indeed," said Hades, slowing to drive his point home as the Oil pulled Hermes the last of the way. "And *did* I"—he took a fistful of chiton and twisted—"or did I *not* instruct you to see her returned to me unmolested?"

"My Lord, I—"

"Consequences, Hermes." He all but growled the words into the Messenger's face. "I warned you."

The æther gave way to the bridge over the River of Fire. Instead of the throne room floor beneath his feet, Hermes now dangled in Hades's grip, legs kicking over the red maw of the Phlegethôn. The Oil receded to its hovering disk, abandoning the joy of control to its maker.

Immortal eyes rolled wild at the sight of the terrible drop.

"Hades!"

It was a cruel mirror to the way Persephone had trusted him to hold her this way, not so very long ago. The goddess had melted into his embrace and altered the nature of his wishes with her surrender. This Olympian jerked, desperate hands choking the coal-dark forearm, the flailing summation of every reaction the reputation of Hades *Clymenus* had earned.

She is the only one. The only one who can see you otherwise.

"She has eaten my fruit," Hades said, accusations booming over the crackling grind of the river. "She is my chosen Consort, and you tell me she is *gone*?"

"My lord!" The voice of Hypnos came from behind him on the bridge. The god must have leapt the æther in Hades's wake, following to mitigate disaster. "He is a son of Zeus, my lord. We will start another war with the Olympians."

The Lord of the Dead reserved the fury of his gaze for Hermes.

"*I* start a war with *them?*" He had never seen the God of Thieves so bereft of his insolence. It fueled some black fire he'd been ignoring, and Hades felt his power unfurl, vast and enticing. "Persephone belongs to me now," he said, "and they have done nothing but come between us. No." Hermes squirmed on his hook. "Olympos has started a war with *me*."

Slate blue eyes were wide, and the god could only whisper. "Please."

Hades's smile curled. "You don't belong here, Messenger." He extended his arm and Hermes writhed over living rock.

"Hades! Don't! No!"

The clutching hand released and the Swift One fell, the boiling vein of the earth pulsing to claim an immortal for itself.

It gave him no small amount of grim satisfaction to hear the terror of a god unaware of the rift Hades had sliced open in the æther. Just above the annihilation of the river, the Messenger blinked out of sight. If Hades's aim was as good as he remembered, the winged sandals and their master would land square in the middle of Zeus's throne room.

Let him pass that *message along. Vacuous fool.*

"*Polydegmon*," came the fearful voice from the bridge, "what will you do?"

His hands rested on the stone railing and the Lord of the Dead swept the Great Cavern in a single measuring look. At his back, the Oil began to shift.

"I have ruled in silence, Hypnos." He felt his desire shaping the weapon. Growing it. Feeding. "They imagine me passive. They will learn."

The *Elaionapothos* unfolded in uncountable directions at once, expanding into something immeasurable. Obscene. Crystal points bristling from the bridge towers warped in the tessellation of power. Stalactites and *paráthyra* distended overhead.

Had the God of Sleep a mortal stomach, he would have emptied it. Had the æther not jangled with disruption, he would have fled. All he could do as his lord prepared to rape the balance between planes, was stand on the bridge and will his pleas to the Fates.

◆

X Equinox

Persephone paced cloud-white stone amid one of the many gardens surrounding her father's palace. It was midday and the brightness made her squint. Her steps carried her back and forth across a mosaic of the great Circle of Houses while hedges and fountains stood about, waiting for her to make a decision. The equinox was upon her. Time was running out.

The Circle bounding her steps lay in the ground in twelve equal portions, rays of bronze dividing them from its center. Different precious stones worked into glittering tiles set apart each of the twelve Houses, honoring a portion of the balance allotted to each of the most powerful gods.

The houses, the houses, the houses. But where am I going to be? Which one is mine?

The first house, in bloodstone and iron, was the House of Ares. The God of War had nothing to do with her.

The second, in glittering emerald and copper, belonged to Aphrodite, the goddess who'd set this disaster in motion. Hermes followed, third, in agate and silver. She skipped forward to her mother's House, the sixth. The warm olive green of peridot picked out Demeter's sigil on the floor, the sickle and cross of the harvest.

And how will there be crop to harvest if you are not here to make it grow in the first place?

Persephone forgot the other Houses, though, and even her pacing as polished obsidian drew her eye. The dark void in the Circle was the eighth House. *His* house.

The arms of the many, bringing the one back into their fold from below, the symbol of Hades, leapt at her in stark white quartz just as it had marked his private chamber doors. Passing through those doors was only the first step of many that had led her here. To this.

Duty or love. Guilt or loneliness. Her mother shamed her to take one course, Hades pled for the other. And Zeus? She made a noise of irritation. Her father was unhelpfully neutral. How generous of him to leave the decision up to her.

And what was she becoming? At Nysa when she'd called the Underworld to stand against her mother ... she should not have been able—

"Troubled, Green One?"

Persephone whirled on a voice like silk and the tinkling of copper bangles. The Goddess of Love sauntered near with a smirk, the æther closing behind her.

"*Troubled?*" It had been some time since she'd been in the presence of Aphrodite, but Persephone had no further use for delicacy. "Why did you do it?" she said. "You could have the attention of any eye on two planes, if you wanted it. Hermes was such a prize you had to turn me into ... into *this*?"

"Into what? An immortal in love?" Her laughter rippled, musical and self-satisfied. "The heart is an irrational master, Daughter of Zeus, as I'm sure you've discovered. Hermes belongs to mine and I did what was necessary to have him back. Just as you will do."

A noise of disgust rattled in her throat and Persephone looked the goddess from sandal to shoulder. "Perfect," she said, hands coming to her hips. "You have him back. And I have nothing but ugly choices. My sincerest thanks, *Fair One*. However will I be able to repay you?"

Aphrodite ignored the lash of Persephone's tongue and stepped around her, beginning a lazy circuit of the mosaic with one dainty foot in front of the other. "There are plenty of unwed immortals in whose path I could have thrown you," she said. "Do you know why I chose Hades?"

"Because his realm would have nullified the power of anyone interested in stopping you?" Persephone said, her voice rising. "Because you enjoy watching others suffer?"

"That's Oizys, and isn't *she* a tiresome thing. No," the goddess said, continuing on her path, "although that first reason *was* rather convenient. No, I only ever make these choices for a single reason."

Helios rode high overhead, and Persephone frowned. The Goddess of Lust strolled as if she had all the time on this plane.

"Lord Hades keeps to his own counsel on most matters," said Aphrodite. "Unlike some, he doesn't spend time flaunting his"—she cleared her throat and wore half a grin—"*proclivities*. But if a god is going to enlist help from Lust herself to fashion certain 'instruments', he cannot expect every one of his preferences to remain a secret. I imagine you've come to understand the inclinations of which I speak?"

Persephone's arms folded across her chest while her face tried not to be red. "And that has what to do with me?"

"By the Fates, you're even beginning to sound like him." Green eyes glittered from across the Circle. "Can you ever recall any rumor, any evidence of Hades pursuing a mate? Now, or in the tales from before your birth?"

Persephone shook her head.

"It is because he hasn't," said Aphrodite. "Not that he confessed to me in so many words, but I do believe the Unseen One never expected to *find* a consort accepting of his particular tastes.

"And you, Persephone." The goddess began making her way back, steps like a clever dance. "I saw your lack of interest in what the other gods had to offer. Even without your mother's edict, I doubt you would have chosen any of them. Not for long, at least."

"Oh?" Aphrodite was right, of course, but her smug certainty had Persephone's hackles up.

"Oh yes," she said. "I know the signs. The hunger. You sought and failed to find a certain type of lover, even if you did not recognize it yourself." Aphrodite's grin showed teeth at what she must have seen as the neatest dovetailing of her many schemes.

"That's all very well," Persephone said, pivoting on her heel to watch the Fair One circle close again, "but I cannot desert my duties *here*. What respect for myself will I have left, if I abandon my calling for the ... the thrill of a bed?" She nearly spat the last words on the ground.

" 'The thrill of a bed', so crude. That is only the narrowest part of what pains you now, and you know it." Green and blue linen fluttered as Aphrodite stepped up to face her. Copper hair drifted on the breeze. "Of all the unwed immortals, you, *Karporphoros*, are the *only* match for our very singular Lord of the Dead. The two of you *must* have this union. Creation demands it."

"D-demands?" The fine hairs on the backs of her arms were standing up as the goddess began circling some unavoidable truth.

"Yes, 'demands'," she said. "Life culminates in Death, Death pushes forth new Life. The Balance is incomplete otherwise. You accept each other for who and what you are in a way no others can. And I tell you, I understand this well, Green One. Do you imagine before my marriage to Hephaistos I had any hope of knowing a mate who could embrace Love and Lust, herself? Knowing what that would entail, and all the very rigid notions of loyalty promising no such thing? But he and I are as much a match as you and Lord Hades. And neither of us cares at all what the rest have to say."

Persephone was backing away, the realities too large to confront. Why would no one, *no one*, let her escape?

"But ... I can't ..." She shook her head. Answers were nowhere.

"I see your struggle," Aphrodite said, pursuing her at a deliberate pace. "But if you force yourself to choose between one unacceptable alternative and another, you will be miserable all the time."

"I *know* that, w—" Persephone swung hard from indignant to anxious as the goddess grabbed up her hands. "Whaaat are we doing?"

The Goddess of Love held her at the boundary of the Great Circle and stilled her retreat with emerald eyes. "Everything is portioned out according to its Lot, my conflicted immortal." She nodded left and right to the Circle's twelve parts. "Perhaps there is a way you can divide your desires according to theirs."

Persephone's gaze followed the Fair One's to the ground. Her left foot stood on obsidian. On the House of Hades. Her right foot, however, rested on the sky-colored turquoise of the ninth House, her father's. She stood astride the two Houses like the horizon straddled the night and the day.

The night and the day. The equinox.

Her knees were weak and Persephone wanted to stagger, but the goddess held her upright. When she could meet Aphrodite's eyes again, the smile beneath them was genuine. Determination tightened her grip.

"Help me gather them," Persephone said. "I will not go and tell him alone."

◆

It could have been moments, it could have been days. Hades had spiraled to such depths within his power, his will so entwined with the amassing fury of the *Elaionapothos*, that all sense of time had receded to a nagging thrum, somewhere at the outermost fringe of his senses.

The wrath built and built, bending reality around it like some black horizon, and once he gathered enough …

Once he gathered enough, oh …

But there was some ripple. Some imperfection coming at a drone, a rumble. From within the sway of the fugue, Hades could feel his face again, and it was frowning.

Closer the noise came, and clearer. Closer, clearer

Closer.

"Polydegmon. My Lord!"

The bridge over the Phlegethôn was under his feet. Kerberos drove his thoughts into Hades's mind with the force of a shout.

The Lord of the Dead turned to the voice and saw with altered eyes. He maintained the Oil in such a state, alive with the vengeance of a Deathless God, that the image of the Guardian appearing before him now streaked away from itself like windblown piles of ash. He blinked and shook his head.

Hypnos lay in a heap at the foot of the opposite railing, no longer able to stand in the vortex, but the three-headed beast ignored him. Ears pinned back and teeth bared against the flux of power, Kerberos managed a growl.

"Hades, they have come," he said. *"The Lord of Lightnings approaches with the Ferryman."*

For several heartbeats, the words were just sounds. A string of syllables. But as his senses continued to merge, they condensed into meaning.

The Lord of Lightnings …

"They dare."

His words still echoed with enough residual power to send the great hound back a step. Hypnos began to stir, but Hades was already drawing in everything he'd extended out into the Cavern.

It happened at a violent speed, and the air of the Unseen Realm filled the empty space with a boom. The sum of his terrible will collapsed back into the *Elaionapothos*, the density of it a gaze-repelling void. Hades wore it about his forearms in the form of twin bracers, its nature concealed, but at the ready.

What they *would* expect to see was his bident, and he had a gateway to the Styx open the moment he drew the now lesser weapon to its length.

"Prepare yourself, Guardian," he said as he stepped through the rift. "The Underworld is about to change."

Black sand was under his feet and the pulsing well of power darkened his brow as the lanterns bobbed nearer through the mist. The ferry approached on phantom waters, inexorable under Kharon's poling, as Hades strode toward the dock.

Kerberos snarled through the æther on the land side of the shore, a recovering Hypnos leaning on the Guardian's massive shoulder. Closer to the ancient pilings ahead, a pair of red lights bloomed into view, followed by the trio of Hekate's overlapping faces.

They all wish to bear witness? Fine.

The *Elaionapothos* all but hummed above clenched fists as the distance closed between Hades and his interloping brother. Zeus had set foot in the Unseen Realm, and for what? To be powerless? To set off ancient rivalries? It was a mistake, and it would be his very last.

The ferry bumped against the dock and, through the clearing mists, Hades could see it carried three. Three aboard the ageless craft, aside from Kharon, and none of them was Persephone.

A void whirled between the tines of his bident as he came, and the Oil began to quiver against the boundaries he attempted to hold. Against the whispers in his ear that he should let go. He should become every terrible thing they all believed him to be.

"You will come here now?" he called out across the narrowing divide. "After you've torn her from my realm?"

The unwelcome passengers disembarked: Aphrodite, Demeter, and Zeus. The one who'd blackmailed him into this disaster. The one who'd demanded an end to his newfound joy. And the one who'd allowed it.

The *Elaionapothos* boiled, unstable, merging with his flesh. It winged out from the contrived bracers in unnatural, parabolic arcs, unable to maintain a form as Hades lost his grip on control.

Then the Olympians parted and the Lord of the Dead couldn't breathe. His bident thumped to the sand, tines dark.

She stepped up out of the ferry, accepting Kharon's gnarled hand for help onto the dock. For a teetering heartbeat, Hades lost all connection to will, and the Oil snapped back along his arms, as inert as its master was dumbstruck.

He had seen her in a torn grey chiton. He'd seen her in the red linen of his own choosing. And, by the Fates, he'd seen her bare and perfect. But today …

Today, the day of the equinox, Persephone came to him in bridal white. The drape of her peplos was intricate, and it hung from her curves sashed in vivid purple. Her hair was mass of dark braids and golden chains, piled atop her head. A whisper of a veil in the traditional yellow brushed the lower half of her face.

She … she has chosen.

What was this feeling? It hurt. It hurt and he wanted it never to end.

She took a step toward him and Hades vaulted up onto the dock, sweeping straight past the others as he would mere shades. Self-mastery was gone and he seized his goddess in an embrace, heedless of who stood by, or what things they waited to say or hear. When she curled into the crush of his arms, he nearly convulsed at the full reality.

Persephone was the Balance. He would *never* let anyone take her from him again.

"Hades. *Sýzygos.*"

Her words in his ear were the sweetest torture. They brought back every laugh, every exquisite sound she'd ever made for him, and channeled them all into a single name: Beloved.

Hades held her and held her, his face buried in her neck, inhaling the scent of green, losing himself to renewed possibility, until a throat cleared behind him and brought him back to the present.

"I was sure they had driven you from me," he said, relaxing his hold to look down into shining eyes. "That they'd forced your choosing."

"*I* choose for me. No one else."

He tipped his head in acknowledgement, accepting the jab he'd earned. When Hades could bring himself to wrest his gaze anywhere else—if only his gaze; his arms stayed locked at her waist—he found Persephone's escorts in a tapestry of states.

Zeus wore a knowing half-smile, tawny arms folded over his chest, sandaled feet planted at shoulder-width. Demeter stood with a silent scowl, arms also crossed, but for far different reasons. Aphrodite flashed teeth in the most satisfied of grins. They could all look however they wanted: the Underworld did not answer to Olympian gods.

"Did I not tell you?" said Aphrodite, twitching a copper brow his way. Hades allowed her the slightest dip of his chin, grudging her the right of her predictions. When the Fair One's eyes slid past him, he followed to see her give a single nod and receive a burning trifold one in return from Hekate. He felt his jaw slacken.

Did they ... did those two ...?

Persephone was trying to untangle their limbs. She'd only just now returned and sought release so soon? But the goddess extracted herself with a purpose, and took a formal step back to stand with shoulders straight.

Before he could ask, she swiped a delicate finger through the air in front of her breast and opened a hand spanning rift in the æther. Hades could have choked at the sight.

The Underworld answers ...

She reached across planes and came back with a handful, closing the tiny gateway in her wake. The Green One splayed her fingers and invited the gathered immortals to see.

"Persephone." It was all he could do not to stammer, not to reach out his hand for the pomegranate. "It *can't* be the same one."

She had a smile for him that had ichor singing in his veins. "Am I the Bringer of Fruit, or am I not?" She palmed the red globe, cupping it in both hands at her waist. "I left with it when Hermes came, and I've preserved it since."

"You told us you'd eaten it, *Daughter*." Demeter's voice rose, and Hades turned to see her taking a threatening step in their direction. "You told us you were *bound*."

Something under Hades's eye twitched and the *Elaionapothos* promised satisfaction with an eager thrum, but the Lord of Lightnings laid a hand on Demeter's shoulder. The god leaned in, murmuring something at the ear of his one-time lover and her arms dropped. Cheeks went red. The Goddess of the Seasons returned to crossed arms and a tight jaw, and if she had any further thoughts, she bit them back into herself.

Persephone, however, stood unperturbed. "I *am* bound," she said, green eyes only for Hades, yet words carrying enough for all. "I'm bound by duty *and* love. You must know this, Consort of my choosing, for my decision comes only with sacrifice."

Consort. Sacrifice. A kiss, then a blow. But Persephone had more.

"I cannot abandon my duties above the earth, but I *will* not exist apart from you below it. My heart lies in two places, and so shall I."

Hades swallowed. "I don't understand."

"I will remain with you here," she said, "until the next Day of Balance, and then I will return to the upper realms. Every equinox I will travel. When the leaves of the trees let go their branches in death, I will join them in the

Underworld. When their time to bud circles back, I will push them up to the Skies again, and I will follow. Please understand, Hades. This is what a union between realms must be. This is the Balance."

Her compromise felled him. How could he keep it all from bursting out through his ribs? She was right. She was everything. And if this was the way she could allow herself to be his, then by the Fates …

Hades tilted her a slow nod, black eyes locked on green, accepting it all. "The Balance," he repeated.

She closed her eyes and exhaled. Some tension left her shoulders and they fell. But when Persephone looked at him again, he saw the intensity of her purpose doubled.

Her free hand came up and yanked away the veil. Yellow linen fluttered to the dock. A stab of her thumbs rent the pomegranate, and she dug her fingers into the pulpy scarlet core, a handful of dripping seeds her prize. She stepped toward him and her voice rang loud and clear.

"I, Persephone, daughter of Zeus, Lord of the Skies, and Demeter, Lady of the Earth, do bind myself as Consort to you, Hades *Nekrodegmôn*, Lord of the Underworld, in the sacred rite of marriage, in the presence of these immortals who do bear witness. May our love endure as long as creation."

In a single clean move, she brought the seeds to her mouth and swallowed. His goddess had bound herself. She had chosen him. Again.

He reached out his hand for his bident, and it flew from where it had landed on the shore. Hades closed the last of the distance between them, just as his fingers curled around the iron haft. As though she already knew what he needed, Persephone brought red-stained fingers to cover his, and the Lord of the Dead spoke his answering vow.

"I, Hades, Son of Kronos, Lord of Time, and Rhea, Mother of the Gods, do bind myself as Consort to you, Persephone *Karporphoros*, Goddess of Growing Things, in the sacred rite of marriage, in the presence of these immortals who do bear witness. May our love endure as long as creation."

The words were no more out of his mouth than Persephone stood on her toes and they met in a bruising kiss. The pomegranate fell at their feet and the ancient surface of the dock erupted with life. Russet moss and bone-white fungi spread in a carpet; along with any sort of live thing as might grow in his realm.

Their realm.

He felt her power well up, even as they consumed each other. The Underworld belonged to her now, as well.

Hades was no longer alone.

The immortals behind them gave up waiting after a time, and departed through the æther, or with Kharon across the Styx. The Lord and Lady of the Underworld had attention only for each other.

◆

Persephone careened past the double doors and into the great hall, grinning and out of breath. The Throne of Tears beckoned from the far end, and she ran to it, catching herself with her palms on its arm.

The chase proved far more sporting when made on foot. No rifts, no æther. Just predator and prey.

Hades followed on her heels, sliding into the space out of the darkness of the hallway. One foot in front of the other, he closed the distance at a deliberate prowl, the line of his mouth wicked with promise. She stood up straight and fixed him with wide eyes and mock horror. Covered her breast with palms in a pantomime of dismay.

Catch me, Darkness. Again and again.

His steps brought him onto the dais, black eyes intent on his quarry. Persephone's heart *whumped* in her chest, some ritual drum, and not from her sprint through the halls of the palace. Here was Hades, her immortal consort, come to claim his bride again. Chest and shoulders dwarfing hers, dark hands ready to circle her arms, her throat. The perfect euphoria of trust—trust and delicious fear—had her thrumming with need and ready to end the game. There was only so long she could play at evading the thing she wanted most.

He took a step forward and she took one back, the air all but crackling between them. Two more moves in this dance and Persephone felt one of the throne's stalagmite columns pressing between her shoulder blades. When Hades closed the gap, she gave up her flight and smiled, sliding her arms around his waist.

"You've caught me, *Husband*."

He peeled her hold away and brought her wrists overhead against the cool, damp stone, holding them in place with a hand. "So I have. *Wife*."

The word still made her skin prickle, from nape to knees. In the last moment, as he tilted his face down to hers, Persephone thanked the Fates.

And then she was meeting his kiss. Challenging with tongue and teeth. He was wedging a thigh between her legs and filling his free hand with the curve of her backside.

She rolled her hips against him now, her part as the fleeing coquette forgotten. His hands were everywhere, palming a breast, thumbing a nipple through the drape of linen. Her moans were in his mouth, the only place left for them to go.

Amid delirium, the supporting column of stone slid away and the polished arm of the throne was at her backside. Hades herded her back and she sat, knees parting around his hips. Every breath of air might as well have left the room for all the urgency with which they stole it back and forth from one another's lungs.

Hades had her face in his hands, and Persephone fumbled, blind, at the fibula to his chiton, tossing it aside as soon as she'd ripped it free. Fabric fell and his chest was bare. The naked soles of her feet pressed to the backs of his knees to bring that scalding heat close.

They ate and drank of each other as though the next equinox would arrive on the morrow and force them apart again. Her head fell back, submitting her throat to the destruction of his tongue, the ungentle claim of teeth. He was going to mark her, and she pressed into it, whining to have a cup filled even as it appeared to be bottomless.

Yes. Yes. His.

His hand was on the back of her neck, the points of his nails anchoring in her skin as he came up to own her with all the volatile possession she'd ever needed to see in two eyes.

"Mine."

Pure and dark as obsidian, his one word called her thoughts into reality. Now she knew. Persephone knew what it was to be loved by the lord of the third realm.

He was pushing the drape of her peplos over her knees now, his free hand seeking, demanding. The moment his fingers found slick arousal, Hades *Clymenus* forgot seduction. He had found the chaos of need.

His hips drove her thighs wider, chiton no more out of the way before his erection slid against the wet promise of union. Her husband would be pushing inside before she could breathe.

No!

"Hades!" She had a hand on his arm, gripping muscle. "My love." There was something unhinged in that gaze, but the endearment was enough to stop him. "Please," she said, every last nerve burning hot, "this is not what I … you know what I need."

He searched her face for a heartbeat, and then sucked in a hiss of air through his teeth. The growl that came after, welling from deep in his chest, was all the warning she had.

Hades hauled her to her feet and spun her by the shoulders, the stone arm of the throne bruising the bones of her hips as he trapped her. Fabric tore and his cock was there, sliding between her legs even as rough hands dragged at her ruined peplos.

Oh, yes. Yes, he does *know.*

A palm was between her shoulders, pressing down, bending her forward over the seat of his power. He was there. He was *there*, hard as granite, pushing and meeting no friction whatsoever. She arched, pressing back to surround him, coming up on her toes.

"Please, *please*, Husband." She sought their coupling, shameless, but he filled her at a tortuous pace, his self-control complete, whatever she'd seen in his eyes only moments ago.

"You can beg as you like, Beloved," he said as he sank in to the hilt. She could hear the depravity in his smile, even as she stretched around his cock, lust slicking her thighs and the cleft between her cheeks.

There was a hand on her left arm, hauling back, stealing her support on one side. Then the right, and he had her wrists at the small of her back, banded together in an iron grip. With the circle completed this way, something supporting fell from her, dragging her stomach through vertigo as it went.

Hades took her with the grinding patience of the Phlegethôn. Ravaging at the speed of molten stone, never allowing their separation, breaking and reforming her until her eyes rolled back, and the noises rattling from her throat were the songs of infinite surrender.

Their entire world existed in the places where their bodies joined. The roll of his hips grew sharp at intervals. Her shoulders strained backward against the rhythm, the pull of his grip on her arms. He snapped into a thrust, and then another, grunting as he abandoned his will.

"*Sýzygos!* Yes!"

We won't last. Too much. Too much!

The Lord of the Dead drove into her, battering her hips against stone. She welcomed the pain again, perfect when it crashed together with the joy, death overtaking life overtaking death, on and on without end.

Too much! Everything! Yes!

The throb came, a deafening rush, and she took him home in that first violent clutch.

"Hades! I love you!"

Her flesh and her cries ended him.

"Persephone!"

He jerked against her, root-deep, and she fluttered around him, wailing, drinking him down. Every muscle in two immortal bodies went tight, and every distraction fled blinding clarity.

Her husband seeded her. That's what this was. Surge after hot surge sought her womb, and Persephone's womb was the earth. The next Day of Balance she would come to term, this year, and every year. She would bear the progeny of Death, up through the soil, reaching and green, this year, and every year. And when her offspring withered and fell away to dirt, she would come seeking their renewal in the arms of her Consort.

This year, and every year.

Tension dissolved and Hades loosed her arms, leaning over her back. He shifted hair from her neck and his kisses fell on damp skin, there and over her shoulders. A hand came around her hip and splayed over her belly, lingering even as he remained inside her.

"This year and every year," he said, the promise brushing her ear. Persephone choked back a sob. He'd seen it, too.

The Fates had been clever, indeed.

He shifted to allow her up, but kept her pinned against the throne, still buried to the hilt. Intimate flesh slipped and stretched, raw from completion, and Persephone shuddered. The sob heaved into laughter.

"Tell me, Wife." A knuckle traced down her spine, and she could feel the trap of that smirk.

Oh yes. Every year.

"Hades," she said, her own mischief curling her lips, "My Lord Husband … do you still have the little bells?"

◆

Persephone journeys at every equinox. Can you not see her passing?

When the year begins on the Day of Balance, her children cry out, green mouths open wide to the skies. The buds and shoots of Spring explode from every vale and branch, petaled trumpets sounding her return to the realm of her birth. They grow for her every year, ripen to fruit and split at the rinds, their love overflowing.

Can you see her leave at mid-year? They called this equinox The Fall, as the goddess once did, from one realm to the next, destined to meet her love. The trees remember her wedding veil; can you see them turn yellow in her honor? Ah, but after the celebration of marriage ... what are they to do? Their leaves can only blush a furious red at each year's passionate reunion. When Persephone descends once again, this year and every year, to find her Lord Hades beneath the earth.

◆

We hope you enjoyed *The Eighth House!*

Like what you read? Why not leave a review on the site where you purchased your copy? Even a short one is always a great help to independent authors, who rely on readers like you to get the word out about their books.

Ready for more?
Sign up Eris Adderly's email newsletter:
(http://eepurl.com/beYqU1)

Get notified about upcoming releases, including:

Upcoming titles in the *Flames of Olympos* series
Bloodnames (After Exile Book II)
The Carpenter and the Deckhand (A Devil's Luck Vignette)
The Merry Widow (Sequel to *The Devil's Luck*)

Eris only sends emails for new releases (both stories for purchase and free reads), no spam. You can unsubscribe at any time and your address will not be shared.

About Eris

Eris writes subversive romance for people who hate romance novels. Her stories are the stomping grounds for badass heroines, untamable alphas, a spectrum of sexuality and a serious disregard for convention. Much like her namesake, Eris likes to make trouble.

When she's not staying up into wee hours writing, Eris also likes to read, baby-talk her cats, exasperate her husband, and obsess about writing some more. Somewhere in the middle, there will be pizza.

Also by Eris Adderly

THE SKULL AND CROSSBONE ROMANCES:

The Devil's Luck – Lust and discovery, betrayal and secrets in the age of sail. Oh yes, and pirates. Dirty, dirty pirates. A young widow from Bristol is ready to sail for the Colonies, but fate seems to have other ideas. A full-length erotic bodice-ripper novel to satisfy your thirst for adventure and pleasure on the high seas.

The Decline and Fall of Rowland Graves (A Devil's Luck Vignette) – A tragic, Gothic romance novella, with a dark, Halloween twist. The origin story of the villainous surgeon who menaced Hannah aboard *The Devil's Luck*.

The Maid and the Cook (A Devil's Luck Vignette) – A light-hearted, bawdy pirate romance novella following Brigit, the widow's maid from *The Devil's Luck*, and her adventures down in the galley when she catches the unexpected eye of the ship's cook.

AFTER EXILE SERIES

BOOK ONE: *An Emperor for the Eclipse* – A man they call 'exile' and a woman they call 'witch' meet their fate on the steps of the imperial palace. Neither will ever be the same. A dark, romantic fantasy.

BLUSHING BOOKS PUBLICATIONS

Gallows Pole – A notorious highway thief makes a dangerous bargain with a hangman in eighteenth century England. A dark, historical erotic romance novella.

Find Eris Online

www.erisadderly.com
www.facebook.com/erisadderly
www.twitter.com/erisadderly

Printed in Great Britain
by Amazon